# The Magic Tale of Harvanger and Yolande

## By G. P. Baker

: : : New York : : :

George H. Doran Company

*To My Wife*

# CONTENTS

# BOOK I.: OF THOSE WHO PASSED BY GREENBANK IN GREENWOOD.

## CHAPTER I.: THE TALE OF THOSE WHO PASSED BY GREENBANK TOWARDS THE SCAUR GAP.

WHEN Harvanger was a boy, and no more than fifteen years old, he used to lie upon Greenbank, beyond the great forest of Greenwood, watching the black-faced sheep that fed there. He was tall and slender for his age, and full of promise of a strength not yet come; he had hair of the fairest and softest, blue eyes, and cheeks and lips that were rich and full of colour. He lived with his parents in a little cot on the hill-side; it was not great, but sweet to look upon, and most of all in spring and summer, when the jasmine was in flower. Harvanger's father owned sheep and pigs, besides a cow; also, he had a little horse to pull his plough; and a cart, when he would fare to some market. They lived much alone, and were not of the kindred of such folk as dwelt nearest to them. So Harvanger knew but little of the world beyond Greenbank; no more, in truth, than he could learn from the few people who harboured with them now and again, and who told tales of wars, and battles, and ill things that were wrought on poor people, and great deeds accomplished by the great.

A brook trickled below Greenbank, and in the pools grew water-cress. Harvanger had no troubles; he lay on Greenbank, watching his sheep, and seeking out for them those places where the grass was freshest. He knew much about sheep, their ways and doings. Then, too, he knew the birds and their names, and their songs and calls, and their nestings and pairings; and the names of trees, and what their timber was good for. He was keen at wood-craft, and loved to stalk the hares and conies that dwelt in a little burg beneath a wood; he knew the foxes, that stole his geese and ducks, and the grey wolf, Isengrin, that came prowling about in the depth of winter, making the pigs to squeal in their pens for fear when they smelt him. It was a fair land in all seasons. Of all these matters that are here mentioned, Harvanger knew: and of corn, and grass, and flowers, of herbs and trees, of animals both the big and the little, wild and tame, fierce and friendly; and of the sun, and moon, and stars, their waxing and waning, their coming forth and departing. There was no thing that grew on a stalk or ran upon legs, but Harvanger well knew all about it. So he was passing wise of wit, even if he knew nothing of the great world, nor of book-learning. And withal, he was very fair to see.

Greenbank was a hill, not great, but wide and

broad; a copse grew on it, above the house, and sheltered it from the northern winds. The sides were covered with thick green grass, whence men called it Greenbank. To the north were the wildwood and the far-away mountains, through which one must travel many a long day to come to any home of men. The forest was mostly of oak. Every beast that dwells in our lands dwelt there; and every flower too.

Towards the east were fair plains and downs, stretching away to the places of the cities. On this side the brook lay.

To the south and west were woodlands. So Greenbank lay right in the midst of the world, open to whomsoever should come; and yet no man seemed to come in these years that I speak of, and Harvanger was much alone, tending his sheep fondly, and sometimes wandering in the forest long journeys, not knowing whither he went, but coming back at last with small tidings. Now he had grown to fifteen years, and this tale begins, concerning him and his seeking for the Best Thing in the World.

One sweet day in the middle of Spring, he lay out on Greenbank below the copse, watching the golden light that shone upon the grass and trees. He looked out to the east, and wondered greatly as to what was there, so far away. It sloped before him, woodland and lawn, down to a level plain, and then rose, till no more could be seen.

Then presently he looked to the north, and saw a man come forth from the Wood, and stride down over the grass. He was a large and ruddy man, rather more like to the Earl-folk than to the Churl-People: for he was straight and big of limb, and walked proudly. On his head was a hat with a broad brim, such as Harvanger had never seen before, and he carried a cloak over one arm, and in his hand a staff. When he saw Harvanger, he leaped over the brook and came near.

"Lad," he said, "knowest thou the road to the Scaur Gap? I am well-nigh lost in this wood."

Harvanger gazed at him, and saw how great and stark he was, and how silky and golden his beard grew, and how keen his grey eyes.

He answered: "I know not."

"It should be well for thee if thou knewest," said the man, gazing back at him and smiling a little. Harvanger said nothing, having nothing to say. The man still looked upon him, not incuriously, as though he saw somewhat in Harvanger that was not common among folk; so, after a while, he cast down his staff, and sat upon the greensward, pulling forth a wallet containing rye-bread and onions.

"At the house," quoth Harvanger, "are meat and ale to be gotten."

"Is that so?" quoth the man. "I thank thee; but I may not stop."

Then he asked his name; and Harvanger told

[14]

it, and they fell into long speech. And the man asked Harvanger many strange questions, as to his heart's desire, and his folk, and his life. And he told him the strangest and most wonderful tales of the Great World; but to all these Harvanger smiled, and shook his head, and answered that he desired them not. So at the end, the man rose up, and thanked him, and said:

"There is one thing in the world better than any I have named. If thou desirest not these things, thou mayest find the Best Thing in the World in that. And it lieth beyond the Scaur Gap. Remember this word of mine."

"Will you not tell me of it?" said Harvanger.

He answered: "Nay; but if another man of my folk passeth by, him thou may'st question."

Therewith he strode away to the east, and was gone. But Harvanger saw how he carried the mightiest slug-horn ever seen at his waist. It was of milk-white ivory, bound with silver, and carved with devices, and it hung from his shoulder by a chain of steel. Harvanger wondered.

The year waxed and waned, and Harvanger saw no more of the man with the horn, nor any man like him, although he waited and watched. Then the next spring came the rains; and after them Harvanger led out his sheep once more. When the new moon after Easter-tide was come, he gazed at the sky, and saw a bright rainbow cast over the arch to the east, against the departing cloud-wrack: and there strode out a man from the wood, whence that other had come, and he stalked up the hill-side like a king in his pride. Mightily tall he was, and ruddy, thick of limb, and bearded with red gold. He wore a broad-brimmed hat, and a green cloak was on his arm. Harvanger deemed him of the same folk as the horn-bearer of yester-year.

The bearded one came anigh and said: "Good health to thee, boy."

Said Harvanger: "If you go to the Scaur Gap, well may you fare on the way."

The man fingered his beard, and looked at Harvanger; fierce grey eyes he had, but nowise evil.

"Which is the road?" he said.

"Truly, I know not," answered Harvanger; "but one of thy folk came to me last year, and departed to the east."

The man sat down on the sward, and asked Harvanger many questions concerning this; he was a strange man, rough and strong, and his eyes sometimes slept, and sometimes glowed with fire. And he asked Harvanger as to the desire of his heart, and told tales very wonderful and strange; but Harvanger said that he cared not much for these things, but would hear of the Best Thing in the World.

The bearded one laughed, but answered naught. Then he took his staff again, and said: "I

[16]

thank thee. Well should it be for thee if thou couldst attain what lieth beyond the Scaur Gap. But if another of my folk cometh to thee, him thou shalt ask."

So he departed, and was gone; and Harvanger saw that a marvellous girthing went about his middle—a belt four hand's breadths wide, rich with gold and enamels; and from it hung a mighty hammer of steel. Harvanger wondered again.

It is to be told that the year wore round again, and no other who could be of that folk came to Greenbank. The summer was very dry, and the grass withered somewhat, save on the hill, which was fed by the brook that never dried up. And autumn was fine, and winter frosty and dry; the arch of blue never clouded for many months. Yule came and went, and still Harvanger watched. But when the full moon of Easter was come, the frost eased gently, and was gone by degrees, without any one being able to say when; and spring came clear and fair. And at the new moon following, Harvanger lay out on Greenbank with his sheep, and he saw a man stride out of the wood, and stalk towards him. He was not so great as the golden-bearded one, but yet a right great man, of middle height and slender, closely knit and stark. His eyes were as blue as heaven; his hair deep ruddy brown; and he was lean and muscular and well-trained, and seamed over his face with ancient scars. On his head was a helm, and he

[17]

bore a great round shield, so that he looked like a man used to faring in war. Harvanger was puzzled at him, for he looked in some manner strange; but soon he saw why this should be, in that the man bore his shield on his right arm, and his sword was bound to his right side, which is against all usage and custom. Thus he came near to Harvanger.

And he said: "Fair boy, which is the road to the Scaur Gap?"

Said Harvanger: "All thy folk wend by the east hence."

"How knowest thou that?" asked he.

"They pass by Greenbank in this season of the year," answered Harvanger, "and they tell me somewhat of whither they go. And when any of thy folk passeth, I am bidden to ask thereof. Wilt thou not tell me of the Best Thing in the World?"

"Right well should it be for thee if thou knewest," quoth the man, laughing quietly.

"Wilt thou not tell me?" questioned Harvanger.

"Yea and nay. Betide there shall come one of my folk, and him thou may'st ask."

"How shall I know him?" said Harvanger.

"Easily," said the champion. "Thou shalt have little doubt when he cometh, for he is chief of us all in craft and understanding. Right old is he withal, and knoweth when to speak and when to be silent."

. [18]

Harvanger pondered.

"Friendly have thy folk been to me," he said.

Answered the champion: "Then luck has fallen in thy way; albeit it is not always clear beforehand where luck lieth."

He sat on the green-sward, and took food from a bag; for neither would he go to the house for meat and ale. Harvanger saw that he had but a left hand; the right was clean shorn away not far above the wrist; and much would he have liked to ask why this should be so, deeming it a hurt gotten in battle. But he forbore; because although the champion spoke him fairly and seemed nowise unfriendly, yet there was a look in his eyes fierce and cruel. He moved little, but gazed afar, like a wolf keen in watching, and ever there flitted across his bronzed and scarred visage a gleam that twitched the corners of his lips. Harvanger thought that he dreamed of war.

They fell to speech presently, and the champion asked him many questions of the desire of his heart; and told him many strange tales of the great world —of wars, and forays, and ford-watchings, and battles—most wonderful they were. Harvanger smiled, and listened eagerly, but said that these things he cared little for. And in the end the champion rose, and said:

"I am quit of thee, then!"

And he strode on his way. Harvanger saw the long blade that hung from his belt; it was richly

[19]

enamelled and wrought; he felt wonder at it. So
the champion departed; nor did Harvanger greatly
long for his company. But now he set himself to
watch for the one who should come. This was the
seventeenth year of his age, and he felt in his heart
that new days were stepping towards him. He
was fain to see the chief of that great folk.

## CHAPTER II.: THE COMING OF WAY-WISE.

THE year wound as before; but the weather
changed, for since that champion departed
the sky was not often clear. Not that there was
much rain; blue mists crept over the bents, and
lay in the wood lawns. The sun came seldom, and
the corn ripened ill and late. Harvanger had less
joy than before, and knew not why. The winter
was stormy and warm and hateful; and spring
brought no better days. Yet Harvanger felt the
rise of the year; for as the sap goes up in the tree,
so rises the blood of a young man.

It was not until the Easter moon was gone, that
the spring gales blew. They rattled down
through the yet bare trees, and waved the grass
that was hardly green yet. After a week the
clouds scudded low, and the wind got to work;
the wildest of storms raged over the land; not seldom Harvanger heard the sound of it in the woods
broken by the crash of some kingly tree. His

father said that it was an ill year; for the land was all sodden with a bleak rain, and things went awry.

On a night near the time of the new moon, they had betaken themselves to bed. Harvanger lay in a loft under the thatch, on a bed of hay and bracken; which was the best of sleeping places, albeit rough. Towards midnight the gale waxed suddenly greater than ever before, till the little house shook and trembled, and from without he heard the snapping of trees, and as it were the confused shouting and crying of many people, and the huge windy roar of the blast sweeping over all the land. He waked and pondered quietly in his mind, and listened to the storm. Not long had he lain awake, when the wind lulled awhile, and he heard a loud knocking on the door below. He sprang up, and down his ladder, and opened the door. The wind came surging in, and he saw a man in the doorway, tethering a great white horse to the door staple. Harvanger beckoned him in, and shut the door.

The man was mighty tall; Harvanger's head came no higher than his shoulder. He wore a hat braided up from his eyes, and a cloak of blue. Harvanger thought that it was as he had been told; for this was the chief man of that strange folk who had passed by Greenbank. When he flung off his cloak, Harvanger was abashed, for never yet had he seen a man so like to what he had heard of the kings of the earth; deep and broad of

[21]

chest he was, full of throat, fine of waist, slim and narrow of hip, and firm on his feet as a stag. A forked white beard fell to his breast; he was gaunt and sinewy, and had but one eye, which was grey and piercing, like a hawk's. Withal he had a nose somewhat hooked, so that he seemed more than ever of the hawk kind. He sat down in a chair by the fire, which he stirred to warm his hands. Harvanger stood by and wondered.

Then presently the man turned round quickly, and looked at Harvanger with his keen one eye. Neither spoke awhile. They measured each other up and down. So the man said:

"What thinkest thou of me, Harvanger?"

"Thou art passing wise of wit," said Harvanger.

"Wherefore?" asked he.

"In that thou knowest my name."

"No wiser than thou art," answered he, "in that thou knowest my folk and my kindred."

"Let it be so," said Harvanger.

The man turned to the fire again, but not for long.

"What shall I pay for my guesting?" he questioned.

"What thou mayst think fit."

"Why so?" he demanded, flashing a hawklike glance at Harvanger.

"I do not measure the wealth of men unknown," said Harvanger.

So he fetched rye-bread, and cheese, and ale, and

placed them on the table, together with a tallow candle. So when the man had eaten and drunken, they drew to the fire once more; they seemed to know that much was to be asked and said.

"My name is Way-wise," said the man. "Thus shalt thou call me."

"Guest Way-wise," said Harvanger, "knowest thou the way to the Scaur Gap?"

"Yea," said he.

"Tell me thereof, if it seem good."

"All ways go to the Scaur Gap," answered Way-wise. "There is land before it and land behind it. Wise men go by fair roads, fools by foul."

Harvanger pondered over this. "Which is the best way?" he asked.

"That which the wise men taketh," said Way-wise.

"Long is thy wit," said Harvanger, shortly.

Way-wise laughed. "Dost thou understand this manner of speech?" he demanded.

"What I know not I will learn," answered Harvanger. "But whither wendest thou?"

"To the Scaur Gap."

Said Harvanger: "Who shall first reach it, thou or thy friends?"

"I shall, by rights; but belike I may turn aside; for many a matter is mine to do."

"Do you all journey by one way?"

"Nay," said Way-wise; "for one will go by

burg and court, and one by farm and field, and the third by tower and trench."

"And thou?"

Way-wise laughed again. "What thinkest thou, Harvanger? Which road ought mine to be?"

"The way of the wise, as thou hast said."

"But which is that?" said Way-wise.

"Did I know, I had taken it long since," answered Harvanger.

"O, thou art already on the road!" quoth Way-wise; and he laughed aloud.


"No man has told me yet that I am wise," said Harvanger, resting his face on his hands, and looking at Way-wise.

"How should they?" he answered; "for then they had been as wise as thou. It taketh the wise to see wisdom. When a man praiseth thee, he is thy master."

Said Harvanger: "Howbeit, I know not the way to the Scaur Gap."

Said Way-wise: "Wait till need comes; for when it comes, thou shalt know it quickly; and when thou hast gained it, thou shalt name the place without mistake. Many a man has passed over the Scaur Gap and known it not."

They were silent a space. Then Harvanger said: "The desire of the heart cometh not to those who abide still."

[24]

"O, true," said Way-wise. "Why prayest thou not for evil times?"

"Why should I?"

Quoth Way-wise: "Because the most joy is on the other side of the most evil. Night comes before dawn, winter before spring, and labour before rest."

"Much do I desire the Best Thing in the World," said Harvanger. "What it is I know not. I only know that I desire it. There is something lacking in life: this land hath a dream cast over it."

Answered Way-wise: "What we know is what hath passed from us; what we know not is that which we have and hold. Go thou and seek it."

Harvanger gazed on him with thought.

"Thou art a strange man," he said, "neither do I understand thy words. But I will bear them in mind."

"Well," said Way-wise, "lay thy mind upon this matter. Treasure the words I speak: for I have told thee of many things little thought of amongst men. That which thou desirest most is the Best Thing in the World; and what thou desirest most is the measure of thy manhood. What it is, thou art. And," said he, "all wise things are cast in the shape of riddles, as was known of old: so that men might learn according to their own wisdom. Only the fool thinks that wisdom is an open book."

Therewith he reached his hand behind him, and drew a small harp from his cloak. He tuned it, and ran his fingers over the strings.

"Shall I sing to thee?" he said.

"Yea," answered Harvanger.

"Have a care," quoth Way-wise: "I may harp the heart out of thee. Dost thou fear nought?"

"I deem thee a friend," said Harvanger: "if thy friendship is fierce, I can abide it."

Way-wise pursed his lips, without smiling, and began his prelude. Harvanger heard the storm die into a breathless quietude, and rise again, as though it stepped hand in hand with that wild and stormful music. For first he sang gently of what was before all worlds, and of the divine wisdom of Buri; and of how the Norns ordained dooms, and Buri crossed those dooms with his own will. And when he sang of Odin and the Aesir, and the strife of the gods that are of will and spirit with the giants that are of clay and flesh, and the making of the green earth thereof, and the building of God-home. Then he chanted a war measure of the strife and stress of men, until Harvanger grew faint with the longing of it; and he sang of the mingling of shields, and the deeds of champions, and the joy wherewith they fall, till nothing seemed so good to Harvanger as this. But Way-wise sang on, and told now of the counting of the slain, and the bearing of the dead to bale, and the returning home of the champions to wife and maid.

And he told of the knitting of hands, and the desire of eyes, and the kiss that was given and taken;
until Harvanger longed for the love of women
that he had never known, and there were tears in
his eyes.  But still Way-wise sang on unpausing,
of the turning of the seasons, and the waxing and
waning of the years; the sowing and the reaping,
and the quiet love in peaceful days, and the ordering of life, until Harvanger changed again and
longed most of all for this.  Then Way-wise lifted
up his voice and swept his harp till the house was
filled with sound; and he sang a great song of triumph in the long wisdom of the hoary elders, and
the years that they had, and the knowledge of the
hearts of men and women, and the great learning
that came with age, when all things are known, and
the cup of this world is at last filled.  And Harvanger yearned for this with the whole of his heart.
And then suddenly he knew not what it was that
Way-wise was singing; all grew dim and misty, but
radiant with light and sweet sound.  And he felt
a great joy and passionate desire, and drooped his
head upon the table.  A cold wind blew upon his
hands, and he sprang up.  Way-wise had lifted
the latch, and was slipping forth into the storm.

"Stay," cried Harvanger.

"I have paid my guesting, friend," quoth Way-
wise.  "The coin is good."

## CHAPTER III.: THE DEPARTURE OF HAR-VANGER FROM GREENBANK.

BUT Harvanger strode to the door. He felt suddenly strong. The fire flickered, but the wind had blown the candle out. Therewith he saw two mice, one red and the other white in colour, that ran over the beaten clay, and so thence out of the door. He rushed forth, and the wind flung his long hair about his face. Yonder was the tall white horse, and although Harvanger cried aloud to him, Way-wise made no stay, but mounted up in haste, and climbed into the saddle. And it seemed as though he and the white horse had dissolved into the driving rain-mist, and a strong wind blew them all away.

So Harvanger stopped at the gate of the garth-wall. He looked to the west, and a single star twinkled. He looked to the east, and the white rim of the dawn was pushing up. The wind began to drop swiftly, and he knew that the storms of spring were over.

At first he doubted that he had been dreaming, for a veil had fallen from his eyes, and a weight from his limbs. He felt fresh, as one may feel in .the early morning. Withal, all things seemed as commonly; nothing was changed. He thought that he must have dreamed of the tall Way-wise

[28]

and his harping. Yet when he fared into the
house, and saw the meal on the table, and the
empty bowls, he fell to thought again, for now he
knew surely that Way-wise had been there. It
was strange.

Then, as the clear light grew, he began to wonder how it was that although he had arisen in the
middle of the night, to open to the knocking, and
talked long to the guest, and heard that mighty
harping, his father and mother had slept peace-
fully, though keen folk of hearing. He doubted
again, and was in two minds over the matter. So
he went to the great locked-bed, and threw it open.
There they lay, cheek by cheek, covered with the
rough cloth that he had thought very fine once, but
that now seemed sweetly humble and poor, as of
pure and valiant lives, but nowise great or fine.
He had never looked into the locked-bed before,
save when it was empty; and he recoiled somewhat
with trouble in his heart. Yet neither started up,
nor opened eye.

Harvanger went back to the stoop, and stood
there watching the light grow. His dog was there,
wagging its tail, and gazing at him with lolling
tongue. After a while he returned, and gazed at
the open bed; he touched his father's shoulder.
A fear hung upon him that was not quite a fear;
he sat down by the fire. But presently he must
needs return again, and pull them by the arm;
for indeed he could not believe that they were not

[29]

sleeping, so quietly did they lie there; and death he had never seen yet, and hardly heard of. Strangely young they looked, and strangely beautiful. He closed the bed.

The day broke apace, and soon all the land was light, and a sun shining—the first he had seen that spring. Harvanger wandered out into the garth, and looked over the pen at the pigs, and round the house he went, many times. All was very silent and lonely; he had not known it so before. Even the woods seemed lonely, which aforetime had been friendly to him. About noon he saw a man coming across the bent; one in a draggled brown coat, carrying a shell in his hat, and singing a stave in some outland tongue that Harvanger knew not. Anon he came to the door.

"In the name of God," quoth he. "I am a poor pilgrim lost in yester-night's storm. I pray you bread and ale, for I am nigh famished."

Harvanger beckoned him in and pointed to the lock-bed.

"God be with them and receive them," quoth the pilgrim, fingering beads on a string, "for I perceive that none other help may they have. How did this come to pass?"

"I know not," said Harvanger.

"Belike it was the close bed," quoth he kindly. And he spoke comfortingly as he might; so that if he were no very wise man, yet he helped somewhat by his good will. He was a small man and a sallow, but he was some comfort.

So when he had departed on his way, after he had offered all his help, and when Harvanger knew that his parents were dead, the young man closed all the doors, leaving the house as it was. Then he called his dog, and saddled the horse, and opened the pens; and when all was ready, set a brand to the thatch. He waited till the house was aflame, and then got an acorn. He made a hole with his knife in the ground, put in the acorn, and covered it up, and said to himself: "Here beginneth a new life."

In the afternoon he set out on his way, driving the sheep and pigs, and his tears fell into the grass as he walked, though he knew it not.

And in this wise Harvanger set out to find the Best Thing in the World.

# BOOK II.: THE SPOTTED DEER RUNS IN GREENWOOD.

## CHAPTER I.: HARVANGER COMES TO THE SIGN OF THE PARTING WAYS.

HARVANGER fared southward over the downs, and in the night slept under the sparkling stars. So long he walked, that at last he met folk who pointed out the road to a market borough, where he could sell his pigs and sheep: and they stared at him somewhat curiously withal, but of that he knew nothing.

He wended on over the downs until they began to slope southward. He could see a forest on the sky-line. After three or four days, he came to the little burgh where the market was; but they told him that market day was Thursday, and this but a Tuesday. So he waited without the town, till Thursday came, and then he entered in with his sheep and pigs, and stood near the cross in the market place. He gazed about and marvelled greatly, and deemed it to be the greatest city in the world, although in truth it was but small; and he watched the people coming and going, and their dress; and all was strange to his eyes. The cross was graven with figures, and much he wondered what that might betoken, for the figures were as if alive.

Many stopped to stare at him, but none bought: and he waited nearly until sundown, when a ruddy-faced carle approached, and said:

"Ho, friend—art thou minded to sell?"

"Yea, truly," said Harvanger.

"Come forth, then, and chaffer."

Now Harvanger knew nothing of chaffer, nor of what his herds were worth; nor would he chaffer much over them. Yet the carle was passing honest, and paid as true a tale of money as any man was like to do in such dealing. So at nightfall Harvanger was glad to be quit of his cares, and wandered over the burgh, ever finding some new and wonderful thing to ponder over. And at last he must seek food and lodging; so he perceived a house with a sign over it, and many little shields above the lintel, painted in colours. He deemed this an hostel; and such it was. He entered therein, and found folk sitting about, and drinking, and talking together. Harvanger sat down apart, and thought over his life, and how times had changed suddenly, as Way-wise had foretold. Bitter was his heart then: for he was lonely and unhappy, and had no friend or fellow. But a short time he had sat when the host marked him. A very stout man he was, and withal cheerful of heart, as stout men are wont to be. He came forward from the fire.

"What!" said he, "thou drinkest not mine ale,
and hast a face longer than a fiddle. Hath chaf-
fering gone ill with thee?"

"Nay," said Harvanger.

"Then little else do I know of, to make a man
sad. Come, drink—and if thou wilt, tell me thy
woes. I am the man to counsel thee in all manner
of things. I know all the roads, and the burghs,
and the names of kings, and gentles, and poor
people, and their fashion of business. I deem thee
a stranger—else would'st thou know John Taberner of the Sign of the PARTING WAYS. I am
all men's friend."

"I thank thee," said Harvanger, wondering.

But John Taberner led him to a seat by the
great hearth, and drew an earthen jug full of
brown ale, and so fell to talking. Harvanger
listened, and presently forgot the keen edge of his
grief, for John Taberner, in his rough way, was
a cheerful man.

Said John: "Now, friend, if thou would'st
know of ways through the world, ask; for it should
go hard but I might tell thee what thou desirest."

"Hast thou heard of a place called the Scaur
Gap?" said Harvanger.

"Nay," answered John: "no place is there,
called by that name, for many a day's journey
round here."

"I journey to seek it," said Harvanger.

"Then go thou into Long Whitewall, where all

men congregate.   If there be such a place, at Long
Whitewall thou shalt hear of it."

Then he told Harvanger of a mighty city that
lay four days' journey to the south; and it was
called Long Whitewall.   He told him also of the
roads that led hither, and of the places that were
on the way.   Harvanger had much wonder at all
these things.   But he asked:

"What meanest thou, by speaking of the Sign
of the PARTING WAYS?"

"Forsooth," said John, "that is the name and
sign of this hostel; and none better there is, within
the whole burgh."

Said Harvanger:   "Never yet have I heard of
a house called by a name, as a man is."

"Thou comest from outlandish parts," said
John, "for all hostelries have a sign, else men
would know them not as such: and the sign has
a name.   Come."

He led Harvanger into the street, and pointed
to the copper sign that creaked in the wind.   It
was made like the letter Y, and was skilfully
wrought.

"Lo," he said, "this sign betokens a road that
forks, and the sign is therefore named the Parting
Ways.   Five golden ducats it cost me, and I deem
it cheap."

"Where are the ways?" asked Harvanger.

"I know not," said John, "nor doth any man
know for a certainty.   But a tale is told that in

ancient times a great folk dwelt here, who came
from the South; and after a while they departed,
and some went to the west, and some to the north,
whence cometh this name and sign. Yet as I say,
I know not truly how it was, for some men deem it
signifieth but the cross-ways in Greenwood."

"What mean these?" asked Harvanger, pointing to the little coloured shields over the
lintel.

"These are small shields," quoth the host, "like
those of which men of noble birth bear, and they
hang up to show that mine hostel hath harboured
great men in its time." So he told Harvanger
their names, and of the men whose armoury was
blazoned on them, and much else, that Harvanger
wondered at even more than before. Then they
went back into the room, and Harvanger ate sup-
per with the folk who abided there, and John
Taberner talked amain, for he dearly loved a
stranger, to whom he might tell all he knew.
But Harvanger presently fell into a dreaming
mood, and heard but little; and some half-remem-
bered, half-forgotten tale formed anew in his mind,
about a folk that had come from the south, and
departed again, leaving some behind. He thought
they were a mighty great folk as to fairness and
valour, and that it might be he belonged to them;
for he saw that the burghers and country-people
were not as he had fancied in his mind they would
be. They were middle-sized and dark, but Har-

[39]

vanger was tall and golden of hair. He knew not where he had heard this tale before.

CHAPTER II.: PARANIDES ALSO COMES TO THE PARTING WAYS.

B Y now the dusk was coming apace, and the evening sky shone blue and brilliant through the little latticed windows, that were flung wide open. A golden star hung in the west, over streaks of quiet purple cloud; and Harvanger saw the spire of the church, with its gilt vane turning round and round. The ceiling of the room was low, and thick oaken beams ran from side to side, with odd tackle hung from them, as bacon-hams, and nets of onions. On the table were earthenware tankards, and pewter polished bright, and tall jugs. Harvanger liked the place well enough.

But as he sat in the growing dimness, he heard a great noise in the street; the trampling of hoofs over the cobbles, the whinnying of horses, besides men laughing and talking—and a strange sound he had never heard before. Therewith a loud voice rang out:

"Ho, John," it called. "John Taberner."

"Hah," quoth John, making shift to run, for all his portliness; "the Seneschal is here."

He went forth into the street, and parleyed; but the folk in the hostel rose up hastily, taking their

[40]

jugs and tankards, and departed by a little door. Harvanger sat where he was, for he knew of no reason why he should go; and he was well at his ease there. Anon a man with a cap of crimson velvet entered, and sat down by the hearth on the same bench, but, because Harvanger was in the deep shadow, saw him not. A strong and bull-necked man he looked, brown of face and heavy of jaw. He was all clean shaven of visage, and besides the crimson cap he wore a riding dress of the same, with golden lilies thereon, and great yellow boots spurred with gold. Round his neck was a golden chain, and his riding gauntlets he had tossed upon the table before sitting down.

Then came ten or twelve men with body-armour, and salets on their heads. They were arrayed in many different colours, as green, and red, and blue; and some had their dress all of one colour, but others had it parti-wise, or in stripes; and all bore on their breasts a badge of blue, with a golden lily embroidered. They crowded in and talked in loud voices, and one sang a snatch of song.

"Bring ale, John," cried the Seneschal, "and candles."

The host set a tankard before him, and he drank. But when the candles were alight, the Seneschal saw Harvanger sitting at the other end of the bench.

"John," he said, "what meaneth this? Did I

[41]

not tell thee to turn out every one, that I might sup undisturbed?"

"He is but a stranger, Messire Seneschal," answered John. "He knew not the ways of the house."

"Amend it," quoth the Seneschal, turning his eyes away.

So John came and whispered to Harvanger, that he should depart thence quickly, into another room, lest the Seneschal take the matter ill. Harvanger liked this little, nor the Seneschal much more.

"Nay," said he, "I am well here."

"How?" said the Seneschal, when he understood that Harvanger would not go; "am I to sup with peasants? Depart, young man."

"Nay," said Harvanger. "I harm thee not."

"Seest thou these men?" demanded the Seneschal, pointing to the men of arms. "At my word, they shall fling thee forth into the street."

He beckoned therewith, and two bronzed spearmen came forward. When Harvanger saw this, he grasped his staff, that lay on the bench; and rose up before the fire.

"Messire Seneschal," said he, "I have done thee no wrong. Better would it be to leave well alone."

It should have fallen out ill with Harvanger then, for all the other men of arms turned as soon as they heard voices raised; but the door flew open,

and the sound of a sweet triumphant voice singing came through it.

> "Full far abroad erstwhile I fared,
> And many a deed of dread I dared;
> 'Neath gilded vanes and burning skies
> I found my foes to fight arise."

A very tall and noble man entered; Harvanger
saw the doorway filled with a flame of steel and
crocus-colour. The Seneschal put down his tankard, and turned half round.

"Ha, Paranides," he said, jestingly, "thou
comest in a good time. Here is a champion to try
thy mettle."

Paranides was a man of the north; he bore his
birth written on his blue eyes and mighty shoulders.
From his neck to his knee fell a tinkling, rustling,
cataract of mail, over which was a côte hardie the
colour of the yellow crocus, embroidered with
many little black ravens. Steel plates guarded his
thighs, and half his legs besides; but underneath
showed hose of purpure, and shoes of the same
colour, with golden spurs of knighthood upon the
heels. As to his face, it was never easily forgotten, partly because of the keen, steady eyes, but
most of all because of its great beauty. Withal
there was something evil in it, and something cruel
and cold in the pure thin lips, and a hard set in
the slim jaw, that was as if carved in marble.
He had long, tapering, flexible fingers, white on

[43]

the back, but hard as horn on the palm side, where weapons had frayed them. And he had thick and clustering chestnut hair, and a clear voice, which now and then rang like a trumpet, or sang with the sweetness of a bird's.

Said he: "Ha, Seneschal, I deem thee over-matched, as thou sayest."

"I said not so," answered the Seneschal, lifting his tankard again.

Paranides looked upon Harvanger where he stood before the fire; then set his salet, with its nodding crocus plume, upon the table, and took up his stand beside Harvanger, laying a hand upon his shoulder.

"Peace," he said. "Put down thy staff, boy. Thinkest thou it were possible to overcome with it all these armed men?"

"Nay," answered Harvanger, reddening.

"Lo," said Paranides, heaving up three feet of glittering blade from his scabbard; "with this sword I have cast down kings. How then may you prevail against me?"

The Seneschal laughed hoarsely.

"That weapon is known through three king-doms, boy," he said, without looking round. "For it is THE DEATH OF MEN."

Harvanger looked from one to the other. Paranides thrust his sword back, but kept his fingers on Harvanger's shoulder, as though he would have him remain, and not depart.

[44]

"Whence art thou?" he questioned.

Said Harvanger: "Erstwhile I dwell on Green-bank."

"Where is that?"

"Four days journey north and west."

Paranides pushed him suddenly, so that Harvanger all but fell back upon the bench.

"Ha, Seneschal," he said, shaking his head, "thou art a fisher of strange fish."

The Seneschal put down his tankard, and turned round to look upon Paranides.

"What meanest thou, Messire?" he demanded.

Harvanger deemed his manner betokened little ease of soul, whatever that might spring from. But Paranides shook his head again, albeit he forbore to make answer. So after a little while the Seneschal took up his tankard, and gazed within it at the spare inch of brown ale left, circled with a ring of foam. Yet he put it back on the board again, and said to Paranides:

"You men of the north are over fond of riddles. I like it less than nothing at all."

Paranides shook his head again, but smiled thoughtfully. He sang in a clear voice:

> "Three kings against me came,
> Three kings with swords right keen,
> Three kings with swords of flame
> As I dwelt in the woodland green."

The men of arms looked over their shoulders

[45]

when they heard his voice, and Harvanger thought they were all smiling. The Seneschal rested his thick elbow on the table, and scowled to himself, as if he knew well what was toward, and found no joy therein.

"Whither art thou going, lad?" inquired Paranides, anon.

"All ways in the world," said Harvanger.

"Which, being translated, meaneth Nowhere. All roads lead to Long Whitewall."

"There are places beyond," said Harvanger.

"Not for every man," said the Seneschal.

"Let be, Messire," quoth Paranides. "Thy tongue would break an ox's back. Hearken, lad, —hast thou any taste in dress? I mean, any liking for one livery rather than another?"

Harvanger thought it wisest to say no.

"Which likes you best," said Paranides; "red, with golden lilies, or gold, semée of ravens sable?"

The Seneschal looked at Harvanger, awaiting his answer with a lowering brow.

"I have mine own ways to fare," said Harvanger.

Paranides clapped him on the shoulder.

"Go they near to Long Whitewall?" he asked.

"I know not, as yet," said Harvanger.

"By Mary of Long Whitewall," said Paranides, "no fairer man could wear the golden gown than thou."

"Messire Paranides," said Harvanger, "thou

shalt not win me with such lures as these. I bid thee good night."

"I thought so," said the Seneschal.

Paranides smiled as steadily as before.

"I wish thee well," he answered, "and not ill."

Harvanger deemed he lied, and liked him no more than he did the Seneschal; for Paranides was an evil man. So, paying no heed to their words, Harvanger betook himself to the inner rooms, and wished he had gone thither at first. When he passed through the door, John Taberner stood there.

"Lad," said he, "it had been better to have abided by my counsel, and departed."

"Truly, John," said Harvanger, "I deem thee right."

"Hearken," quoth John. "To-night thou shalt lie here, and the quarter of a silver penny shall be thy reckoning. But to-morrow, rise early, and depart hence or ever the Seneschal is abroad."

"I thank thee," said Harvanger.

John was silent awhile, gazing upon him.

"Thou bearest strange tales, and stranger deeds that have been, and are yet to be, on that face of thine."

"How so?" said Harvanger.

"O, nay," he answered. "I mean nought at all more than thou knowest thyself."

Harvanger thought of many things.

[47]

## CHAPTER III.: PARANIDES WALKS IN THE GARDEN.

HE slept well that night, on a bed of thick hay, and when the dawn was breaking gloriously over the woods he arose, and stepped forth into the garden. A trellis of creeping roses ran across it, with the roses just budding. Harvanger had but just issued into the flowery close it made, when he was aware of Paranides standing under the trellis. He had been plucking buds to stick round his yellow bonnet; but no sooner had he espied Harvanger than he donned it, and cast the remaining buds at him in a handful.

"All joy fall to thy lot, as do these roses," he said, smiling.

"What art thou doing, Messire?" said Harvanger.

Said Paranides: "Three joys there are in the world, and I name them thus: War, Song, and Flowers. Song is best at eve, war at noon, and flowers when the dew is on them, which cometh to pass in the morning. Therefore am I risen, that I may gather them to my heart's content. How say ye?"

"I thought there were more things of worth to be gotten than those," said Harvanger.

"As what?" demanded Paranides.

"Men . . ." said Harvanger, coming to pause.

[48]

Paranides ran his arm under the arm of Harvanger, and paced him slowly up and down before the roses.

"I know what is in thine heart, boy," said he, "for once I thought so too; but times have changed, and the world is different to me. Thou would'st say, that there is love of men and women, kind looks and loving thoughts; the hand pressure of friends and the heart pressure of mistresses. Yea, it is true; I need none to tell me, as though it were a wisdom I had not known before." He said also, drily: "What would ye, friend, when I am grown so base, and have so dulled the fountains of my life, that I ride with the Seneschal? I did thee wrong last night. Thou art not a man to be caught with a flutter of silk and steel. Hearken, then. Hast thou heard my name spoken of?"

"Nay," said Harvanger.

Said Paranides: "I deemed as much, or else would ye not be walking here, thine arm in mine. I am the captain of a Free Company. No eye is so keen as mine for the chances of war; no onslaught is so dreaded in battle as that of my gold and sable banner. I have cast down great kings, and trampled on the bravest and the proudest of lineage; yet once I fared forth from my father's house in like manner as thou. I dreamed of love and friendship, and the hope of waxing years; but the dreams faded one by one, till in these days I hold my place by the terror of my name,

[49]

and the strength of my right arm. It may be so with thee."

"Nay," said Harvanger.

"Hearken again," he answered. "Not soon shall ye find a man as great as I, who will dream of his past youth when he beholdeth thee. I say, join my company, learn the craft of war and the ways of men. Learn the manner of harping and singing, and the bearing of a knight; for my heart goes out to thee, and I wish thy luck in the world, and to behold thee growing in might and manhood." He said: "How seemeth that? Good or ill?"

"I have other guides," said Harvanger, seeing again in his heart the vision of those who passed by Greenbank.

They turned round, and began to walk back, between the rows of lilies white and tall. As the sun rose higher, it sent rays down athwart the close, and they smote with sudden brightness on the silver and steel of Paranides' war-web.

"All that ye can desire of love and friendship," he said, "lieth in Long Whitewall. There shall ye find waiting all those gentle battles that are the savour of living. There dwell men and women, both fair and foul, good and evil, rich and poor; all that a man needeth to wax in power of love and hate. If ye truly desire the company of men, that ye may love and be loved by the good and noble, and hate and be hated by the evil and base, I counsel thee to follow my leading, and be my man until thou can'st walk alone in the world. Ye shall bear my shield and be my esquire; for presently, I see in thine eyes, thy wisdom shall make thee a leader of men, a ruler of lands, a disposer of menfolk as it were God himself. Would it not be a joy to thee, lad, to gaze abroad from thy tower, when thy beard is waxen grey, and know that all men loved thee for the beauty and the splendour of thy days?"

"Such a thought was in my mind," answered Harvanger.

"Well, what answer do ye give me?"

"I have other guides," said Harvanger.

Paranides' glance strayed over the flowers; he looked up at the little white blossom of a pear tree that shed faint fragrance over the garden. Between its branches a golden ray shone full upon his yellow bonnet and the plume therein. Then he turned and they walked back.

"If it were wisdom, then," he said, "in Long Whitewall men meet together from the four winds, and there dwelleth many a man learned in wise things. Long Whitewall is fairly placed. No harsh snow, no bitter rain, no rough storms come near it. It lies in a fair meadow land, and its towered ramparts go round about, with four great gates therein. Its streets are paved with cobbles; its houses are strange and pleasant, with many carvings upon them; and there are fine fountains,

[51]

and a mighty minster that rises against the blue
of the sky like a thing beheld in dreams.  All the
days of thy life might ye wander in Long Whitewall and its blossoming closes, and never come to
the end of the carven tale and the painted story,
nor even to the end of thine own.  Night by
night should the harp tremble in thine ear, and the
ghosts and dreams of joy begin to march and live;
day by day should the sweetness of sky and earth,
and the work of men's fingers, grow dearer to thee,
and life lovelier; even the map of men's fate
should be unrolled before thee, till the manifold
ages past and to come should be as one tale soon
told.  O friend,—all these things thou may'st
find in Long Whitewall; but without it are cold
heart and hard hand, and the ear that soon for-
gets, and the eye soon turned away from thee.
Thou knowest not," he said, "how grim the world
is, nor what triple brass must sheathe the heart of
him who would prosper in it.  Bitter and deso-
late days will be thine till that lesson is learnt;
I know, for once they came to me.  Take the
beauty of life while ye may, for to-morrow it
may be far from thee."

He had a tongue of gold; Harvanger listened,
and was torn with hope and fear, for it shone before him like a dream that was, and yet was not.
How greatly he longed for such a life; how happy
he would have been in it.

"Then come with me," said Paranides.

[52]

Harvanger looked at him almost fiercely; most fair was Paranides, with the glitter and fall of his mail, and the joyous colour that shone in the golden light; and all about him were flowers and sunshine and the fragrance of the morning breeze, till he flamed and glowed like a fighting angel. But when Harvanger saw his face, a cold fit came upon him; for there was craft and cruelty of heart, as well as strength and gaiety in it, yet not so much that a man must wholly hate him. Harvanger turned thence.

"Nay," he said; "other guides have I got, and other friends in this world."

"Thou knowest not thy loss," said Paranides, "nor mine. Yet I wish thee well . . . being withal a fool for my pains, as I see."

Harvanger answered: "Messire, never will I be thine enemy, if thou art not mine."

Paranides smiled. "A like oath I make to thee," he said. "But it shall go hard if we keep the peace."

He said no more, and Harvanger did not understand his words, but felt rather like one who is hedged with things not clearly seen or known.

## CHAPTER IV.: HARVANGER LIETH OUT ON THE CROSSWAYS IN GREENWOOD.

HARVANGER took his staff and fared forth in the early morning. The streets of the burgh were still and deserted, but spring was wide abroad, and all the world sweet with mingled scents. He felt happier as he moved further away, and Paranides became a dream; happier still when he issued without the burgh, and saw the long white road, and the distant Greenwood, with the blue haze of early morning lying over the tree-tops, as he had known the world before. So now he fared on briskly, his heart grown strangely light. But better was his mood when, after an hour's space, he came to Greenwood's edge, and found the stout oaks and the flowers multitudinous beneath the brake. There he sat down, and gazed back whence he had come. The Little Burgh lay with its roofs shining red, the tall church spire rising from the midst, and its gilded vane wavering at odd moments. Folk were abroad in the fields afar off, and he saw little white specks on the green, that were geese and ducks marching towards their cool green pond. But a short while did Harvanger sit there watching with a smile on his lips. Then he took up his staff and fared on into the shade of Greenwood.

The path was wide, some ten paces or more, yet not so wide as to let the sun grow hot on it. The trees lay on either hand; the deep golden-green shadow behind, with brake that was now blooming, and beds of wild flowers thereunder. There was great plenty of hares and conies, which

[54]

sometimes scurried over the path, and scurried back.

When it had come to noon, Harvanger found himself at cross-roads; for here the way forked, one path going to the left hand, one to the right. It was a pleasant little dell in the wood, covered with thick green grass, and had a brook, that made a pool. Harvanger knew not which way he ought to take if he would reach Long Whitewall; for he had clean forgotten what John Taberner taught him. So he lay down on the grass amid the flowers, and ate, and drank a little wine out of his bottle, and had no care for the morrow. He deemed himself a good twelve mile into the wood. He waited for folk to pass.

About an hour after he heard squeaking and grunting; and lo, a peasant wended up one of the roads, driving pigs that made this music.

"Good day, friend," said Harvanger, when this man was come nigh.

"Good day, friend," quoth he. "What do ye here?"

"Which of these roads goeth unto Long White-wall?" asked Harvanger.

"This that leadeth west away," answered the swineherd.

"Thither I shall go," said Harvanger. "But I know not these parts; whence I waited here for folk who should tell me."

"More folk dwell in this wood than thou deem-est," quoth the swineherd.

"Will they do hurt to good people?"

"For one thing," said the swineherd, "they take no man's oath as to his own virtues. For this they are not held dear by the rich."

"Who be they, then?" demanded Harvanger.

Said the carle: "THE SPOTTED DEER."

Then he bade Harvanger a good morrow, and departed on his way with his pigs.

Harvanger had no haste to be on his feet, but lay kicking his heels, and watching the birds and beasts of the wood. Once there came forth a mighty stag from the thickets, to drink at the pool. Huge and sleek he was. . . . And he saw a band of yeomen pass by on stout nags; and towards evening, in the dusk, Harvanger lay half in dream, and saw a party of burghers ride by him on hack-neys, and ride quick, for that they feared the Spotted Deer. And with them rode a dozen ser-geants with the golden lily of the Duke on their breasts, and long spears. Presently the round red moon rose over the trees, and shone in the blue-black sky. Harvanger wrapped himself in his cloak, and slept sweetly amid the grass and flowers: which was better than at the hostel, and cost nothing.

He awoke in the morning, under the bright sun. He thought he would fare on now; but he lay idly awhile, for the place was sweet, and he had no pressing business, nor much dread of the Spotted Deer. So an hour passed, and he broke his fast, and dreamed day-dreams; and then he heard folk riding.

Therewith two men at arms hove in sight between the trees, as if coming from the Little Burgh. They were mounted on great destriers, and Harvanger saw, by their glittering salets and golden lily badge, that they were of the Seneschal's men. Then he sprang up, and would have slipped into the wood; but the riders had perceived him.

"Ha, Samson," quoth one, "behold the young cockerel of John Taberner's hostel."

"I doubt but he hath been over close to the Spotted Deer," said Samson.

They drew their heavy horses thwartwise across the road, and sat awhile, looking down at him without speaking.

"What shall we do with him?" said Samson.

"Ride thou on," quoth the other. "I will have charge of him."

"Nay, there be those in the wood that are good at shooting, as I deem. I have no mind that the Seneschal should stumble over his avant-guard, stuck through the throat . . . as hath been. The Spotted Deer will not draw on two men."

"I know not as to that," said the other, glancing amid the wood. "But be it as ye will."

[57]

So they waited, while Harvanger lay kicking his heels idly, and smiling at them.

Not long it was before arms glittered amid the trees, and Harvanger saw how the Seneschal came riding with his men, with Paranides by his right hand. They rode over the lawn, and came to stand about Harvanger.

"Whom have we here?" quoth the Seneschal.

"I deem it one of Rafe's folk, Sir Seneschal," said Samson. "But ye should know him best, having had speech with him aforetime."

"Yea," quoth the Seneschal, "and full high shall he hang, if he be of the Spotted Deer."

He turned his brown seamed face round to Paranides, who looked on gravely, but said nought.

"Dickon carrieth a rope, Sir Seneschal," said Samson.

"And yonder do I perceive a good tree," said the Seneschal. "Ask Dickon to fetch his rope." So they fetched it, and the Seneschal said: "A grievous thing it is to hang so fair a youth; but justice cometh before all else."

"By thy leave, Messire," said Paranides, drily, "thou hast as yet put no question to the prisoner."

"What availeth it?" demanded the Seneschal. "He is caught red-handed. Did we not see him at John Taberner's hostel?—and do we not now find him in the very haunt of the Spotted Deer?"

"Then thou must needs hang us all, on that

[58]

evidence," said Paranides. "For we are all in the same boat."

"Truly," quoth the Seneschal, "but we are known men. If Dickon and Samson hold of the Spotted Deer, then even I and thou are not exempt. Fetch the cord."

Harvanger heard all this, and liked it little. He rose up, and picked his staff from the ground; and when he was on his feet, there was none, save Paranides only, who was so strong and tall.

"Seneschal," he said, "retract thy tongue, or thou shalt retract more than it."

"What do ye say?" said the Seneschal.

"I say, Messire," answered Harvanger, "that if Dickon trotteth over fast to me, thou shalt trot faster to Heaven. My staff is iron-shod, and thou art not mailed."

The Seneschal reddened and paled. "Lo, now," said he, "dost thou hear that, Paranides? Now the tale is proven, for well I deem that no man save one that holdeth of the Spotted Deer would speak so boldly."

"Long Whitewall must rule over a starveling land if thou rulest it, Seneschal," said Harvanger.

Then they fell to arguing and talking, all but Paranides, who smiled scornfully from his high seat in the saddle. But anon he caught the Seneschal's bridle, and wheeled their horses away out of ear-shot. They spoke together a short space, while Harvanger stood eyeing the men at arms, and they him. After a moment the Seneschal turned about, and gazed on Harvanger.

"Forsooth," he said, bitterly, "Messire giveth us such fair words as we may not lightly brush aside. So thou shalt go free; but keep clear of Long Whitewall, boy, for when next we meet I shall see to it."

"I thank thee, Seneschal," said Harvanger; "and when next we meet I also will see to it. I will buy something better than an iron-shod staff."

"Ho," said the Seneschal, pausing. "Let Dickon rip his purse up. This is Greenwood, and woodland law runneth here."

Harvanger looked at Paranides, who kept his face averted; he looked at Samson, who had an elm-wood face, scarred and bronzed.

"My money is my own," said he; "and I go on a far journey."

"Thou art a fool," answered Samson, showing his white teeth. "By rights had ye been swinging ere now. Thank Mary of Long Whitewall, and give the money as ransom."

Harvanger thought over the matter; then took out his florins, and threw them under the feet of the Seneschal's horse, whence Samson rescued them. The Seneschal was as black as thunder, but gave Samson his purse withal, into which the florins were put; and then they moved off at a foot's pace, up the western road. Samson caught at his own rein, and turned towards Harvanger.

"Thou art a game-cock, youngling," he said; "but not all game-cocks win their battles." He laughed and spurred after the Seneschal.

Harvanger took his staff and walked along the road that led to Long Whitewall, angry of heart. A little way from the dell the road narrowed, and the trees all but met over-head. Harvanger had not gone far, before he sat down on the bank, and rested his chin in his hands. Sorely he longed to have vengeance on the Seneschal; there seemed no thing so hard but he would do it, and no way so long but he would wend it, if he might have revenge on the Seneschal. But he thought of the great Paranides, and knew that it would take long to bridge the gulf between him and them. They were mighty, and he was feeble; strong men of arms rode behind them, and he was but one, and lacked their wisdom, and knowledge, and skill. He thought that now he would go to some place where he might learn the ways of the world, and how battles were fought, and things brought to pass. The anger in him was good; it made his heart rise; and he felt strong and fearless, and as though there were nothing that could beat him down. And he thought that he could rule the land of Long Whitewall to more profit than the Seneschal; and that this might come to pass. So he felt and thought, when he heard a voice behind him saying:

[61]

"Ho, young man,—what do ye here, sitting by the way?"

He started up; and in the long grass behind, half-hidden by the bole of a tree, stood a tall and lean man with a scanty beard, and keen black eyes, and a long, thin nose. Forty years of age he might have been; and he was clad in a faded green jerkin, and thereon the likeness of a spotted deer of the Greenwood, all but worn away. He stood knee-deep in the flowery bracken, leaning on the lengthiest and thickest bow Harvanger had ever seen. A sheaf of arrows peeped over his shoulder.

## CHAPTER V.: THE GREENWOOD MEN.

HARVANGER gazed at the bowman awhile, and then said: "I deem thou art of the Spotted Deer."

"Who knoweth?" said he, coolly.

"If it be so," answered Harvanger, "an enemy of thine hath passed close by, and thou sawest him not."

"What mean ye, young man?" demanded the bowman. "By what name is this enemy called?"

Said Harvanger: "His name is Seneschal."

Light came into the bowman's eyes. "Ha," said he; "and is this true? Hath the Seneschal veritably passed on this road? How many of men had he?"

"Some twelve, as I have seen," said Harvanger; "and they have despoiled me." Then he held up his empty wallet.

"Yea," quoth the bowman, grimly. "That looketh somewhat like business. The Seneschal would hang himself for a rogue, if he did justice to all men. Knowest thou woodcraft?"

"Passing well," said Harvanger.

"Then follow thou me."

Harvanger climbed up the brake, and plunged into the long grass and the hare-bells. The Greenwood man set out swiftly through the thickets, and Harvanger followed him. Now they slipped along by a tiny path, and therefrom broke across the wood, creeping under bushes, and climbing past fallen trunks. The trees were great and thick, and the underwood full of thorn, and berry-bushes; and the ground rose up and fell down into all manner of cunning nooks and dells, so that a man must needs have good knowledge of the place, or else would he have been utterly mazed and lost. The Greenwood man looked behind him often, but when he saw that Harvanger was able to follow hard on his heels, he went more and more swiftly, till Harvanger panted with the creeping and running. Then, after about a quarter of an hour, they came into a little dell, wherein was a brook. This they crossed, climbed up the bent, and so down into a lawn, which spread out fairly, bordered with tall forest trees. Harvanger per-

[63]

ceived a pavilion of blue and yellow pitched at the further end; and in front of it a lady sitting in a chair, and a knight lying on the grass at her feet, playing on a harp.

When they came near, the knight ceased his harping, and sat up.

"Ha, Will," said he; "do ye bring tidings?"

"The Seneschal and Paranides are in the wood, Rafe," answered Will, "and eleven men of arms. This youth hath seen them."

Rafe put down his harp and arose. A short man he was, and not lovely, but dark of eye and hair, and strongly built; and his face was bronzed and seamed with scars. Withal, he was marvellously strong and fierce of mien, and Harvanger thought the lady passing fair.

"This cometh of feasting and revel," said Rafe. "We were long abed this bright morning. Come, Kate, arm me; and thou, boy, tell me what thou hast seen."

So Harvanger told him; and anon Rafe was armed at all points in mail of black steel. Then the lady kissed him, and placed a plumed basnet upon his head, and bound a sword to his side. And Will blew up a great horn that hung from a chain. Therewith came a short man with red cheeks, called Roger of Cold Haven—a man in a green coat, with the Spotted Deer on it. He strode round the pavilion and stood before Rafe.

"Roger," quoth he, "the Seneschal and Paranides ride in Greenwood. We missed them at the Crossways. What shall be devised to remedy it?"

"They cannot pass the Four Oaks but we shall know of it," said Roger. "I sent five good bowmen down to the Hermitage, and if they see not to Paranides, by Mary, I will see to them."

"Let us go to the Four Oaks," said Rafe.

Now the Spotted Deer began to run. Roger and Will struck through the thick of the forest, taking Harvanger with them. The sun was half-way up the sky, and nearing noon; all the dells and glades were full of golden light, and the tangles were flecked with rays that filtered down. A gentle wind stirred the leaves, and blew in Harvanger's face. It was a day of gold.

Such speed they made, that in half an hour they were creeping down a wooded slope that was piled high with bushes. A little path wound thereamong, and the twisted oak-roots made as it were steps. All the odour of the forest was in Harvanger's nostrils and beneath his feet he saw black earth. The bowmen pulled the bushes apart, and climbed and crept until they came to the bottom of the dell. Then they saw the road winding along; and there were other men lurking in the brake, with great bows.

Said Roger: "Lo, the Four Oaks." And Harvanger beheld four ancient trees set circle-wise, not far from the road. Roger went out into the road, and presently returned, smiling. Thereupon the bowmen took up stances, scattermeal among bush and tree, some on the slope, some on the flat, but all as still as mice, and well hidden, yet with space to draw and loose. Harvanger crouched down on the grass. So they waited in the hot morning tide.

Not very long had they waited, when Roger appeared from behind a bush, making a sign. Then came two men at arms, in their salets; Harvanger saw their golden lily badge. They passed by unharmed, ever searching to left and right watchfully. When they had gone, there was a dreadful stillness for a while; even the forest fell quite silent. Then sounded the clink of harness, and the black and yellow of Paranides flamed amid the bushes, as he rode at a foot's pace beside the Seneschal. Before and behind were the spearmen on their huge war-horses, and with long lances rising fifteen-foot overhead; but Paranides and the Seneschal stood out before all. The Seneschal rode silently, with head down-bent, and plume nodding forward; but Paranides gaily, singing little staves of song, and ever he caught idly at the stray leaves which trailed across his polished headpiece. The little black ravens were marshalled throughout his yellow surcoat; the mightiest and boldest of men he looked; and Harvanger held his breath to see him.

Therewith came the short note of a horn; and the shower of shafts, and the up-rising of the

Greenwood men. Quick and hard they drew; the arrows flashed over and through the brake, like beams of light. The coursers plunged beneath the bitter fleeting shafts; they rose up and fell down screaming, so that Harvanger heard them for many a day after; and the riders came crashing to the cold earth, with a great wavering and entangling of the long lances, and blood ran over the grass. The Seneschal was the first to fall, and lay pinned, and across him fell more than one other, and the lance staves. But Paranides was, as ever, in arms of proof. While the shower rained into and about him, he closed the ventail of his helmet, and stood stiffening and tense, fingering his bridle reins, and all about his horse's hoofs was wrack and ruin. . . . Then the Greenwood men ceased of their shooting, and scrambled out of their covert, and waded through the brake of thorn and hare-bell. Not till they were running to catch at his bridle did he move. Then he pricked on, and issued forth of the wrack slowly, and turned his head to see what had come to pass. He saw Rafe, on a tall bay steed, just framed in the greenery. So he touched his destrier with the spur, and broke away with a sudden demi-volte that was quick and smooth as light; and he passed on down the road at the fastest gallop, and was gone; the only man unscathed from that bushment in Greenwood by the Oaks.

Harvanger watched him, and stayed even after

[67]

he was gone. It was hard to believe great evil of Paranides, when he was so gay, and gallant, and bold, and so much like a god. But presently he climbed the bank, and returned into the wood, where the men of the Spotted Deer were congregated about an oak-tree; and in the midst was the Seneschal. There stood Rafe with his basnet off, and the bowmen stood round in a circle under the shade.

Rafe spoke somewhat thus: "Friends, justice runneth slowly in the Burgh; yea, it wriggleth on its belly. Therefore we should speed it in the Greenwood, lest it fail amongst men for ever. Good fellows, look upon this man that standeth before you, and judge what penalty should be enforced on him, were he but a poor man and friendless."

So they all answered: "Death, death."

"I deem it so," quoth Rafe; "now, what manner of death best befits his crimes, that we all know of too well to spend many words over."

Then spoke Grafton the miller: "Let us burn him alive, for he burnt my mill that stood on Deep Hay, and all my folk therewithal."

"Nay," answered Rafe; "that may befit him, but not us."

Then said Dick of the Red Ditch: "Let us cut off his hands and feet; for so he did to my brother that lived by Still Fosse that is under Greenwood to the south."

"Nay," said Rafe, "we will not copy his own deeds."

Then Simon Redskirt spoke, saying: "Let us starve him to death with hunger and thirst, for he drove my father and mother to death, who dwelt up in Tofts, and else had been alive now."

"Nay," answered Rafe, "we may not do that." But he smiled none the less.

So then Roger of Cold Haven spoke, saying: "I would that we might cause him to work from dawn to dusk, and yet never have the labour of his hands for himself; and so toil wretchedly year-long, and year after year, seeing every hoped for thing wrested from him; and so die in the end. For this he caused my folk to do, that dwelt at Cold Haven by the Sea."

"Hearken, young man," quoth Rafe, turning to Harvanger, who listened at his side: "I would that I might take from him his gross soul, and make him a gentleman that loved love, and grace, and handsome life, and wide lands, and fellowship, and children, and flowers. And I would that Paranides might set eyes on the lady that he loved, his wife; and I would that he and she might be harried from pillar to post, and his house burnt, and his children slain, and the name of his pride written up as that of a robber and a wolf's head; and vengeance slow to come. For this came to me. Only one thing I should not wish him: namely, stout fellows and a free life in Greenwood.

But I deem that we may not wreak this vengeance on him, for he is but a churl, and hath no soul higher than a full belly and a long purse."

So they were all silent and grave, and looked at the Seneschal. But he, for his part, kept his eyes on the ground.

"He it was," quoth Rafe, pointing quietly, "that while I was away burnt down my manor house, and Yolande my babe therein."

"By God," said Will, "ye make many words. Fetch a rope and hang him straightway; for if justice runneth not swiftly, belike it shall not run at all."

Thereupon they hitched a rope over a bough, and slung the halter round the Seneschal's neck. But while they did this, they heard a horn blown in the wood, and paused awhile to marvel; and before they could pull at the rope, they saw something gleaming and glittering at the end of the dell. And there came a man on a tall black horse, leading another horse. Then they knew him for Paranides, and sprang to the bushes, all save Rafe. Paranides drove heavily across the lawn, cut the rope in two, and the bonds that bound the Seneschal. Rafe sprang at him from the quarter, crying:

"Thy life, Burner, or mine!"

"Valour goeth ill with a bare head," quoth Paranides, quietly. "Let it be thine." And he smote a terrible back-stroke at Rafe, who fell into

the grass, and so lay. By now the bowmen had
drawn their bows, and the Seneschal had clambered
into the saddle of the spare horse; but their shooting was infirm. Paranides looked round again,
and galloped away after the Seneschal.

Harvanger heard Roger shout: "To the Hermitage"; and he stayed not, but took his staff
and ran swiftly through the wood after Paranides,
caring not who followed. Paranides had gone by
the forest paths, as could well be seen by the hoof
marks, and the tufts of hair on the bushes. Harvanger ran breathless for nigh an hour, and as he
threaded through the trees he deemed that the
day was changing, for the sky grew dark, and
bright drops like diamonds came scattering down,
trickling over the dry leaves, and lying upon the
thorn brushes and blades of grass. Therewith he
came to the end of the wood; for he was at the top
of a high bent, nigh seventy feet from the road, and
all the slope was set with fair timber, and many
poplars that rose up far higher than his head. Beyond was another wooded hill, not so high; and
beyond that, open sky, with a rag of filmy rain
cloud passing above, letting fall a few silvery
drops of rain; but in other places it was clear blue,
and the sun shone gloriously over a clear meadow
country, and on somewhat far away, that gleamed
and glittered—he knew not what it was. So as
he looked down, it seemed as if a great rainbow
spanned the dell, and one end rested hazily on the

road.   And his heart leaped, for at the foot of it, shading their eyes against the sun, stood two men with wide hats, and cloaks, and travelling staves. One was mighty big, and had a curling beard of gold falling down upon his breast; the other was not so big, but ruddy and yellow-haired, and a vast horn peeped under his arm.   The bow began to fade, and the cloud passed over; but those two abode.   They waved their hands to Harvanger, and presently he got down the bent, what with climbing and sliding, and came out into the road. And there they were, standing before him.

## CHAPTER VI.: OF A MEETING IN GREEN-WOOD.

SAID the horn-bearer:   "This is well-met, Harvanger; and ye are grown wondrous big, forsooth."   The golden-bearded one smiled, but said nought.

"Whence are ye sprung?" said Harvanger. "Almost I deemed ye were come across the bridge of the rainbow."

They both laughed, and the golden bearded one answered:   "No more than when we met in aforetime."

"Well," said Harvanger, "I shall be surprised at nothing ye may do; for Way-wise sang songs to me, and drew my father and mother away after

[72]

him as two mice; and when I followed, he was gone, save mist wreath. A strange folk are ye, truly, and all that ye told me hath come to pass."

"Ye shall tell us what befell, Harvanger," quoth the horn-bearer. So they all three sat down on the side of the road, and Harvanger told them, and also of all matters since he had gone from Greenbank. When he had done, the horn-bearer clapped him suddenly on the shoulder.

"Have better cheer, Harvanger, for I ween that the times are not so evil. Let us all seek the Scaur Gap; and thou shalt see what thou shalt see. We are like to fall upon good things in thy company."

"Yea, truly," quoth the golden-bearded one.

"I know not where it lieth," said Harvanger.

"It shall be contrived, I think," said the horn-bearer. He stopped, and said again: "The world is wondrous wide and big; and somewhat it hath, that ye were born to hold."

"What is that?" quoth Harvanger.

"I know not," said the other, "but thou shalt find it."

The golden-bearded one looked up and down the road a while, and afterwards partly closed his eyes and fell to whistling. "Of a truth," said he, "the wonder of the world is greater than its wideness. The strings stretch all abroad, and are gathered together at the Scaur Gap. My name is Goldbeard the Hurler; for so am I called."

[73]

"I am named Horn, the Watcher," said the other. "Now are our names told."

So they made friends wisely, and made an oath to seek the Scaur Gap in company.

Not long had they been speaking together under the trees, when they heard the sound of horse-hoofs, and straightway saw Paranides and the Seneschal riding towards them round a bend.

"A crown counts many, in the Burgh," said Goldbeard, "but only one in Greenwood—and a Seneschal's bâton less than a long bow and a three-feathered shaft."

"What shall I do?" said Harvanger. "It were ill to stand idly by."

"O, take thine ease," answered Goldbeard, "for there be long bows up in the wood. Let each man do his own work."

So they walked beneath the trees, until Harvanger was ware of a Hermitage that peeped forth of the leafage above the bent; and the brake was thick thereabout. After Paranides and the Seneschal had passed hurriedly, Goldbeard flung himself down on a small grassy lawn, because, he said, he wished to see what would happen. Then anon they perceived them come to the top of the road, where it began to slope down; and it was a likely place for bushments and entrapments. Paranides saw it, but could not avoid it. He

[74]

pressed on warily, keeping the Seneschal on his leeward side.

Therewith came shot out of the wood, and the Seneschal's horse fell, smitten with three shafts. Paranides reined in; but more shot came from the wood—Paranides was smitten over his mail, but the Seneschal was pierced in breast and throat.

"Ha, friend," said he, "I fear that I am hurt to death. Go thou on."

"Nay," said Paranides, "I am no craven."

He sprang from his horse, and strode lightly back. They saw him stoop and speak to the Seneschal; and men were coming down the bent with gisarms—but no more shafts were shot. They held speech awhile; no man might ever tell what they said, nor what it was that passed between them. But then Paranides strode back with his drawn sword in his hand—and there was blood on the blade.

"Lo, now," quoth Goldbeard, nodding, "Paranides hath slain the Seneschal."

Then the battle began; but the three stayed not to see it. They walked onwards under the trees. So when they had gone a pace, they found the end of Greenwood, and a bridge that spanned a river. Thence was a fair view over the land, for below them was a meadow country, and corn-land, and copses, and winding streams, with here and there a red roof. But on the sky-line gleamed

[75]

and glittered that something which Harvanger had beheld from the bent over the Hermitage; and now he understood that it was the clustered spires and towered walls of a great city.

Said Horn· "LONG WHITEWALL."

It lay in the golden glare of sunset, as if it would fade away with the light; and soon after, as they looked on it, a man rode past them over the bridge. His mail was torn and his plumes scattered, and he was binding up a wide wound in his arm. It was Paranides that rode by the river's edge. He looked upon them earnestly.

# BOOK III.: HARVANGER COMES TO THE CITY OF LONG WHITEWALL.

## CHAPTER I.: OF THE CUSTOM THAT THEY HELD ON MAY DAY.

I T was a fair morning when those three came unto Long Whitewall, and saw its roofs of scarlet clustering high in heaven, and thereover gilded vanes, and globes of gold. The scent of apple and pear blossom hung heavy over the land, where the closes and orchards were breaking into milk-white bloom. The sun shone down, but as yet the morning was early, and the air fresh. When they drew near, they heard the faint swinging of hidden bells, that ceased never during the day in Long Whitewall; and the blast of silver trumpets. Many folk fared inward along the shady road, with whom went Goldbeard, and Horn his fellow, and Harvanger; but none spoke to them, nor took heed of their presence, save that some would gaze at them awhile, and straightway fall to their own thoughts again. So the three walked on, and came to a mighty gateway; but it was closed.

Then said Goldbeard: "The gate is shut, but the wicket may be open. Let us knock."

So he knocked, and the wicket was opened, and

a man garbed in steel and crimson stood there, who said to them: "This day is May Day in Long Whitewall. Whence come ye?"

They put forward Harvanger, and he answered: "We come through Greenwood from the north."

Said the Guardian: "Such is the custom of this land and burgh of Long Whitewall, that whoso cometh hither from Greenwood on May Day shall either turn back from our gates, or stake his life on four casts. Of which the first cast is at play of chess, and the second at reading riddles, and the third at play of wrestling, and the fourth at stroke of sword. If ye fail, your lives are forfeit. Also, I deem that ye three shall count as one; for that is the custom. Therefore go back, and enter not, or consent ye to this custom."

"We will well," quoth Goldbeard.

"If ye fear," said the Guardian, "go your ways forthwith in peace."

Howbeit they went in; and there was a page clad in crimson satin, who tripped on before up a stairway, and anon brought them out on the battlement of the wall—and thence they might see all the land and burgh, for it was passing high. They followed the page along a balcony that ran round a tower, and so along the rampart; and ever, at due spaces, they saw big men of arms, who spoke not, but stood grimly in alcoves, and in depth of windows, and all manner of cunningly devised hiding-places, holding long pikes. But the page led Goldbeard, Horn, and Harvanger up stone steps to a door, the which he opened with a key. And then they were in a great tower, hung with blue tapestries. So, to be short, presently he led them out of that tower by ways that led to a fair garden full of first bloom of lilac. Therein lay a pavilion of crimson; and in that, a table; and on the table, a board for chess; and on the board, chessmen of wrought gold and carved ivory. But of people there were none.

Then they were aware of a book upon a desk; and it was a goodly book, bound in a cover of white vellum. Horn put his finger upon the cover, and read the words that were written in letters of gold: THIS IS THE BOOK OF THE CUSTOM THAT IS HELD ON MAY DAY. So he opened it, and they gazed on the pictures that were painted therein, and wondrous finely they were painted, with dragons of gold and blue and red, and devils and angels playing amid the floriated letters, and fair black writing to tell the tale the pictures showed forth. Some were very old, and the people dressed differently; but some were not old, and there were blank leaves at the end, to take more pictures; but when Horn counted the blank leaves, there were but four.

He said: "There are but four leaves left. We shall each have a leaf, and the fourth shall be for another, that as yet we know not of."

They fell to looking at the pictures; of which some were dolorous, telling of nought but failure among the men who came on May Day, and some were happy and victorious, and among these was Paranides. Horn presently took the book, and read it; but what he found in it he would not tell them.

When they had waited there a little while, they had sight of a company of folk coming into the garden, fairly clad in diverse fashions. And the first was a little lean man, brown of skin and dark of eye, and he was dressed in crimson velvet, and leant on the shoulder of a little page. Then he came and sat down in a chair, and all the other folk ranged themselves about, who were great lords and ladies, passing wonderful to look at. And of these, one was Paranides. Thereupon the Duke gazed at the three and spoke:

"Ye are the May Day men?" he demanded. "Well, which of you playeth the game of chess?"

"That do I," answered Horn.

"Fall to, then," said the Duke. So a stool was set for Horn, and they began to study the chessmen—he, in his great hat and thick-soled boots, and the Duke, in fine velvet, and flashing jewels.

The Duke moved out a knight, and so began the chess-playing. A cool and calm man was Horn; and ever the Duke looked at him keenly. They pushed and placed the chessmen all over the board.

No great time passed before the Duke lifted up his eyes.

"Thou playest unfairly, fellow," said he; "for the pieces are not as I put them."

"It should be no easy matter to cheat, with all these lords and ladies about," answered Horn. "Will ye that we begin afresh?"

"Yea," answered the Duke.

So they gathered in their pieces, and began afresh. Yet the time was over-short before the Duke frowned, and studied the pieces; and anon he leaned his chin upon one hand, and gazed upon Horn. Howbeit, he said nothing. Then Horn mated the Duke with ease, and rose up smiling, to retire. The lords and ladies came closely to see; for this was a great marvel to them, considering how notable a player of chess the Duke had ever been held.

"Messires," quoth the Duke, deeply vexed. "I wonder greatly at this defeat to-day—for I am well, and not out of health. It seemeth that some glamour is over the pieces; for ever when I look, they are otherwise than as I had willed. Wherefore I will play a third game, while ye shall watch and see that no unfairness be done."

They assented to this, and Paranides took up his stand by the Duke's elbow. Then the board was set again, and the play began. Horn neither smiled nor frowned, and the lords and ladies took

[83]

good heed. They played on for a time; and ever did Horn win on the Duke, who at length smote his hand across the board, and dashed the chess-men on the ground.

"There is magic in it," said he, rising up.

Horn bent to gather the pieces.

"Have I won, lord Duke?" he questioned.

"O, yea," quoth the Duke. And he departed with all his company.

"It is not well to entertain strangers," said Horn, putting the chessmen back into their box. "One may entertain men of sorts."

Towards noon, meat and wine and fruit were fetched, and they ate, and spoke together of the riddling. Horn said that this should be Har-vanger's deed; for Goldbeard must do the wres-tling. Harvanger was not well at ease over it. Horn and Goldbeard smiled, but told him little, save that he should answer simply. And when they spoke of the wrestling they laughed the more.

So a little after noon they saw the Duke and his company returning; the Duke now wore blue velvet, and a medal of silver on his breast, hung from a chain. Amidst the rout was a lady, wimpled so that her face might not be seen; and for the rest, she was clad in fairest blue silk.

"Sirs," said the Duke, pointing to this lady with his wand, "here ye behold mine own daughter. She is of wisdom mateless among women. Take

heed, therefore. Which of you doth the riddling?"

"That do I, Duke," answered Harvanger.

"Well," quoth the Duke, "bear in mind that
ye three count as one man; and if one fail, all
forfeit."

He sat down in his chair as before, and the
lords and ladies stood around. Then they put the
wimpled lady in their midst, on a fair seat, and
Harvanger facing her upon another. But when
the Duke made a sign, and the lady drew her veil,
lo, that was a wonder, for she was as fair a maid as
man could conceive. Harvanger looked upon her,
and she on him; and she cast her eyes down, and
so did he. And the Duke chuckled drily all to
himself.

"Now beginneth the riddling," he said. "And
three riddles shall be asked by either."

The lady crossed her hands and said: "O,
young man, what is the height of wisdom?"

Harvanger knew not, and was confounded. But
presently, when he had pondered, he thought of
the answer that seemed most meet, and said: "To
know the Best Thing in the World."

"That is no proper answer," quoth the Duke,
sourly.

"By thy leave, Sir Duke," said Horn, "it is the
best answer that ever I heard."

"And it is the flat truth," said Goldbeard.

The Duke scowled, but could not deny it.

[85]

"Well," he said at length, "let it go. We shall see the next riddle."

The lady said: "Fair youth, where is the Best Thing in the World?"

"It lieth beyond the Scaur Gap," said Harvanger, becoming very confused.

They were all still at that.

She said sweetly: "But what is it?"

He answered, thinking of Way-wise: "It is one thing for one man, and another for another; for the desire of the heart is the measure of manhood."

Then the Duke was astonished, as if he could hardly believe his ears.

"Ha," said he, "thou answerest patly."

Said Goldbeard: "The girl will be lucky to answer as well."

"Silence," quoth the Duke. "Messires, ye shall listen to the riddling of the May Day men."

Then Harvanger said: "If I praise any man, what am I to him?"

She answered: "A friend."

"Nay," said he; "a master, for I can only praise him when I comprehend his wisdom."

They wrangled over this; for the Duke held otherwise, and Horn would not allow it. But at last Horn gave way.

Then Harvanger said: "Who was the best friend of the Seneschal that was slain in Greenwood?"

She answered: "Paranides"; and they all assented to that.

"Nay," said Paranides, "I cannot claim that."

"O," quoth the Duke, "we know well how good friends ye were."

"Sir Duke," said Paranides, "there were men better friends with him than I."

The Duke shook his head. "Then ye must have quarrelled in Greenwood," said he, smiling. "Now to the next riddle."

Said Harvanger: "Who cut the Seneschal's throat in Greenwood?"

She answered: "The men of the Spotted Deer."

"Nay," said Harvanger, as the Duke set down his staff to arise. "Thou art wrong."

"Nay, she is right," quoth the Duke. "Or who was it?" he demanded, suddenly.

"It was Paranides," said Harvanger.

"Believe him not, Duke," said Paranides, coolly. "He is a liar."

"I saw the deed done," said Horn.

"And so did I," said Goldbeard.

The Duke looked at them, and then at Paranides. He said: "Well, we will consider these matters anon; for I must see into this. At evening we will have the wrestling. But mark ye— I say not yet that ye have won the riddling."

And he departed.

"Pride destroyeth Princes," quoth Horn.

[87]

"One riddle begetteth many," answered Goldbeard. "But to-night I shall wrestle."

"How deem ye of that?" asked Harvanger.

"O, less than nought," returned Goldbeard.

So they ceased talking.

At evening the Duke returned, and Paranides
was with him. He came anear, leaning on the
shoulder of his page, and behind him stalked a
mighty big man, black as coal, who had a loin-
wrap of bright blue about him. So when the
Duke was seated, he pointed to the black man with
his wand, and said:

"Sirs, this is my wrestler. He is the mightiest
man of his hands in this world, and hath never yet
been defeated. I have great hopes of him. Who
will have to do with him?"

"That will I," answered Goldbeard.

So the black man stood on the lawn, quietly.
Then Goldbeard unloosed the tie of his linen shirt,
and drew it off; and when he was clean stripped
thereof, he was a bigger man than the black man,
for chest, and arms, and shoulders; and his skin
was as soft as a maid's cheek. Thereupon they
faced each other on the lawn; the black man was
like a huge elephant and had a small head—but
Goldbeard had the face of a god.

"Fall on," quoth the Duke.

They sought a grip, and anon found one, which
presently Goldbeard broke, for he did not like it.
Then after a little feinting and sidling, the black

man got his grip in upon Goldbeard, and they strained in silence. A minute or two passed, and then Goldbeard set his lips and threw the black man up, so that he turned over in the air, and Goldbeard drove his head and shoulders flat into the grass. Goldbeard walked back, and began to put on his shirt.

"Ha, he is slain," quoth the Duke.

"That may well be," answered Goldbeard.

But soon the black man arose, dizzily, and they led him away.

The Duke considered in his mind as to how things had befallen, and he was heavy. He gnawed his lip, and tapped with his staff on the ground.

"Well," he said, turning beady eyes upon the three, "ye have won this game also. The day after to-morrow, one of you must do the jousting."

"We claim our forfeit," answered Horn.

"In what wise?" demanded the Duke.

"We have forfeits three: one for the chess-play, one for the riddling, and one for the wrestling. Thus our accompt is made: for the chess, we shall walk freely in the city, for the riddling, we shall have a champion, and for the wrestling, all the gear that he may need for his joust."

"How say ye, Messire?" asked the Duke of Paranides.

"I will well," quoth Paranides, drily.

[89]

"Then do we grant it so," said the Duke. And thus ended the three first bouts.

## CHAPTER II.: HOW THEY GOT BERNLAK OUT OF PRISON.

THAT night they slept in the tower that was hung around with blue tapestry; and when morning came, they broke their fast and issued forth into the town of Long Whitewall, to seek their champion. The page let them out of the garden with a key. They went down steps and along a lane that was between walls topped with ivy, and presently they came into a great street. It was paved with cobbles, and the houses were big and fair; for they had roofs of silvery lead and scarlet tiles, and tall gables, and gargoyles wrought like griffins, and dragons, and imps, and all manner of demons and unheard-of things; from whose mouths fell a few silvery drops of rain—albeit the morning sky was clearing, and was all but pure blue by now. And in the street were shops, over which hung signs of iron and copper, telling of what was made, and what was bought and sold within. Many folk walked to and fro, of diverse kinds, common people, and knights riding, and ladies in fair array, sweet visaged. So they walked up the street amid the folk, and wheresoever they went, the people stared after them, think-

[90]

ing it a marvel to see men so big and fair; and the young men gazed at Goldbeard, because of his bigness, and the older men at Horn, because of his steady eyes and calm brow, but all the women at Harvanger, because of his beauty of face and his noble mien. But of that Harvanger perceived nothing.

They went along the streets, and looked on the houses, and the churches, and every place they might attain; too long it would be, to tell of all they saw and said. All was fresh and sweet after the spring rain over-night, and the sun shone over all. And when they had passed along the streets, and Harvanger had gazed his fill upon the marvels there, they came by wide ways to a market-place, wherein was no such cross as he had seen in the little burgh beyond Greenwood aforetime, but the mightiest of minsters, triple-towered and wrought all over with carving that was coloured and gilded. And it looked like a thing seen in a dream, so strange it was, and he could not choose but linger before it somewhat, and think and wonder.

But they left the minster after Harvanger had stood on the steps and gazed up the wide street that led from the market-place; (he knew little of when he should next stand there and so look). And they came to a huge gate that spanned the way from side to side, and was set under a tall tower. The gate was so high, that an armed knight could ride thereunder without lowering his spearshaft; and all about the tower were galleries, and turrets with pointed roofs, manifold and multitudinous. From the topmost turret floated and flickered the Duke's crimson banner, and painted shields hung above the gateway. There, too, stood a tall man of arms.

So, first having gazed well thereon, they entered the gateway, and came into a long tunnel as it were, built all of huge stones. On each side were gratings, like the gratings of dungeons; and such they were, for voices cried from them dolefully. For this reason the tower was named the Doleful Tower.

Horn walked slowly on before; and when he had almost come forth upon the further end of the tunnel, he stopped. They heard a voice come from a grating, and it said: "Sirs, I am Bernlak of the High Marches, King Orvan's son of Varraz. If you will wend or send into Varraz to him, and tell this to my father the king, I will gladly repay you, either in gold, or gear, or deeds."

Then the voice ceased; but presently it began again, and spoke the same words as before. Horn turned about to Harvanger and Goldbeard, and said:

"Well, I deemed that we should belike find a champion here, and so it seemeth to have fallen out. For if any man in this world can overthrow Paranides, he is here."

[92]

"Let us speak with him," quoth Goldbeard.

Horn stooped to the grating in the wall, and spoke through it.

"Sir," he said; "we hear thy words. Now it is needful that we have a champion to encounter a champion of the Duke. Wilt thou fight for us?—for then we may deliver thee from this prison."

The voice came from the grating and answered: "Sirs, I know not whom you may be; nor out of this prison may ye lightly deliver me, for it is sealed up. Nevertheless, if your cause be just, I will fight for you."

When he had spoken thus, Horn and Goldbeard consulted together. Then Horn stooped to the grating and said: "Friend, thy name we have heard, and thy deliverance will we encompass. Be patient, and shortly we will return."

So the three companions sought out the Duke, and named Bernlak of the High Marches as their champion. The Duke answered, that it was well.

Said Horn: "Wilt thou not deliver him out of prison for us?"

"Nay," said the Duke; "I made no covenant about letting anyone out of prison. But see that your champion is ready at the summons," he said, drily, "for I shall admit no excuses."

And they could get no better answer from him than that; so they departed.

[93]

Then said Goldbeard: "We have made no covenant with the Duke but that we might dig our champion out of prison."

"True," said Horn.

"Let us gather tools," quoth Goldbeard, bluntly.

"What," said Horn, "art thou minded for such a game as that?"

Goldbeard answered: "Since the Duke will not dig, let us do so. But hearken," said he, taking Horn by the shoulder, "I think we can gain our point if thou canst be subtle enough. Go and ask craftily; the Duke will give us leave as quickly as though we asked leave to dig holes through the moon."

Horn smiled somewhat, and assented. He went back again to the Duke, while Goldbeard and Harvanger waited.

"Ye are all mad," quoth the Duke, when he heard this new demand; "but if ye will dig, dig and be damned. I deem ye will not be far forward at nightfall."

"Wilt thou write that down, Sir Duke?" asked Horn.

So the Duke bade his clerk write, and sealed the writing with his ring. Goldbeard was well content.

"I will answer for the digging," said he.

Thereupon they went and bought tools and baskets, and a wheel-barrow; and they put the

[94]

tools in the wheel-barrow, and wheeled it back to the Doleful Tower. They showed their writing to the Seneschal, who was newly appointed; his name was Naiman.

"Well," quoth Naiman, "if the Duke wills it, ye may dig; not that ye are like to get much from it."

"What wilt thou lay on that, Naiman?" said Goldbeard.

"What wilt thou?" asked he, smiling.

"Seventeen golden ducats that we are done by nightfall," quoth Goldbeard.

"A hundred to it," said Naiman.

Now the digging was begun; and soon a great flock of people was gathered to see, and the Duke himself presently heard reports of the digging, and came likewise, scarce believing what he saw. Goldbeard took crowbars, and mattocks and sledges, and Horn shovelled, and Harvanger wheeled the earth and fragments away. First they pulled up the pavement of the tunnel, and made a deep trench in the ground. Goldbeard drove his bars, and smote huge and swift strokes, and Horn shovelled as swiftly as he might, but was ever a little behind Goldbeard; and Harvanger fled to and fro until his body ached, but was ever a little behind Horn. Then more folk came, and the Duke parleyed.

"Ye had best seek another champion," said he, angrily, "for although ye have done a part of the work, the hardest part is yet to do; namely, the wall and basement of the tower."

"Thou art never content," quoth Goldbeard, looking out from his trench. "Thou wilt not dig for us; therefore let us dig."

When he had rested, and drunk a flagon of wine, Goldbeard braced up the wide girth at his waist and fell-to again, harder than ever; till it was a wonder to see. Hardly could any man have shown such force and strength; he hammered home his crowbars, and tore out the stones, and shattered those that were too big to move, and brought out the wrack in clouds of dust, like smoke. Horn shovelled and shovelled, and cleared up the fragments as fast as ever he could. As for Harvanger, when afternoon was one-third gone, he knew that to stop would be to fall down; for every limb of him ached, and yet Goldbeard attacked the wall with the strength of one possessed and stopped only to brace up his belt, and call for wine.

"The man is a bottomless pit," quoth the Duke. "He can swallow more wine than any I ever saw."

"We will swallow Long Whitewall too, if thou canst get it into a cup," said Goldbeard, pausing between two swings of a sledge. So the afternoon wore on, and Goldbeard had driven a great breach into the wall by the grating of Bernlak's dungeon. Swiftly he toiled, till sweat ran down from him, and mingled with the smoking dust.

[96]

And half an hour before sunset, he drove his bar through, clean into the room where Bernlak sat and waited.

" 'Tis done," said he.

"Nay, he is not out yet," quoth the Duke.

Goldbeard took another bar, without answer, and began to break through the last foot of stone. He drove, and pulled, and shattered, and cleared out the fragments like a giant, never pausing once, but working on throughout the evening tide. And last of all, he was left smiting and pulling alone, for Horn sat on the bank of the trench, and smiled, and Harvanger lay down upon his back, and looked up at the roof. When the bell began to toll, and clash to and fro for marking of sunset, Goldbeard threw down his sledge.

"Lo, our champion, Duke," he cried out. "One hundred ducats from Naiman, and a burg from the Duke."

Then they were aware of a man that had issued forth of the breach, and stood before them, dressed in a suit of blue, ragged and faded, and bearing in his hand a harp. He was not big, but broad and strong; jet black as to his bushy hair, and brown of face. So short he was, that his head scarce came to Goldbeard's shoulder. He stooped somewhat also, and had keen, dark, fierce eyes, and a sharply pointed chin.

"Ho, Messires," he said quietly, "now have ye

[97]

set me free of prison. I am at your service."
And first his eyes sought Harvanger's, and he said:
"I thank you."

They cast a cloak about him, and led him into
the street. No man stayed them at that time;
but presently one looked upon Bernlak, and another cried his name, and a third started forward,
and soon a great concourse of people followed
them, knights, esquires, burghers, and common
folk, and people ran out of houses and shops, and
came running from all quarters, all crying the
name of Bernlak, and staring at the three who
strode around him.

As for the Duke, he fell into a great rage, and
said: "I know not who these men may be; but
I know that their champion is born of a mortal
woman. Of them, I cannot say so much."

When they had come into the streets, as afore-
said, and found so great a multitude of people
around them, Horn said: "Now hear my counsel. Let us seek out a hostel, for we may never
return whence we came, in this press, and the
Duke hath such a holy fear fallen upon him, that
he will try all he may to fore-do this."

To his counsel they agreed, and after they had
cast about, they found a hostel that had a sign of
THE CHANTICLEER, and a red cock that
crowed to the morn. It lay in a great wide street.
Then they hurried in, and Goldbeard stood in the

doorway to keep out the press; and anon they were brought into a large room over the street, where they deemed themselves safe. They could look forth of no window but they saw sights that pleased them; for at the back was a garden close full of flowers, and trees, and the apple blossom was pink and white in the afternoon sun; and through them peeped the red roofs and white walls of houses and towers, with the three blue spires of the minster vast and faint against the sky. Then at the front was the street with its cobbles, and tall gabled houses with gilded signs. The sky was mainly blue now, and mighty clouds were marching over it, sparkling in the sun.

So they looked round the room, which was passing well done, for it was panelled and carved in oak, and had a deep window that opened outward. Lozengy panes were set in it, some thick and green, but others of bright coloured glass; and on either side of it were curtains to draw at need.

"Here we shall make our stronghold," quoth Horn, "and none shall turn us out."

After they had eaten, and arranged themselves a little, they fell to gathering gear for Bernlak. First Horn called to him the host, that they might make consultation with him.

"Messires," quoth the host, "I will get you the cunningest armourer on this earth; his name is William of Whitewall. If any man can prepare array for you in time, he is that man. And for

[99]

greater safety, I shall presently bring him to you here."

Said Horn: "Will not the Duke presently wreak this on thine own head, friend?"

"Well, I may not gainsay that it might fall out so," answered the host. "Yet the Duke we fear not over much; rather it is Paranides whom we fear. And I deem this knight to be one of the men now living who are able to overthrow him; wherefore I shall do my best." He said, further: "These times are passing evil, sirs; for the Duke is crafty and cruel, and Paranides hard and orgulous. Between them we are as between the upper and the nether millstone; but Paranides is the one we fear. Many a man fleeth to the Greenwood, and of those who stay, few are glad."

"Even so I thought," said Horn.

The host sent for the armourer, who came privily after dusk. He was a short man, black of hair and beard.

"Ha, messire," he said to Bernlak, "now I have hope that times shall mend in the burgh of Long Whitewall. Many a helm of thy cleaving I have mended, and few were ever cleft deeper."

"Can ye get me arms?" asked Bernlak.

"Sir, I can do so. I can arm ye as neatly as ever ye were armed; for I have the mail of Flacandrin: also his sword, and three great spears. Item: his shield, which I will get a clerk to blazon.

Item: I can find you a horse. To-morrow at noon ye shall be armed in the field."

So after a little more speech, he departed. Then said Horn: "Now all is done that we can do before-hand. Nought else is left but to wait." Which they did with grace and hope.

## CHAPTER III.: THEY DWELL AT THE SIGN OF THE CHANTICLEER.

**B**UT after night had fallen, there arose a sound in the street. Harvanger knew well now what it was: to wit, the trample of horses and the clash of mail. He rose up from the table where they sat, and leaned forth of the window.

"What is it?" asked Horn.

Said Harvanger: "The Companions, and Paranides."

Horn looked grave, and Bernlak glanced at him.

"Deemest thou that he is coming up to us?" said Horn.

"O, yea," said Harvanger; "he is dismounting, and passing in. What shall be done?"

"We will speak with him," answered Horn.

It was not long before the host came, and knocked on their door, which was shut.

[101]

"Messires," quoth he, "Paranides is here, and desireth company of you."

Goldbeard arose, and unlocked the door; and there came into the room the tall figure of Paranides. He had on a coat of yellow satin, and a cap with a feather set in a jewelled brooch. Very mighty he looked, and ever he held himself like a king of the earth, and smiled softly and proudly, as his use was. Then Goldbeard closed the door, and stood over it.

Paranides touched the pendant that hung on his breast, and bowed. Then he nodded and smiled to Harvanger, and said: "Good things come out of Greenwood."

"And some ill things stay there, and some not," answered Harvanger.

"Well," said Paranides, "every dog has its day, but to deal with its master is a different matter."

"As to that, I know nothing," said Harvanger.

Paranides seemed to muse a little, gazing first on Harvanger and then upon Horn; but he turned to Harvanger at last.

"I know not," he said, "why we are not better friends, Harvanger; for surely I have never been a foe to thee. Nay, I have ever been a good helper; for thou hadst not been here, save for me."

Horn said nothing, nor did Goldbeard.

Paranides spoke again, still to Harvanger: "I am not come," he said, courteously, "to breed ill-will amongst friends, nor to draw thee away from where thou desirest to remain. But see thou—it is not to be thought that in this matter thou art doing thyself any great good. This game is but a game; it comes to no end at the last. I desire to be thy friend, Harvanger; I have never been otherwise, it is true, but I would be more so."

"A gift-bringing Greek," quoth Bernlak; but Horn stilled him with a gesture, and they waited.

"In what way wouldst thou be a friend to me, Paranides?" demanded Harvanger.

He answered: "Thus; thou art becoming entangled in a trap, which no man but I will reveal to thee. At first I thought thou wert walking into it wisely, and with understanding; but since then I have perceived it is not so. Thou knowest not what is meant by the custom held on May Day, and these thy friends have not told thee."

Horn and Goldbeard listened, but said nothing.

"I have trust," said Harvanger, "that wherever I walk with these friends, I shall walk wisely. If not, let the blame be mine."

"Thou art giving up ways sweet and safe for those that are strange and unsure, and full of peril," answered Paranides.

"If I love strange paths in the world," said Harvanger, "I do no otherwise than as thou didst."

Paranides continued: "Thou hast seen somewhat of Long Whitewall. If it pleases thee, I

[103]

would have thee stay in it; if not, yet stay and better it. I much desire thee, Harvanger. If thou wilt be an esquire of mine, be sure that I will make thee a great man and a strong."

"Oil and water do not mix well," said Harvanger.

"Tell me, then," said Paranides, "what thou wilt do better than this; for it is no small friendship that I offer."

Something began to arise in Harvanger's heart. He knew not what it was; but it formed itself, and took shape in those few moments.

"I have heard much of thee, Paranides," he said, "and seen somewhat of thee. Thou art not a man to buy gold with gold."

"However good thou art," answered Paranides, in a very clear and certain voice, "thou wilt be spoken of as I am, when thou art a man of might. I have not been an evil governor of Long Whitewall. Thinkest thou that I would offer thee friendship, if I hated thee?"

Harvanger answered, no less clearly: "Of a truth, Paranides, I should fear thee less if it were enmity thou didst offer."

"Why so?" asked he. "Surely I have never shown any ill-will to thee."

"I care not," said Harvanger. "I have but one desire of thee; and that is, to be thy master. And," he said, "this shall come to pass presently."

Paranides smiled. "Nay," he said, "be not so

[104]

rash and hasty.   Yet the desire is a good one, and I praise it.   Courage is the best of things."

"I will not deal with thee, Paranides," said Harvanger, with a new fierceness in his heart. "Go thy way, for I am not of thy kindred.   Thou canst not entice me; and I see well that thou wouldst not have come hither for any purpose save only that."

"Why so?" demanded he.

"I know not," answered Harvanger, "but thou and I were not born to be friends; and I will not take thy friendship."

Paranides paused; then he looked at Harvanger sharply, with a coldness and threat of eye that could not be hid.   He gazed at Harvanger's clear, full eyes, and knew that indeed there could be no friendship between them; for there was growing up a new force and passion in Harvanger, swiftly day by day.

"Well," said Paranides, "tell me where thou wilt go."

"I will not do even that," said Harvanger. "Dost thou prejudge the issue of to-morrow, while it is still to-day?"

A flash came into Paranides' countenance.   He began to look at Horn and Bernlak, and fingered his pendant again.

Now Goldbeard stalked over from the door, and set his hand on Paranides' shoulder.

"Listen," he said.   "What was it that thou

didst bring from the chapel of the Hermit, that is by the Scaur Gap? The Death of Men, or the Death of Kings?"

"The Death of Men," answered Paranides grimly, but somewhat thrust back into himself by Goldbeard's manner.

"And why didst thou take that?" asked Gold-beard.

"It was my desire," he answered.

"Then stand to it," said Goldbeard, dropping his hand. "Stand to it like a man, and try no more to shift the issue, as a craven does."

"I am no craven," said Paranides.

"Of that, I am sure," said Horn. "But to-morrow, the luck will change, for a new man has come, and the old days are no more for thee, Paranides. And he has spoken."

Paranides ground his teeth quietly, but soon took heart again.

"Springs and summers have gone," said he, "and I have changed my heart more than once. Still, man for man, it should go hard but that I had the victory to-morrow. Many are called but few are chosen, as the book saith: and of the chosen, some are cast down again." Then he turned suddenly on Bernlak. "Ye should gaze over Greenwood, Messire, were ye but alone. Howbeit, this boy shall do greater deeds than thine, and be thy master for many a day. See thou to it; for my time is not over."

[106]

He bowed to them, and walked thence lightly; and Harvanger understood that he deemed his overthrow drew anigh, but why that should be, and what that should import, Harvanger knew not. Yet it was in his mind that Paranides had been to the Scaur Gap, and gained somewhat there, that was now over-blown and dying. He thought it strange. Then he remembered the words of Way-wise, that he had given as answer to the maid's riddling. So he sat there studying in his mind, while Bernlak talked and laughed gaily, for there was never a man easier of heart than he. And he devised a little song, and good music to it; but Harvanger did not understand it well.

"Thou oughtest to understand it, being young," said Bernlak, "for it is of love."

"What is love?" demanded Harvanger.

"The Best Thing in the World."

Harvanger looked up, and remembered things that he had heard aforetime; he knew not how long ago, but it seemed very long. And he began to look at Bernlak more closely.

## CHAPTER IV.: THE BATTLE IN THE LISTS.

NOW came the day of the combat, and it was as clear and fine as the yester day; the sun flooded down into the streets and broad spaces of Long Whitewall, and the swallows twittered and swung round the eaves. Harvanger found that he could reach a swallow's nest by leaning far out of the window; also, there was a stork in the out-buildings. So he took and showed a little swallow to Bernlak, and after put it back in its nest. They began to be good friends, for although Bernlak looked cruel and fierce of visage, there was great courtesy and nobility in his heart, and Harvanger liked him well.

Before noon came, they were apparelled; and there came a great company on horseback, with pennons and long spears, and heralds. Then these brought the three and Bernlak through the streets with great pomp and noise of trumpets, till they came to the field of jousting. There were the pavilions all pitched, of silk and cloth of gold, and the devices of lords and great men set out on shields and banners. All was gay beyond wonder. Erstwhile Harvanger would have been abashed; but now he was not, and knew not why. And he saw Bernlak, in that faded suit of blue, walk and speak easily, and gracefully and courteously; and it seemed most good to him.

Now they sat in their pavilion at the barrier, and waited; for as yet came neither mail, nor weapons, nor horse. The Duke observed them, and sent to learn if they required ought, but they answered no. And presently they grew anxious, lest mishap had befallen William the armourer, but ever would Horn bid them be of an easy mind, for all should go well. So, when an hour had gone, they perceived William draw in, and men that bore a chest, and long spears, and a shield; and incontinent the gearing and graithing was begun.

William the armourer pointed to a cloth laid for Bernlak to stand upon while he was being armed. "Sir," quoth he, "I shall arm thee lightly enough, and I deem that it will be best so. For Paranides rideth half as heavy again as thou, and will most like have the better of the running. So use thy skill there; and I shall arm thee lightly for the sword play, wherein thou art swiftest, and also as strong as he. Do I speak well?"

"Most well," said Bernlak.

So William swiftly clad Bernlak in a close suit of blue leather, and armed thigh and leg with plates of steel before, and hose of mail behind. Then he cast over him the great hauberk of mail, and armed his limbs with plates, and laced up the camail, and put on him a short coat of blue silk, broidered with golden flames. Then he drew leather shoes on Bernlak's feet, and fastened the golden spurs thereto, and belted him with a great belt. When it was done, William said: "I will lay a golden ducat on thee, Messire; for thou lookest promising."

Then he stooped to the chest, and drew forth a long sword with a scabbard wonderfully wrought with inlay of gold and blue enamel.

"Messire," said he, "this was the sword of

[109]

Flacandrin; keep it well, for it is a good sword, and it is called the Seeker after Strange Deeds."

And all the arms on Bernlak were inlaid with gold and blue, till they glittered and gleamed. Then William gathered his tools, and took the basnet in his hands, and waited.

Said Bernlak: "Is there no destrier for me?"

"Messire," answered William; "I have promise of a good one, which shall be here shortly." Therewith a trumpet blew, and all the folk were ready, and the scaffoldings filled, and the Duke seated.

"Ha," quoth Bernlak, "we are shamed."

"Messire," said William tranquilly, "be not over hasty. There are yet two more blasts to blow."

Suddenly a great horn was winded, and an esquire clad in white rode into the lists; three varlets followed, leading a tall milk-white courser. The esquire rode up before the Duke, and sprang to earth, and ascended the scaffold lightly. No other cognisance had he save a golden rayed sun on his breast.

"Sir," he cried out, "I seek Bernlak of the High Marches. Show him to me."

"Lo, yonder," said the Duke, pointing. The esquire turned, and ran to Bernlak, and touched the ground with one knee.

"Messire," said he, "this courser shall ye ride

[110]

this day. It is a gift from him who brought you over Mill Weir into Long Whitewall."

"I remember him," said Bernlak, "and I thank him." So he gave the esquire quittance, and the esquire mounted again and rode forth; and no man ever knew whence he came and whither he went.

Now was the courser brought to the mounting stage, and they saw that it was fully trapped and barded in mail; never was a horse better caparisoned, or fitter for a king's son to ride.

Then the trumpets blew and flourished, and every man tingled and braced himself. William set the basnet on Bernlak's head, and laced it, and trimmed all to a point of nicety. So anon he was in the saddle, and a long spear in his hand.

Paranides came first into the field; for his esquires leaped over, and threw open the barriers, and his horns blew, and he issued forth all armed, riding on a coal black destrier. And he was one flame of gold and steel, like hoar-frost on the faded brake in winter, or dew on the yellow crocus. So he moved round the lists quietly, and in deadest silence; and he turned but once, to salute the Duke on his high seat. For the rest, he made no sign to man or woman; and they none to him. Yet most glorious he looked, and beautiful.

Then Bernlak started forth fiercely, and passed round the lists curvetting and prancing. He saluted the Duke with his great spear, and kissed his hand lightly to the ladies on their scaffold, and managed himself so gallantly that presently all folk there were laughing and waving to him; and he laughed back again, and his heart rose high with joy and strength. And Harvanger's heart rose too; for he began to like Bernlak well, and all the courteous ugliness of him.

They took their range presently. Paranides sat at the further end stroking his gauntlets. Bernlak flung round into place, and volted and demi-volted ceaselessly, as a swallow circles in the air. And as the trumpets blew up a third time, they laid spear in rest, and rode together in the lists.

Harvanger's heart stood still; for they met like thunder, and smashed their spears to shivers. The white horse went on its haunches, and its fore-hoofs up into the air. Then they wheeled round and returned, and William handed up a fresh spear.

The second time they met more fiercely than before, and now Paranides had found his eye, and came down so heavily and so truly that he rolled the white horse clean over, and Bernlak out of the saddle; and he rode on with a shout, and then himself reeled and went over, till there were two men and two horses mingled, and all the folk rose up, but silently.

This was but a moment of time, for swiftly Bernlak got to his feet, and drew the Seeker after

Strange Deeds, and Paranides arose, and flourished the Death of Men, and they sought one another amid the struggling horses. And then began the greatest battle ever fought in those lists of Long Whitewall.

Paranides set on fiercely. His sword flashed and swayed, so that no man could fail to see the strength and skill of his arm. He followed and pursued, and Bernlak tricked and retired, crouching low and subtly, and ever swift on his feet. The blue and the yellow mingled, and parted, and shifted, and passed, and the silvery blades circled round them. Then at length Paranides found home with his blade, and Bernlak bled fast, but still leaped to and fro quickly.

Paranides followed up, and now the battle was fierce and fast. They hewed one another's shields in twain, and gave great wounds, and one slipped down after the other, but rose up again. At last a mighty shout came from all the folk, and Harvanger saw that Bernlak had at long length smitten in the helm of Paranides with one great stroke; and Paranides stopped, for blood was flowing fast and fast over his brow, within his helm. When Bernlak saw this, he sprang in, and tempted Paranides on; and Paranides swore an oath and came on, and smote Bernlak grovelling, and rushed to trample him down. But ever Bernlak was wise and watchful, and retired and avoided; and ever he fled before the blinded giant, smiting great blows that crushed in helm and crest together, and cut through the camail to the shoulder. And ever the blood flowed into Paranides' eyes. He stopped again, and strove to wipe the trickling drops away; but he wore a helm with no ventail, and his gauntlets would not serve. He would have appealed to the Duke; but could not gain time to do so. Then he would have torn off his whole helm; but he might not do that either. Then he cursed God and man alike in the very drunkenness of rage; for he could see only through a red mist. And he came on, and sought to strike Bernlak down by sheer force, and followed and pursued, and smote blows that would have cut iron bars in twain; but ever Bernlak departed on agile feet, and returned, and avoided, swiftly as ever, until Paranides was all but foredone. Then Bernlak sprang in and struck a blow that cut through the linked rings on Paranides' leg, beneath the plate—yea, to the living bone behind— and Paranides was left with one foot hardly on the ground, and the pain of hell in him.

Bernlak rested a moment, and said, grimly: "I have heard that knowledge is good, Messire. Thou art learning fast." Then he rushed round, and in, swiftly as ever, and hewed amain, and overthrew Paranides; and blood and fire mingled in those blows. Paranides waited for him, if he might seize and hold his enemy; for he was far bigger and stronger than Bernlak. But Bernlak cruelly smote the waiting hand, and the Death of Men he struck away, so that it flew through the air like a fiery comet. With that, the end came.

Bernlak strode round, and put his sword to the eyelet of Paranides' helm, from over his head.

"Yield ye, or die, Messire," he said.

"Is my sword broken?" demanded Paranides.

"Sir, it is whole," answered Bernlak.

Paranides was silent for a long space.

Then he said: "I yield me; namely, of the guardianship of this burgh, and all the rights that fall of it; and of forfeit I declare you all free."

Bernlak tossed his sword in the air, and caught it, and began to walk towards his pavilion. And for a while there was a half silence, and only a broken sound in the air.

## CHAPTER V.: HORN AND HARVANGER SPEAK TOGETHER.

SO they fetched Bernlak home to the Duke's palace; and much ado they had, to push through all the crowds and the press. The bells were rung, and there was much joy in Long White-wall, because of the casting down of Paranides. When the surgeons had put Bernlak at ease, and bound up his hurts securely, the time fared on to evening, at which time Naiman came to them.

"Ha, Naiman," said Goldbeard; "thou owest me one hundred ducats.  What hath befallen to Paranides?"

"He is sorely wounded," answered Naiman, "but shall presently be whole.  I have seen his harness laid out; and truly, never did I see mail so evilly entreated, for the work done to it is more like a devil's than a man's.  Also, the Company, that guards the citadel, hath shut itself up there with him.  Hardly have we escaped battle in the burgh.  Forsooth, the Duke rueth the custom held on May Day, and is fain you had never been born."

"I believe you well, Naiman," said Goldbeard, laughing.  Then Naiman turned to Bernlak.

"Messire," he said, "ye have done a great deed; how great, I know not yet.  The Luck of the Burgh is fallen this day, and Paranides will depart."

"What then, Naiman?" quoth Bernlak.

"Why, sirs," he answered.  "I do not know; but these are great matters.  The Duke had dread lest the Companions should have seized upon the whole burgh by force of arms; as I think they might have done, for they are stronger than we, who were born and bred here.  Howbeit, Paranides would have none of this counsel.  He will depart."

Said Horn: "Therein he is wise; for he may never come to mastery in this burgh."

"Well," said Naiman, "take heed to yourselves. Ye have done great deeds, and the Duke is wroth. As for myself, I know not what manner of men ye may be, save such as it may be better to help than to hurt."

So he departed, and left them. Then said Goldbeard: "This meaneth treason, my masters."

"The Duke beateth the air," answered Horn.

"Whatever may come," quoth Bernlak, "I will not go from you. We four should yet win to safety."

Harvanger said nothing then; so Horn turned to him.

"What sayest thou, Harvanger?"

"Having come so far," answered Harvanger, "the tale must be told to an end. I have seen greater marvels than that we should escape scatheless out of this place."

"And then?" said Horn.

Harvanger answered: "I have not yet found the Best Thing in the World. I desire to seek the Scaur Gap; and thither will I fare. If ye will come with me, I shall deem that luck."

Horn laughed. "True," he said. "Ye found much wisdom running about loose on Greenbank." But he went into a study, and spoke no more.

The dusk fell, and the stars shone in the sky. From the town came a great brightness of light, and the sound of music, as if the folk rejoiced, and made no stint. Bernlak slept on his couch, and Goldbeard slumbered in a chair, but Harvanger leaned out of a window, and drew deep breaths of the fragrant air, that was fresh with the scent of flowers and open land, and its trees and fields.

But in a little while he felt someone near him; and it was Horn. In the dusk he seemed grown to the stature of a giant; his frame was vast, and full of iron strength, and there was a smile in his eyes.

"Harvanger," he said, "tell me truly what thou deemest of our life this past week; for we have seen a little happen."

"What shall I tell thee?" said Harvanger.

"Thou knowest well, friend," he answered, "that there are more things in the world than a coming forth from Greenbank. Thou hast laid but one finger upon life. Look upon the light and noise of the burgh. Men dwell there, and work there; there men are born, and grow up, and love, and beget children, and die, and depart to a new life. Friend, what is in thy mind now?"

"It is but a little while," said Harvanger, "since I dwelt on Greenbank, and one day was much like another day. But then time changed. O, that is very long and long ago."

Horn gazed out of the window into the spangled dark, but said nothing.

"Friend," said Harvanger, "I have lain beneath the stars full many a night in spring, even as this night; and in summer and autumn when the moon hung over the trees. I learned the ways of the sheep, and the deer of the wood, and the flowers and the birds. I was of them, and they of me. But afterwards, when I came amongst men-folk, it was different. I know not rightly; but the world is not as it was before. Then I had only my father and mother, but they loved me, and were as the rising and setting of the sun, that came every day, and were ever good, and sweet, and pleasant, and never swerved. But the great world has many a man; and yet what is it to me?"

When he had said this, he suddenly laid his head down upon the sill, and the tangle of his hair was around it.

"Harvanger," quoth Horn, "ye shall find those that love you; for such am I, and such are Goldbeard and Bernlak, men who are fierce and strong, and swerve not. Friend, I know thou art courageous. Take thought, and consider the fewness of my folk. Yet for the love we bear to one another, and the love we have for men, the world is sweet, and we are strong. But such there be, who are poor, froward, and mean, and oppressed by themselves and by others; nor is there love among them, but each for himself. There are many things to be done in the world; many deeds, many things to be sought, and felt, and known. How well it were, that thou shouldst feel proud life, and joy in the mere living amongst men, so

[119]

that every day thou shouldst wrest good from the passing of it, and let it follow on into a great store of pleasant memories, that grow greater from year to year."

"Yea, truly," said Harvanger; "I would seek to encompass that."

"Every man according to his might," said Horn quietly. "What wilt thou do again, friend? For bethink thee; what thou gainest of the poor, turneth to dust and ashes in the mouth; but what thou givest them, it returneth more sweet than it went forth."

Said Harvanger: "Sweetest of all things, friend, it would seem to me, to feel the strength of life in me, if I might but order, and achieve, and appoint, and smite and restore. For so my heart crieth out, and may not be stilled. I sought fellowship, and have found it not; for fellowship abideth in the Greenwood with outlawed men, and is not here. But I have no wisdom, nor strength, nor skill to bring it here; yet for that my heart crieth; I desire it, and may not be satisfied."

"These things we may help thee to," quoth Horn; "but wisdom must be thine own. For many gifts may be given by a friend to a friend, but wisdom is the man, and no man may give or take himself."

Harvanger pondered in his mind awhile.

"I may not amend that," he said; "I deem it true, for as a man is, so worketh the desire and the

[120]

heart of him, and so falleth his life. Yet I do not think I am afraid. Give me the help that thou art able to, good friend; and when I can make of it, that shall come to pass. As for the rest, thou canst not prevent it nor force it, nor can I. Let me touch all things that there are, and turn them to whatsoever it is in me to make them. None can do more."

Horn smiled, and showed a sudden radiance of strong, milk-white teeth, like pearls.

"That is well spoken," said he. "It shall be as thou askest. I do not fear for thee."

"When shall we begin again the quest for the Scaur Gap?" said Harvanger.

Horn answered: "In three days' time."

They spoke long that night, but at last Harvanger slept. Horn moved not from the window, ever gazing at the coal-black sky and gleaming stars with strange eyes that had seen many things, and beheld the earth in constant watchfulness. It was not easy to say whence he came, nor whither he went, and his folk no man knew.

## CHAPTER VI.: OF THE WHISPERED TALK IN THE PLEASAUNCE, UNDER THE STARS.

THE galaxies of that glorious night were still sparkling; no sign of dawn had come, when Harvanger opened his eyes, and found himself gazing over the dark pleasaunce, and saw below him someone who glimmered faintly through the dusk. While he sat wondering, another little pebble struck his cheek; and it seemed to him, as he thought about it in his mind, that there was one who desired to speak to him secretly, although, indeed, he could not imagine what thing they could ever speak about together. But he rose up, and put his elbow upon the casement, and leaned forth, striving to see who it was in the pleasaunce.

"Who walks in the garden?" he asked softly.

"Hush," said another voice, still more softly. It was a woman's voice; and Harvanger deemed he knew it. It said: "Art thou the boy? I wish to speak with thee, if thou art."

"I am he," answered Harvanger.

"Wilt thou come to me, or shall I come to thee?" inquired the voice.

"I will climb down the ivy, if it will bear me," said Harvanger. "How couldst thou come to me?"

"O," quoth the Duke's daughter, lightly, "I can climb at least as well as thou. See, else. . . ." And she began to climb up the ivy very quietly, and cleverly, until she was sitting in the window in front of Harvanger, with one foot on the sill. The softness of her silken gown was close to him; the faint fragrance of its perfume mingled with the fragrance borne from the garden. "Thou seest, I can climb," she said.

"I would not have believed it, had I not seen it," he answered, in great wonder.

She laughed; it was a most beautiful and musical sound, this her laugh in the dusk. Harvanger began to smile also, for he liked her a little, and thought her new and strange.

"I could tell thee many things, sitting here," she said. "But not all that I now desire to speak of. Here is a key," she continued, placing it against his cheek, and then putting it into his hand. "I know the ivy will not bear thee. Unlock the door of thy room, and descend the stairs, and cross the pleasaunce to the pavilion. I will be there waiting for thee. Wilt thou do this?"

"I will do it," answered Harvanger.

"Go softly," she whispered.

As she bade him, so he did. He unlocked the door, and gently descended the narrow stairway, that wound steep in the thickness of the wall. At the foot was the door. He opened it, and passed across the garden in the deep dark that is just before dawn. He paused when he came to the pavilion, for he could see no one; but two hands caught his, and drew him to a seat, and there they began a whispered converse that lasted long.

"Fair boy," she said, "thou knowest who I am?"

"With thee," he answered, "I did the riddling."

"I am the Duke's daughter," said she; "and thou art the May Day man."

[123]

"What of it?" he demanded.

She said: "I desire thee to forego thy forfeit."

"It may be," he answered, "that I am not a wise man. Tell me, therefore, what the forfeit is."

"I am not wise either," she said, painfully. "I know they say I am; but I should know best. I cannot hold cunning speech with thy friends, for they are strong and terrible men, if they are men at all, but thou art gentle and kind, and not yet cruel with the world's wisdom. Who were thy sire and thy lady-mother?"

"Truly," answered Harvanger, "they were poor folk, as I am poor. We drove a little plough in Greenbank that is in Greenwood."

"That I may not believe," she said, "for ye have the figure and the face of a noble man."

"It is as I say," answered Harvanger.

Said the Duke's daughter, after thought: "Well, I deem customs and usages vary between different lands; our general father Adam was an husband-man, clerks tell us. And ye are verily a man of flesh and blood, of like nature with us?"

"I trow no otherwise," said Harvanger, smiling.

"For," said she, "I have doubts of the man that calleth himself Goldbeard; also of Horn. But these matters are not my business. I deem that sorrow has never come thy way, nor trouble. Is it not so?"

"I cannot say," he answered. "Sometimes it seemeth as if there were worse sorrows in the world

[124]

than any I have endured; and if it be as I think, then it is not for me to reckon up my troubles."

"I have thought this too, for my own part," she said. "But what wouldst thou have, pretty boy? It is our own sorrows God gives us to deal with, not those of other people; and indeed, even the lightest are enough to make us busy." When she had said this, she drew a breath, and her voice changed somewhat. "Dost thou love me very much?" she asked softly.

"I had not thought of that," said he.

"O," she said, half-laughing, half-discontented, "thou art a boy; it is so easy to make a boy hate one. I could soon devise that thou shouldst do so."

"I do not hate thee," he answered, wondering.

"I am glad of that," she said; "for it is a safeguard. But thou art not a fool either," she added, musingly. "I see how it is, and I am glad again. Then thou couldst not love me, even if I were to smile upon thee very sweetly, and give thee every grace thou couldst desire?"

He answered: "Indeed, I am not skilled in these things, and know not what to say. How should I know the right answers, that would seem courteous and kind, and satisfy thee?"

It was quite dark in the pavilion, so that they could not see one another. Their heads were bent close together; her hair brushed his cheek now and again, not unpleasantly. But if he could have seen her, he would have perceived that she smiled.

"But," she said, "I desire true answers. It is not a game, as thou seemest to fancy. Wouldst thou slay men to win me, and pursue me to the ends of the earth, and think the labour of thy days well repaid if I smiled upon thee?"

He pondered this over in his mind. "I do not think," he said, "that I feel any of these things in my heart. None the less, I will gladly do what I may to give thee pleasure."

"Thou wouldst not harm me?" she asked.

"Nay," said he; "I would never do that, if I might avoid it."

"Is that a true answer?" she demanded.

"It is a true answer," said he.

"But how true?" she inquired. "A saying may be true if it is half true; but tell me a whole truth from thine heart."

"Dame," he said, "be assured that there is in my mind no wish to do ought that should give thee hurt or sorrow. And this is a whole truth, free from falsehood."

"To how many women wilt thou say this?" she asked.

"To all," he answered; and she believed him, for there was frankness, and no guile in his voice.

Then she said, her voice changing afresh: "O, but if that be true, why art thou doing me this injury that will destroy all I care for most?"

"What is that?" said he. "For I know not any."

"To-morrow," she said, "they will give thee thy forfeit, and I am the forfeit."

"How so?" he demanded.

"I am the Luck of the Burgh," she said. "He who wins the May Day Games wins me as the forfeit, and weds me, and is the guardian of the Burgh, and its ruler."

"What then dost thou wish?" he questioned.

"Hearken," she said. "When Paranides came to Long Whitewall, I loved him; and it is through me that he has ruled here. Fair boy, thou wilt some day love, and when that day comes, thou wilt know more than my words are able to tell thee thereof. If thou takest thy forfeit to-morrow, Paranides will depart, as I think he will in any case, for a short while, but then he will depart wholly, and I shall be wedded to thee, and thou wilt become the guardian, and step into the shoes of Paranides. . . . Ah," she said, suddenly, "I know now what thou carest most of all for; thou art as he is, a lover of power and rule. But hearken still. If thou takest that forfeit for the sake of such ends thou wilt not long enjoy them."

"Dame," quoth Harvanger, "I bid thee let me speak before thou sayest ought else. It is not in my mind to wed thee."

[127]

She said: "Not even for the rule of the Burgh?"
He answered: "I have other guides, and another
pursuit to make."

"Wilt thou make that answer to-morrow?" she
asked.

"Even so."

"Well, hearken, none the less," she said. "I am
older than thou; not an ill woman, it may be, but
thou art a boy, and I have been the wife of a
mighty man and a gallant lover. Thou dost deserve a happier love than ours would be; and I
might put venom in thy wine, fair boy. Also,
thou hast not the power to rule in Long Whitewall. Be sure they will understand how to
smother thy will, and entrap thee in crafty meshes,
and overthrow thee by the strong arm if need be.
Take heed, therefore, and refuse the forfeit."

He answered: "Dame, my roads are already
made over the world; and those that are not yet
made, shall shortly be made. Be at peace; for I
shall not take the forfeit."

"Why didst thou come hither?" said she. "Lo,
all thou hast done is destroyed already."

"Nay," he said, "I do not deem it so. Take
heed, Dame, lest in serving thine own ends, thou
dost help me to ends thou hast not thought of."

"I care not if it be so," answered the Duke's
daughter. "But what would they be?"

"I know not," said Harvanger.

She smiled, saying: "It may be so, for thou art

a strange boy, and hast wise counsellors. Have I gained my point?"

"Yea," he answered; "thou hast gained it."

"Forgive me," she said, "if I have been a fool and a child. I am not wise enough to be Paranides' dame."

Said Harvanger: "Thou art at least wiser than I in some things."

"Kiss me, then," said she. So he bent and kissed her, and afterwards passed over the pleasaunce while the birds twittered to herald the dawn; he locked the door, and tossed the key forth again into the pleasaunce, where the Duke's daughter found it amid the grass. He was a little confused with that kiss, as a youth will be who has never kissed a woman before; and half he repented of it.

The next day came, and they all went down again into that garden where the pavilion was. A thrush ran on the lawn, and there they waited, till a postern door at the further end opened, and forth issued the Duke, leaning on the shoulder of his page. Amid the company that followed him was his daughter; and she walked with her arm through that of a great lord, her eyes downcast, till they were all gathered in a half ring about the three companions and Bernlak, who stood awaiting them.

"Which is the master amongst you?" quoth the

Duke. For a little while they said nought, but remained silent, till Horn laid his fingers on Harvanger's hand, answering:

"This is he whom we serve; this is the May Day Man." So Harvanger stood there in front of them, the goodliest man in that garden, and the most serene of brow.

"Messire," quoth the Duke, "I commend to you my daughter, and this lord who will speak for her and for Paranides, since Paranides may not himself be present. I pray you attend to them."

Now the lord advanced, and led the lady before Harvanger, and withdrew her veil, so that they might gaze upon one another.

"Messire," quoth the lord, "I speak with the lips of Paranides. Here is the Luck of the Burgh, and the wife of its guardian. I surrender it to you, for such is the custom held on May Day."

"I thank thee, Messire," answered Harvanger. "I refuse this forfeit."

The Duke started. "How—ye will not?" he said.

"I will not," answered Harvanger. "I declare this forfeit invalid."

They were astonished, and the Duke most of all. He looked about him, as if seeking counsel. Nothing seemed to have happened quite in the way he expected. His fingers moved, and his brows bent.

"Well," he said, presently, "let it be as ye will.

Ye remain in my custody, messires; for you have surrendered your forfeit."

"We are content," answered Harvanger.

## CHAPTER VII.: THEY DEPART FROM LONG WHITEWALL.

ON the third day of their life in that soft prison (for they understood now that it was a prison), they stirred in the early morning, all save Bernlak, who slept soundly. So they looked forth of a window, and beheld the departing of Paranides. Fine and clear and balmy grew that day, and all the roses opened in the sun, and their scent hung sweetly in the air that played through the courts and gardens. Over all that mighty burgh shone the quiet rays, and over the hundred towers, and dreamy courts, and quiet pleasaunces of the Duke's palace. The wrath and evil seemed gone, and a great peace had fallen upon it. Very near, now, drew the end of their sojourning in that place; but it grew the sweeter therefor, and deeper grew the wonder that men had wrought it, who are so evil, and yet in whose work is so much of good.

Then as they looked, they saw tall gates of wood, bound in iron, open silently; and the spears went forth two and two: three thousand gleaming men of arms; and presently they were clean gone.

[131]

So they saw again how the black destrier was led out; and it was no long while before Paranides issued through a postern door, and mounted upon it.  He walked slowly, and with pain, and was wholly unarmed, for as yet he might wear no gearing of war.  Beneath his yellow silken bonnet were great swathes of linen, and one arm he bore slung in a silken kerchief; and his leg also was bound, and halting, for the Seeker after Strange Deeds had bitten the living bone.  But when at last he was mounted, he rode trampling forward over the stones, and as he passed he caught a rose from the trellis, and put it in his breast.  So Paranides departed, and went his ways out of Long Whitewall in the golden morning of May.  No man sorrowed for his going, who was so brave a knight; none wished him back again, who was so wise in counsel.  Howbeit, the Duke was heavy, for he had dreamed evil dreams.

Then towards noon the Duke arose, and called the captain of his guardians, that was newly appointed since Paranides went.

"Forsooth," he said, bitterly, "I see none but new faces around me now; and yet it is not so long ago that my friends and true servants dwelt with me."  So he took his steps to the chamber where were those three and Bernlak, fast bolted and barred.  And they lived not over heavily; for Goldbeard and Horn played chess together, and

Harvanger sat gazing out of the window, and Bernlak ran his hands over the harp strings, and sang songs of love and battle, for the very joy of life that he saw without and felt within him.

The Duke gazed around, and was not glad to see them so well at ease. He had rather have seen them in pain and hardship.

"In right good estate do I find ye, messires," he said, "and more like to welcome guests than to foes that lie in durance."

"In some places we are welcome, and in some we are not," answered Horn.

"I have dreamed strange dreams," said the Duke. "And the dreams I dreamt told me that ye were not such men as ye looked to be."

"What didst thou take us for?" said Goldbeard.

"At least men," quoth the Duke, sourly, "and not fiends or warlocks."

"Well," cried Goldbeard, with great laughter, "be at rest, Duke, for we are neither, as I trow."

"I would that I had surety thereof," said the Duke.

"Thou art an old dotard," said Goldbeard, roughly. "Fetch hither the bishop, and dip us ten feet deep in holy water. Of a truth, Duke, thou art liker to see the bottom of the bottomless pit than ever we are."

"Thy speech is not courteous," he said.

Goldbeard shrugged his shoulders. The Duke stood biting his thin lips in an uncertain way.

[133]

"Sir Duke," quoth Horn, "thou talkest evilly in saying that we are fiends and warlocks. Here is Bernlak of the High Marches, a king's son of Varraz. He shall witness that we deal in no matters of necromancy."

"Truly," said Bernlak, "I have not observed such."

"Ha," quoth the Duke, "I have been to see the Doleful Tower, and I dare to allege that no mortal men could have stirred its stones as they have been stirred. Who be ye, sirs, to accomplish tasks which no men erstwhile have accomplished?"

"If we deal in enchantments," said Horn, "then art thou and Paranides also guilty thereof."

"None the less," answered the Duke, "I purpose to detain you in my prison, till surety hath been had. Ye have done me great hurt and injury, for which I shall presently have revenge."

"As thou wilt, so thou mayst do," said Horn.

"And, sirs," said the Duke, "ye shall not depart so lightly from this business as ye deem."

Said Horn: "We will take that risk.

"Sirs," said the Duke, "I see well that ye think no man able to overcome you; but, sirs, I shall attempt it, for I have great power in this land."

"As the tree grows, so does it stand, and as it stands, so does it fall," said Horn. So the Duke departed hastily, all a-tremble with his wrath; yet, indeed, he knew not why he was angered so.

[134]

Then rose up Horn and said: "My friends, ye have heard what the Duke saith, and how he purposeth to do us treason, against his oath to us. It shall afterwards be to his injury, and our profit. But now is our labour here accomplished, and tomorrow we shall depart. Let us be ready."

"Whither shall we depart?" said Bernlak.

"Messire," answered Horn, "we depart on a quest, whose end we know not yet. And first, we must follow Paranides."

"I am content to go where you go," said he.

Then Horn fetched Harvanger forth, and said: "My friends, this is our comrade and fellow, for whose sake we go on this quest. Thou and I, Goldbeard, have fared over the earth many a day, seeking that which we found not; but he shall find it for us. And thou, messire, should bear him great good will, for it is from him, and not from us, that all fortune floweth. How sayest thou? Wilt thou take him as an esquire, and learn him all manners of war and courtesy, as befitteth a gentleman?"

"Yea, truly," answered Bernlak. "That will I do with all mine heart; and I do not know whom else he may have, better than I, as a teacher."

"Now," said Horn, "I will teach him the craft of governance, and the ordering of folk; for in these matters I have wisdom."

"And I," said Goldbeard, "will teach him the
[135]

wisdom of the green fields, and the good that groweth out of the ground, since in these things I have some understanding."

"What sayest thou, Harvanger?" said Horn.

Harvanger was pensive awhile; but then he lifted up his head, and answered: "Friends, I know not why ye do this, but certainly it is out of your goodness and love, which I will not refuse. I will learn from you, and when I may repay you, I will do so to the uttermost of my power. Since I have such noble masters as ye be, I think I cannot fail to be a noble man."

"I will answer for thee, on my part," quoth Bernlak. So they agreed together, and afterwards made ready for their journeys.

While it was yet dark before dawn, Goldbeard laid his hand on the latch, and opened it; and they followed him silently through many passages and rooms, and out into the courts of the palace. And it seemed as though every door were unlocked. Then they came to a postern, and it was open, and they issued out into the street. Still Goldbeard strode on before, and spake no word, and they followed him through the dim grey streets, where no men were, and passed by the smooth minster, all silent and great in the dawn. Over the green close they went, and towards the gates of the burgh. The gates were closed, but Goldbeard opened the wicket and stepped forth, and when they were all come forth after him, he closed the wicket again. Then they were on the white road, and beheld the green fields before them, and the rim of the sun pushing up amid a glory of light and colour.

# BOOK IV.: HE JOURNEYS OVER THE FAIR PLAIN TO WHITEWAYS BY THE MILL WEIR

## CHAPTER I.: THEY COME TO A FAIR LAND, AND FIND MANY CITIES THEREIN: AND THAT PARANIDES HAD BEEN BEFORE THEM.

NOW the tale tells of how those three and Bernlak entered into one of the fairest lands in all the world where men dwell together. They came into it over a great flood of water, by a stone bridge. Here were no deep forests, nor wide wastes, but all was fair and green, with copses dotted over it, and long scored fields, and great waving seas of corn rippling in the wind and sun, and poppies red and white and blue gillyflowers therein, so that nought could be pleasanter. And also, there were farmsteads, with grange and croft, and wide sweet meadows for grazing of sheep and kine, and ever they came upon villages, and towns big and little, that were under no hard dominion, but free, and the folk fierce in upholding their ancient customs. It was a sweet and fair land, and none could be better to live in.

They went on their way after passing the bridge, and saw how good the land was. So they came unto a burgh, not very great, but of good substance, and it was called the Burgh of the Green Crofts. Here they stayed one night, and asked after Paranides, and his company. Then they were told:

"Sirs, such a company as ye show us of passed our town two days ago, and laid toll upon us, to the sum of five thousand golden florins. We knew of no war, and had not heard of any; and we might not do otherwise than as we did."

They departed, and left the Burgh of the Green Crofts, and did so much by their journey that they came to another burgh, which was called Langton. And here they were told as before. They departed from Langton, and followed such roads as the folk showed them, and after a day they came before a greater town than they had as yet seen thereabouts, for it had two great churches and a gild hall, very nobly built. It had been evilly mishandled, for the gate was all broken, and lying askew on its hinges, and part of the town was burnt and smoking. So when they had made inquiry about these matters, one said to them:

"Sirs, this place is called the Burgh of the Three Sisters; and ye shall understand that yesterday there came a great company who demanded toll of us. Sirs, this town is a free town, both by written charter and by ancient use and custom, and we were in no mind to yield us to robbers. Wherefore we closed the gates, and rang the common bell, and assembled together with weapons; but

[142]

these Companions anon broke our gate, and stormed the town, doing great injury as ye perceive. So when we saw that we could do no otherwise, we paid them what they asked, and they departed away."

Horn asked what they meant to do.

"Sirs," answered the man, "we know not whence these aliens come, but our best men are already assembled, and I think they will send messages and letters to other towns, and do all they may to recover our florins, and save the country."

Bernlak said they must needs make haste; so then he departed with the three, and they travelled till they came to a burgh called Meadham, which lay amid fair meadows, by a river. And there on the green slope of a hill they saw many folk gathered with such weapons as they could bring, pikes, and old swords, and scythes tied to poles. They inquired again of these folk, who told them that they held of the bonded burghs, which were three in number, namely, Meadham, Whitewaterford, and South Marling: and these three burghs were gone into the field to fight the Companions. The folk on the hill were the young, and the old, and such as knew not how to fight well, so stayed behind to guard the town.

They left them, and fared on; it might be a mile or more that they went, before they came by a timbered road to a great meadow. Goldbeard said it was a water meadow, and showed how the

[143]

water was let run in at flood time. As they stood talking, they saw a man come towards them at a great pace, all dishevelled and wild of eye.

"Sirs," he called out, "take heed to yourselves, for the foe be hard behind." And he ran on swiftly, and after him came many others, some of whom said likewise, but most ran as hard as ever they could, paying no heed to ought else. Then came a burst of men flying into the meadow, fifty or a hundred at once, casting spear and buckler away on either hand; and then more, so that they might not be counted, and mingled in their rout were mailed men on great horses, striking and hewing. Anon there came a banner, which was green, with yellow flowers upon it; and ever the banner-bearer rushed hither and thither, calling to his comrades, until a mounted man smote him through the body, and trampled upon the banner. Then the others fled the more, and more men at arms came galloping and more of the burghers breaking into the meadow, till Horn said: "Friends, we are best out of this. Whither shall we go?"

Bernlak answered: "Let us go forward, for that is the wisest counsel."

So they went forward, and awhile saw nothing of the battle, albeit they heard it afar off. When they left the road again, they saw that they were upon a low hill, that sloped down into a wide green place, and over against them rose up a town set high on a rock above a river. In the plain was a great battle, which was the Whitewaterford battle, arrayed with its banners and foot men against the Companions. The standard of Paranides was planted amid bushes, and near it sat he, ordering and directing how matters should be done. It seemed like to go ill with the townsfolk, for they of Meadham were broken, and driven clean off the field; and the rest were breaking quick. None the less, they fought right well, and there was one who stood in the forefront, and smote with a huge sword; he was clad in red, and might be seen among them all.

Now came certain of the Companions, returning from the pursuit of the Meadham burghers; and they assembled, and were at point to assault the Whitewaterford battle in flank, which should have destroyed it without hope. But as they were making ready, and marshalling in the green meadow, a sound began in the road under the burgh, and all men might behold the array of a third battle, that moved up all new and fresh with its banners, and a company of pipers and drummers playing before it. It advanced slowly, and in good order, every man in his due place, to the sound of the pipes and the rattle of the, drums, and the armed men unrolled and displayed the great banner of their town, and gave three loud cheers.

"What is this?" said Harvanger.

After looking at them a little while, Horn said:

[145]

"Unless I am mistaken, these are the South Marling townsmen. I deem they have been delayed by the breaking of the bridges. Let us watch what they do."

Now began the fight; which, after it had been set going, went confusedly, as fights will. Those three and Bernlak sat down on the grass of the hillside that was dry and yellow with the heat; and thence they saw all that befell, for the plain was under their eyes, and beyond was the town with its pinnacles and many spires, as though it were the stage of a Corpus Christi play. Paranides troubled not to wait. They but turned their glance to see him guiding his black destrier over the greensward, and crying on the long lines of horsemen that wheeled out from the rear of his array. Bernlak sat with dark brows, watching intently. Now they came on, tall riders armed at all points, half a spear-length each from each; and they went passing by, at the charge, with spurning hoof and springing steed, and their captains ahead, whose shields were scored with quarters and rich with colours and gold. Most gallant men they were, and Paranides waved on each rank as it passed. The townsmen of Marling thronged tight together, and there was turmoil, and shouting, and a great press, and no man knew what thing chanced, save to himself, and even of that but little; but the hedge of steel and colours never wavered, and the mailed men rose and fell crashing amid it as they burst in upon the townsmen. They cried "Saint Mary of Long Whitewall," and the townsmen cried "Marling," and each had trouble to escape his neighbour's weapon. Harvanger saw the lines of mounted men come to pause; and the rearmost stopped, and waited, so that below him were men at rest, curbing their restless horses; and in the front glittering figures were on the ground, and steel clad legs stuck out from between the burgher's trampling feet. Then the second line charged in, but the deadly turmoil continued, and spear after spear went over into the press, and Bernlak sprang up fierce with excitement.

" 'Tis over," he cried.

"Watch, Messire," quoth Horn.

The third line went in, but the turmoil continued; a grim struggle of which no man knew the true story. Soon Harvanger saw isolate men on foot run forth, and the riders of the fourth rank move to meet them. Then, as they gazed, that fourth rank wavered and shook; and slowly at first, but anon more swiftly, the mass of the Marling battle came on at a run, and opened out, and all at once it was a rush and a flood of flight and pursuit over the meadow, the Companions giving back yet fighting fiercely, while amid and behind them came quick and furious men, mad with the rage of battle and anger, who cut down the horses with to and fro sweeps of their long gisarms. One captain came down so at the foot of the hill,

[147]

and was pinned by his destrier; there were twenty pikes at his throat before he could move, and already the fighting front of the Marling men was far ahead. So they came into the meadow, and were sparkled abroad somewhat, and lost their array; and driven down the field still were the riders, giving back but hovering like hawks for the rally that might yet scatter the townsmen as chaff. But now suddenly appeared leaders of the townsmen, rushing hither and thither to marshal them; and the banners were set up and displayed. After that the horns blew, and order was wrought out of the chaos, and the battle gathered again.

"What think ye of this?" said Horn.

"Of a truth," answered Bernlak, "I think this an unlucky day for Paranides. There are those on the field who will yield much to strip, and more to ransom."

"Few will need ransom," said Horn, briefly.

For a little while all things were in flux, the burghers crowding the meadow below, while beyond, the strife had ceased a moment, and it was hard to tell what the Companions were doing. But when the pause had lasted a short time, the Marling townsmen began to advance across the meadow, and the tall man in scarlet who led the Whitewaterford array was seen standing with his sword raised high in air.

"Ha," quoth Bernlak, as they watched, "I have

[148]

not seen men of common blood so bold and so well led as this."

"They have much to lose," said Horn.

"Men play high for a great stake," said Gold-beard.

Harvanger heard much wisdom spoken in those few moments, concerning the art of war, for all three of his friends were men expert in judgment, and they bade him heed all that he saw and heard. The Marling townsmen fell on all they might, and they entered in amongst the Companions and over-threw many by cutting the horses' legs. So fiercely they fought, that the Companions began to recoil back. Then they raised their shout, "Mar-ling," and pushed on, and the Companions re-coiled back further, and were thrown into disarray, for many were on the ground. Paranides sought to bring more riders round from his rear, to strike the Marling townsmen in flank. Then came the Whitewaterford battle on the right, with axes and swords, and smote down whomsoever they could reach.

The Companions, being once disordered, could not easily recover. Many fought on foot, but were presently smitten down, and the two battles of the bonded burghs pressed on against those who kept up. The moment of victory for Paranides had gone by now, and the burghers waxed stronger, and bigger of heart, as they saw the mailed men give way before them. The Companions rallied

[149]

into knots, and the man in scarlet came in fiercely amidst them, bursting them asunder for his axe-men to finish. And for their part the townsmen showed little mercy to those who lived by plunder, and ransom, but slew them all. So, fighting, they came out of the meadows to the rough ground.

Then a loud trumpet blew, and the Companions turned and fled at a trot. There was a small compact array on a hill just above, and in that place was Paranides. While the greater part retired, these moved forward slowly, their spears rising like a sapling copse. The burghers halted, and clustered.

When the three and Bernlak saw this, Horn said: "Come, let us go to Whitewaterford, and hear the news."

They went down the hillside; but Harvanger wished to see the end of the fight. Bernlak took him by the arm, and pointed across the land.

"The fight is now over," said he. "It was won and lost in that moment."

"I beg you to explain this to me," said Harvanger.

"When these Marling townsfolk made their onslaught," answered Bernlak (while Goldbeard and Horn listened), "Paranides made attempt to bring round his rear to enwrap them, and fall upon their flank; which was a good and prudent action. But the battle beyond, which is of Whitewaterford folk, pressed in so hard, that for every foot he gave in doing so, they won a foot for themselves. So he changed his movement into one of retiring; and while the fight went on, he withdrew all but two small parties. One party then turned and fled. If the burghers had then scattered in pursuit, the second party would straightway have charged them, and driven them like chaff before their onfall, and I think they might have retrieved the day, even to the storm and sack of this burgh before us. But the burghers stayed in their ranks, and the Companions are now departing, as you may well see."

"It is a game of chess," said Horn.

"There is the mark of the skilled captain," quoth Goldbeard.

The leaders of the townsmen were running up and down before their lines, praying all men to hold fast their array. Even as Harvanger looked, he saw the tall riders enter the high road far away on the left, going two and two together; and those who had lately fled, were setting themselves in order, and making ready to follow. A tall mailed man rode to and fro with a warder in his hand, and soon they had wheeled and moved after those that had gone before. When the last spear had vanished in a dip of the ground, Paranides rode along the front of his small company on his coal black destrier; and his banner was planted, and

[151]

the Companions wheeled round past it, and so towards the high road, into which they turned. So they departed and the land was left bare.

It was dusk before they came up the steep road to Whitewaterford, and met the battles of the burghers marching back. First went the White-waterford battle, a strong array of swordsmen and axe-men, and then the Marling battle, a great stream of spears. The gates were opened, and those within came forth to meet them. The town was built on a rock, above a river that bent round the rock, and where no river defended them the folk had built walls with towers. All that night the gates and the road and the meadows flared with torches, and waggons and litters came in with the slain and the wounded. Harvanger saw the aftermath of a great battle, and grievous it was, and terrible; but men rejoiced for the defeating of Paranides, and the hostels and churches were alike bright with light, until dawn put it out. These things he saw and remembered, and forgot nothing.

But they entered into speech with certain of the Marling folk, and heard so much that Horn coun-selled that they should depart with them, and go to Marling. Among others, they met the tall man in scarlet, who had led the Whitewaterford array. He stood in the porch of a church with some of his people.

"Nay," he said to them; "I am not of Whitewaterford, but of Marling." When they asked why he had led the Whitewaterford battle, he answered again: "I am the hereditary guardian of Marling: I accept all challenges, and lead its battles. When the three burghs made agreement to be one in attack and defence, they chose the guardian of Marling for their captain. Therefore I came to Whitewaterford without staying for my folk to follow me."

He was a fair, blue eyed man, as tall as Harvanger, and not unlike him, save that he was of middle age. From his speech, they judged him a keen and skilful captain, expert at arms.

So they took Horn's counsel, and on the morrow left Whitewaterford, and came to Marling.

CHAPTER II.: OF THE BROTHER WHO SOUGHT OUT ANCIENT BOOKS; AND WHAT HE TOLD THEM.

THEY deemed it a good place and fair, for it lay in the midst of a wide plain of meadows, with plenty of streams, and tall poplars, and fields of corn. And in that spring-tide the waste was covered with dear and homely flowers, daisies and buttercups amid the grass, and dandelions which the husbandmen dug up with little spades; and the wild roses were in flower. But for the most part all was delved and ploughed and

[153]

ordered by men's hands, so that things ran not wild very much, but were as clean and prim as any garden. Beside a stream was a little white abbey of monks; there may have been ten or fifteen brethren therein.

Goldbeard had great joy in all these sights. He loved the corn-fields and the meadows, and could speak to the churls as though he were one of them. He would walk forth into the fields, and show Harvanger how they were ordained and carried out; but Bernlak stayed with the lawmen, and conversed with them about ancient wars that had befallen in that land, and the goodness of the times; and Horn tarried chiefly with the monks, speaking of strange things written down in books.

So on a morning he took Harvanger by the hand and said: "Friend, whither will ye go to-day?— for I have somewhat to show you." Harvanger said he would do as Horn willed.

"Then we will go to the monks," quoth Horn.

The abbey was fairly built among the fields, outside the burgh wall. It had a kitchen garden, where the brethren laboured, and a garden of flowers; and all around the buildings went a circle of tall poplars, through which the roofs and walls peeped. One of the brethren was a carver, and had carved a part of the walls, as well as the chapel. Horn showed his carving to Harvanger, and the brother looked on and blushed for pride at their praise. But one was a great collector of

[154]

books. He lived in a cell that was full of all manner of written things, and he knew how to write and how to devise the floriating of letters. Nothing did he love so much as to be told some tale or history worthy to be written down. So when they had come to him, he showed Harvanger all his books, and made a narration of how he had gathered them together; for he had travelled in far countries, and when at any time he heard of some new book, either an old one or one newly devised, straightway he would go thither to see whether or no he might obtain it or copy it. Harvanger wondered at the books, and at the pictures in them, and the scrolls of leaves and flowers that ran round the margins; howbeit, he understood no more.

"Friend," said Horn, "fetch forth the book we read yesterday. I desire you to show it to us."

"Willingly," quoth he, as a man well pleased at the asking. He brought a book bound in blue leather, with clasps of gilded brass, and opened it on his desk before the window. Then he said: "Of a truth, friends, this is an ancient and veracious history, which I prize above all other books, for it holds the tale of Marling itself, and has been written in by many men before me. Now ye shall behold it."

Thereupon they beheld it, as he turned the pages. Harvanger gazed upon the pictures, which were of

[155]

many men faring over the sea in ships; and presently the pictures changed, and showed a land full of trees, small and strange and beautiful, wherein that folk dwelt as in a garden of Eden. And anon were more pictures; of which the first was of a great ravine of rocks, and that folk wending out with waggons drawn by long-horned oxen; and the second was of a great forest, and some of the folk wending as before, and some lingering behind as if they would remain, and go no further. Harvanger said: "Why do these people tarry behind?"

Answered the brother: "The writing declareth it to be that they are weary of marching, and desire to remain in the place wherein they are."

Then the pictures showed the folk making a burgh; and anon they were departing from the burgh, leaving some behind; yet thereby they were in nowise diminished of number. Another picture showed them making a new burgh elsewhere. Then said the brother, proudly:

"What burgh is this, young man?"

"I know not," said Harvanger.

"Then I will tell thee. It is Marling, where we dwell. And I deem that my fathers were of this folk; for I am like them."

Harvanger gazed upon him, and thought it might truly be so; for the brother was like unto the folk in the picture, tall, and fair, and fresh of

[156]

face, and like the man who had called himself the hereditary guardian of Marling.   He wondered at this strange tale.

"Turn to the next picture," said Horn.

When they had done this, they found the folk departing in their waggons, leaving some behind; and next they made a new burgh, which the brother said he had been to see.   But the folk left that place as before, and founded a new burgh; and after a while they had no rest there, but departed.   Yet not as before; for those who went away did not march together, but divided into two parties; and the name of the picture was THE PARTING WAYS, and over it was an escutcheon, with a great Y, as on the sign of John Taberner's hostel.

"I have been to this burgh," said Harvanger, "and it lieth over beyond Greenwood."

"Yea, it should be so," answered the brother, "but never yet have I been so far that way."

The folk having divided, one part thereof wended through a wood; and these were the chief men of the folk, with a few followers.   They founded a burgh bigger than ever before, and its name was written above it: LONG WHITE-WALL.   These of the folk marched no more, abiding in that place for ever; but the rest fared on into a great forest, but now it was without its leaders and kings, and some lingered behind, and

[157]

desired to go no further for weariness; and after that the book ceased, and he who wrote the history said at the end, that neither he, nor any man he could find, knew what had become of that part of the folk, but deemed them all lost, or else that they had come over the mountains towards the great sea. Wherewith this part of the book was finished, and the tale of Marling begun, save for a picture of Adam and Eve, and the serpent wound about the tree; but the brother said that this picture was no great matter, and of rights belonged to another book.

Then said Horn: "What became of those who tarried in the forest at the last? How sayest thou, Harvanger?"

Harvanger ran his fingers through his hair, and smiled, answering: "It may be that one or two thought Greenbank no ill spot to dwell in."

"So I deemed," said Horn.

But Harvanger added: "Friend Horn, it may be, too, that of those who passed the great mountains, some have returned in these days."

"Who knoweth?" said Horn. "But what burgh did that folk found, before they built Marling?"

"It is now called Whiteways," answered the brother; "but it is not large, and is now mostly deserted, since Pike of the Weir established his stronghold therein."

"To Whiteways will we go," said Horn.

Presently they left the brother, who was sorry for their departing; and they thought him a good man. Harvanger gave him a florin, towards the buying of books.

## CHAPTER III.: DAY DAWNS IN THE ANCIENT CHAPEL OF WHITEWAYS.

SO they took their leave of the Marling folk, and followed the road to Whiteways; a long road, as it proved. But it was little dull. Ever the fair plain stretched before them and on each side, flowery and green and smiling in the early summer, with grassy banks, and paths white in the sun's heat. They followed the track of the Companions, who passed on taking ransom, where they could, of big or little, fighting where they must, but chiefly avoiding the stronger towns, because the letters of the bonded burghs had run on ahead of them. As they went, the three and Bernlak made inquiry of such folk as they encountered; and some stared, and some smiled, but all told them that their journey should be as that of those who go out for wool, and come home shorn. Then Goldbeard said wrathfully:

"Who is this man, Pike of the Weir, of whom we are told so much?"

"Do ye not know him?" they demanded. "His name is bruited well abroad. Well, we might

[159]

have guessed that ye knew him not, or ye would not seek him."

"What doth he do?" said Goldbeard.

"Sirs, he dwelleth by Mill Weir, which is the chief entry into this land, and he holdeth all passers to ransom or death. Surely he is right evil of manner and custom; for since he came to dwell in that place, the country thereabouts hath dwindled of its folk; he holdeth the ancient towers of Whiteways by the river Bordering, beyond which lie other lands, of which we know little in these days, albeit our fathers used to know them well. That time was different. Pike hath many a knight and squire, of diverse countries, in his livery; he keepeth all his neighbours down by fire and sword, and scat and tax. Right cruel is he also, and expert in deeds whereof men speak largely, but not loud. In truth, sirs, few go that way, and little do we know of how the place looketh; howbeit, men say that there are wizards, and all kinds of marvellous things in it; and a knight garbed in silver and scarlet, who rideth about a wood—we know not why or wherefore; and there is a scarlet banner set on a hill, we know not why, nor who set it there. And men say, moreover, that Pike is established there by a great and mighty one, to hold the passage lest men find out his haunts; though who he is, and what he does, we know not either. In all ways, sirs, it is a strange place, nigh to the beginning of the world."

[160]

"I desire to see the beginning of the world," quoth Bernlak.

"Thou art as like to see the end of it," said Horn.

"Then this Pike is a robber?" demanded Goldbeard.

"As Barabbas was," answered Bernlak. "But honest men's dwellings are seldom strange. If ye would seek adventure, seek out evil."

"For the evil and the good are at the beginning and the end, and the middle is mostly neuter," said Harvanger.

"The boy is right," quoth Horn, laughing. "Evil and good lie in extremes, yet close together. A hair divideth them; which is why men err so greatly."

"In all this," said Goldbeard, "I see no reason why we should not seek out Pike."

"Another is also seeking out Pike," answered Horn, "and his name is Paranides."

So they fared on, in hope to discover why this should be so. And some folk would not speak to them of Pike, but others would; from whom they heard tales that they deemed strange. As they journeyed further, they heard more of these tales; and there was a man of arms, a squire, who stood in a market-place, and said:

"Ho, messires!—I have fought against Pike in old times. He is a mighty big man of his hands, not lightly to be undertaken. But as for what he

[161]

can do, I count it not a fly. The sun shineth over
Mill Weir, and Whiteways is full of flowers in
summer. The Devil is present in all places, I
understand. So ye are no liker to meet him there
than here; at the worst, all men must die. If I
deemed death so evil, I should be a monk."

"Ye say truly," answered Goldbeard.

"Well, sirs," quoth the squire. "Ye shall find
force and fraud and great marvels at Whiteways;
but since ye shall find force and fraud everywhere, the marvels are the only new things ye
are like to see."

They thought this talk better to their minds
than anything they had heard before. Then they
met a cleric, who told them for certain that Pike
was a great heathen, and persecuted the Church;
at which Bernlak was grave, but Goldbeard
answered that he knew not what the church was
like, out Pike's way. And the more that men
spoke of the dread of Pike, and the horror of his
house, the more desire had those three and Bernlak
to behold him.

It came well into August before they knew, from
folk whom they fell in with, that they drew near to
Whiteways. The towns ceased as they approached it, and the country was given over to
wide green meadows, and marshland, and copses
of wood. Still, it was good to see, and very fair.
Upon a day they came to cross roads, and no man
was near to direct them. Then Bernlak said:

"It comes to my mind, friends, that we must sunder for a while. Let two take one road, and two another; we can meet again at Whiteways."

"Ye ride a horseback, messire," quoth Goldbeard, "and we are afoot."

So at last, after speaking long, it was settled that Bernlak should ride west, and the three wend east; whereof great adventures befel; but they swore to meet again at Whiteways.

Now let us speak first of the three that journeyed east. They walked seven days, and on the seventh day came down over a ridge into a river land, and a white road, bordered with goodly trees. About the hour before dusk they saw a house with white walls and red roof, planted amid trees. A garth wall ran thereabout, and over it grew lilac bushes, poplars and elms. So they approached; and the house was near to a river, great and wide, and full of water. Then they understood that it was a mill; for there was a weir, over which the water slid and tumbled in foam, and a great still pool above it. The weir was made to turn a water-wheel; but it seemed as if the mill did little work.

"This must be the MILL WEIR," said Horn.

"What of that?" demanded Goldbeard.

Said Horn: "The Mill Weir is a great entry into all the lands we have passed, even to Long Whitewall itself, and Greenwood. Not far hence should be Whiteways, for it is from here that Pike of the Weir getteth his name."

"It may be so," answered Goldbeard.

They also perceived that a ferry boat ran over the river, and they went upon the landing-stage, and saw the reeds and flags growing around the edges; and the posts and piles were green with weed, and tench and dace flitted in the water.

"If one had a line, one could catch fish in this pool," quoth Goldbeard.

"Pike, maybe," answered Horn. Then he lifted up his hand and pointed beyond, to where somewhat, like a dark cloud, rested on the sky-line. "Behold," he said; "that is Wildwood."

"Black as a sleeping bear," said Goldbeard.

"It is a mighty big forest," said Harvanger. "I deem we shall see it anon."

"O, yea," answered Horn, "ye shall have as much thereof as ye list, and belike more."

While they stood on the landing-stage, and gazed, they saw a rider on a horse, beyond the river. He issued from a dell, and was armed all save his head in glittering mail, which flamed suddenly whenever the light struck it. His horse was white, and his bonnet of scarlet. He entered a small wood, and they saw him no more.

"Ye see," quoth Horn, "that not all men are liars."

But since the boat was not to be found, they left the landing-stage and returned to the mill,

[164]

where they found a door, and knocked.  An old man came, and opened the door.

"Friend," quoth Horn, "can we pass the river?"

"Yea," said he, "if ye love swimming."  They thought this unfriendly.

"What should hinder us from taking the ferry?" Horn made demand.

"That there is no boat.  Ye must needs go to Whiteways, for the boat is there, and hath been this long time."

"Well, show us the road to Whiteways," said Horn.

Suddenly, a man of arms strode out of the dusk of the room.

"If ye will go hither," said he, "I will show you the road.  I am here to show all wayfaring men to Pike.  But it waxeth over late of the day; wherefore ye had best sleep here to-night.  In the morning I will lead you to Whiteways."

After taking counsel, they agreed to this, and entered the mill.  The chief room was large and low, paved with flagstones and beamed with oak; from the beams hung onions, and bacon-hams, and fishing-rods.  But they saw nought of evil.  The old man fetched them ale, and trout well cooked, and rye-bread, so that they were well content, and thanked him.  When they had supped, the old man took a taper, and showed them each a room. Harvanger had a small room with a window.  He knew not where Horn and Goldbeard slept.  The

[165]

window was open, and the fresh scent of the country came through it, and he deemed himself well lodged.

So it fell dark, save for the stars, and a new moon. Harvanger leaned forth of his window awhile, musing and dreaming. When he was weary, he lay down upon his couch, and slept; but it was not yet midnight when he heard a bell clash and ring, and awoke, and looked out of his window. Thence he could see the garth, with its trees and lilac bushes, and also the road beyond; but the other side of the house was hidden, nor did he know what it might be like. And it seemed to him that he saw a knight in arms of silver, and a cap of scarlet, who rode along the ways, and looked upon the door, and afterwards departed. Also, he thought that this knight was the one he had seen across the river.

The bell rang no more, and he fell into a light slumber; all was dark when the horned moon had set, but the night air was balmy and sweet. So at some time he awoke, and listened; for he fancied that a door was opened, although he could not see it, and there was a wind upon his face. But it was dark, and Harvanger had forgotten where he was, and thought he was in his house at Greenbank. Therewith he started up suddenly, and found a man within his grasp, who struggled, but said no word. Harvanger kept silence, and

[166]

they wrestled mightily in the dark, until he flung the man over, and something clattered on the floor. As to the man, no one knew what became of him; but most like he was stunned by his fall, and lay there till morning.

Harvanger drew his long shepherd's knife, for he deemed that some treachery was afoot; and felt for the door. He soon found it, and went through in search of Goldbeard and Horn; but when he had gone a few steps, he found that a change had come, for this was not the entrance he had come in by, but another. He touched a great wall of huge stones; and steps ran up. Along this passage he went slowly, feeling each step. Anon he saw a faint beam of light, and knew that it was from a lantern in some alcove in the wall. He began to marvel afresh, and doubted but he dreamed. Then the light circled and flashed, and a man issued from the wall. Harvanger saw that the stair wound, and descended into another passage. There flashed out a great blaze of light, which, indeed, was but from a lanthern, and an armed man in yellow livery was aureoled in the glare.

He had not time to move or speak before Harvanger leaped upon him like a lion, and they both reeled and fell to the bottom of the stairs, and rolled against a door. Harvanger was uppermost, and thrust home with his shepherd's knife. The man lay still; and Harvanger's voice sounded

[167]

strange as he asked: "Who art thou?" But he got no answer, for his stroke had been mortal. So he stood up in the darkness, and listened. There was no sound; so he felt for the door, and found it unlocked, and pushed it open, and passed through.

Then he fell on one knee, for he was no longer in Mill Weir. Dawn came breaking over White-ways, and its first beams glowed like fire through a window. He gazed, and saw Saint Michael all bathed in a glory of gold and red, trampling down the Dragon, and about him fighting angels, richly apparelled in all the colours of Heaven. He thought they lived and moved; and he watched the vast irradiance that glowed and shone before his eyes. And the dawn grew, and the sun's rim rose above the blackness of Wildwood, and the birds began to twitter. But Harvanger remained as one in a trance, amazed. He stood up again, as it grew lighter, and saw that he was in a chapel, vaulted and pillared; and Saint Michael was but a figure in a window.

## CHAPTER IV.: HOW THEY DEPARTED FROM WHITEWAYS.

HARVANGER rose up slowly from the floor of that chapel, on whose level flags now shone the clear light of day. Now as he looked, he saw a door with a lock, and in the lock a bright star. He marvelled that a star should shine in a door. As he approached, he saw that the star was light coming through a key-hole; so he gazed through, and saw Horn sitting by a window. Then he said: "Friend, be ready, for I think it time and tide that we departed."

"So much the better," said Horn.

A bunch of keys hung on the wall. Harvanger tried three, and the fourth unlocked the door. So Horn issued out, and they held quiet counsel.

"I know not," said Harvanger, "where we are come unto; nor how we got here. Yet thou hadst best devise a way by which we may escape."

"Yea, presently," answered Horn. He looked round, and beheld suits of mail, and all kinds of weapons hung up on the pillars, as though the chapel were used as an armoury. "Let us arm ourselves," he said, "and then seek a way out, while I awaken Goldbeard; for I know not where he lieth, nor how we may easily go hence without him."

Thus they did, and soon were arrayed. Then Horn went to awaken Goldbeard. Harvanger found the door of the chapel, that was big and wide, and he opened it, and so came into a hall, in the calm light of morning. And as the chapel was, so was the hall, mighty with shafts and pillars, but beamed with oak, and hung around with tapestries of old tales. Great tables ran up and

[169]

down, and along each table sat many men. Harvanger gazed upon them; but they were all as dead folk, who neither speak nor move; for they slept, heavy headed with wine. Some were old, and some were young; diverse was their garb in colour and cut; and before them were cups of gold and silver, and beside them, weapons. Harvanger gazed long, full of wonder, and then betook himself back into the chapel, where Horn was; to whom he said:

"Here is a mighty great feast hall; and the folk armed and sleeping. I know not who they are, nor what place this is."

Horn answered: "Goldbeard is asleep also, and I cannot awaken him. Someone has taken the key; I cannot guess why."

"What then shall we do?" said Harvanger.

"Depart," answered Horn; "for Goldbeard will follow us. Now be silent."

They entered the hall, and the feasters slept on; and all the sound therein was their breathing, and the chirping of a linnet in a cage. Upon the dais lay a cross table, behind which sat three men. He on the right was a small man, whose white beard swept to his waist; but he was delicate of build, with long white fingers, and on one finger a ring set with a beryl. He in the middle was bigger; he had a cheerful, laughing face, and his beard was auburn and curling. And on the left was a tall man of fine feature and great strength; it

[170]

was Paranides. Then Horn mounted the dais
and beckoned to Harvanger. First he pointed to
the sword which lay loose on the board beside
Paranides; and Harvanger took it. Then he
pointed to the cup before the man with the auburn
beard; and Harvanger took the cup. Then he
pointed to the ring on the finger of the third man;
and Harvanger drew off the ring. Then Horn
strode off the dais, and Harvanger followed him;
but both kept silence. They went down the hall
between the sleepers, and none said any word till
they came to the end. But then the linnet
chirped, and clattered wildly on the wires of its
cage, and one man stirred and said: "I have
slept long. Is it morning?" And when he had
spoken these words, he yawned, and stretched
himself, and drove his elbow into the ribs of the
man who sat next; and that man woke suddenly,
and said: "What o'clock is it?" And so he
knocked over the cup of the third man who opened
his eyes in a sleepy fashion and said: "I have
dreamed that the clock struck thirteen. The Silver Knight has taken off his bonnet, and put on a
helm with a leopard crest, and the leopard's eyes
are two great emeralds." Then a fourth man
awoke; but by now had Horn and Harvanger
reached the door of the hall.

Therewith the first man perceived them, and
cried in a voice of thunder: "Ho, my masters,
awake, for the two wizards are departing." And

[171]

all the men at the tables awoke in great tumult, each gripping his arms.

Then quoth Horn to Harvanger: "Saddle three steeds." Harvanger rushed into the court, which was large and square, surrounded with grey walls of ancient stone. On the right were the stables, whose door was open. Harvanger took down saddles and bridles, and dight three horses for riding; he belted the sword to his waist, and drew the ring on his finger, and stowed the cup in his saddle-bag. Upon a nail was the key of the great gate. He took it, and rode forth again, leading two horses with him. And from the hall came the greatest tumult ever he heard, for the sleepers rose up all together, some still drunken, and thronged to the door; but Horn had turned the key in the lock, and cast the key over the wall. They who were within struck upon the door with their weapons, and made a huge din, as though all the fiends of hell were loose. Then Horn said: "Goldbeard is a hungry and thirsty man, and he ate and drank over well last night; but if this does not wake him, only the Trump of Doom will."

Yet, for all that, Goldbeard slept on. Now Horn turned to a horse, and put his foot in the stirrup to mount; and at the same time a bell began to toll, and other of Pike's folk came thronging by diverse ways into the court, with spears, and axes, and swords, so that they filled the place. Horn cried out in a loud voice: "The gate!— open the gate!" Harvanger heard him, and rode for the gate, leaving him struggling to mount. Anon the gate was opened, and Harvanger guarded it with the Death of Men in his hands. By this time Horn had mounted, and essayed to follow; but he was met by so mighty a rout that he could not. Then befel a great battle and a fierce, for the doors of the feast-hall gave and swung on their hinges, and through them poured the mailed reivers of Pike, and the flaming companions of Paranides, and Pike himself, in gold inlayed armour, and a coat of blue with three silver fish thereon.

"Where many meddle, least is done," quoth Horn; and he pressed through the raging crowd, which strove to grasp his bridle and pull him down. Then when the others in the court-yard beheld this, they fell upon those who issued from the feast-hall, deeming them to be his friends; and these last, being largely drunken or half drunken, fought right well with them. So their enemies did battle with one another in the gate-yard of Whiteways. Those who were slain were as many as the leaves that filled the dykes and hollows of Wildwood after the autumnal gales, and their blood was as July rain. And before Pike and Paranides could part the fighters, and show them their error, Horn had won free from those who assailed him, and had joined Harvanger; and they rode through the gate, and so departed.

## CHAPTER V.: OF BERNLAK.

NOW, concerning Bernlak, that was seven days parted from his friends. Far he journeyed, and swiftly, and things came so to pass that on the fifth day he looked upon a wide river and a deep; which men called Bordering, because it divided the Fair Plain from Wildwood, and the strange lands beyond. Bernlak heard that Whiteways was upon this river. A sweet land it seemed, and well wooded, with green grass like velvet, and the river was deep, and reedy, and green. Withal, the land was somewhat burdened with a blue haze, not to be seen close, but fleeing before and closing behind, as though a glamour of illusion hung over the place. And so men said of it; for whomsoever he met, implored him not to enter that land, and said that none did so, and yet returned whole, but were as those that go forth for wool, and come home shorn. But he paid no heed, for his mind was troubled with doubts lest his friends had come to ill; so he forded the river.

And it was the greenest country he had ever seen; he thought he had not seen such fair grass and such bright leaves, and the flowers were nodding and brilliant with a rain that never dried, and yet never fell greatly, but was like a dew from morning to noon, and noon to twilight.

Too long it would be here, to tell of all his adventures; for he took three days to press up the river to Whiteways; but there was an adventure of a ragged man who left him in fifteen feet of green water, to sink or swim back to the ford: and the knight Ossaise who held a passing at a little house for Pike, and was overthrown by the man of Varraz: and the daughter of Ossaise who brought him up to the passage which was nearest to Whiteways, and there the guardian had been reinforced, and Paranides had set his captain, Alyot Courtain, with others to hold the ford. But he forced it, nevertheless, and dealt with them so, that they said to Alyot: "We have done enough for one day. If Paranides is our leader, it is because he is the best man amongst us. Let him do it. We are spent." So they departed. And after that he fought a fight with Alyot and the guardian, and slew the guardian, and smote Alyot down upon the grass. Then Alyot said. "The Devil is in you, I think, messire"; and rose up, and presently was cast against a bush, and lost his glaive. So while he was grasping the bush and getting the sharp thorns in his hand, Bernlak put an iron shoe upon his throat.

"Alyot," he said, flourishing his long sword,

[175]

"thou art the prize I was fainest to have. Now I may have my will of you."

"That is true," quoth Alyot.

"But, Alyot," said Bernlak, "I would rather that you went to Whiteways on foot, as you are now, and told Paranides that I will fight his whole company with the Devil his sire for banner-man."

"I will tell him," quoth Alyot.

So Bernlak let him rise; and after a space he walked off to Whiteways, round the loop of the river. Then Bernlak caught his horse, and kissed the damsel, Ossaise's daughter, on the cheek, and sent her back to her own home. And she would willingly have accompanied him further, but that he said nay: for she thought him the mightiest man on earth. After this, Bernlak was in the domain of Whiteways. He forded the water and rode till he came to an inn. And there he saw two men riding towards him.

CHAPTER VI.: OF THE APPLE-ORCHARD, AND THE INN, AND THE DEATH OF PIKE OF THE WEIR.

BERNLAK gazed, and as they approached, he had great wonder, for they were Horn and Harvanger, and they seemed to have been in the biggest fight ever fought. When Harvanger saw who it was, he leaped from his horse, and ran and

[176]

embraced Bernlak; and Horn smiled. There was many a question asked and answered, and the more each knew, the more marvel he had. So after they had spoken together a space, Horn pointed to the Inn's sign, that swung above them. And it read thus: THE BEGINNING OF THE WORLD—with a picture of God creating the earth and the heavens.

"Ye have your desire now, friend," said he, "for we are verily come to the Beginning of the World."

The road passed in front of the Inn, and an orchard stood behind it, and on one side was a green bordered with trees and bushes. A tall white horse cropped the grass; it was barded and trapped in mail, and cloths of scarlet broidered with silver, now somewhat faded. Very rich and stately were all those garbings, and Bernlak, having wonder again, went to the Inn and knocked; and there came out a burly red-faced man wearing an apron.

"Ha, sirs," quoth he; "why knock ye at this door? It is sixteen years since any stranger entered here."

"We desire food and drink," said Bernlak.

"There are apples in the orchard, and water in the river; death in Mill Weir, and the Best Thing in the World beyond it."

"Have ye no meat or ale?" demanded Bernlak.

"Sirs, I have none," said the host.

[177]

"It may be," said Harvanger, "that thou hast somewhat that is dearer bought."

"True," said the host again.

Said Horn: "If he who last entered here is the man I deem him, it is Harvanger who should enter next."

"I will not say nay," answered the host.

"And it is neither the apples in the orchard nor the water in the river that I want," said Harvanger, "nor the death in Mill Weir; but that which lieth beyond it, which I have no monies fit to buy."

"Thou speakest well," said the host. "I will not shut this door to you, lad."

Then said Horn to Harvanger: "If the Silver Knight is within, give him the ring and the cup we took from Whiteways."

So Harvanger pushed open the door, and had to stoop to enter; for he was far taller than the folk of that land. The Inn had no more than one room, and walls bare, and a floor of beaten clay; thereon was a table and a chair, and on the table a sword, and in the chair a knight. The knight was all armed save his head, in burnished steel; and his côte hardie was of crimson; but had no armoury upon it. As to the man, he had a pale, fine face, thin lips, and hair blacker than a raven's wing; Harvanger thought he had seen it before in dreams, it was so pensive and delicate and yet so strong, more like a woman's face than a man's.

The Silver Knight said: "Who art thou?—and whereto goest thou?"

Harvanger answered: "My name is Harvanger; I come from Greenwood, and go to the Scaur Gap, seeking the Best Thing in the World, although I know not its name."

Then the knight saw the ring on his finger.

"Ha," said he, smiling suddenly, "I perceive that thou art well furnished; for thou hast my ring. Hast thou also the cup?"

Harvanger set the cup and the ring on the table.

"Truly," said the Silver Knight, "I thank you for them." He set the ring on his finger, and the cup in his breast. "Thou art welcome to my friendship, and thou shalt be free of the way to the Scaur Gap. And the sword thou wearest, thou shalt deliver it there for thence it came." He rose up suddenly, girded on his sword, and departed. He mounted on the white horse, and rode through the ford, out to Wildwood.

After he was gone Bernlak said: "Well, since there is no food, let us eat of the apples; for it is better to eat fruit than to starve."

"Much better," quoth Horn, "for I would sooner eat fruit than meat, any day."

"It is the great example of our Father Adam that lieth on my mind," answered Bernlak.

"Be of good cheer," said Horn. "It is not a woman that tempts you. And," he said laughing,

[179]

"I think you avoid the example of Father Adam in more ways than one."

"How so?" demanded Bernlak.

"Forsooth," answered Horn, "Adam was an husbandman, and ate bread by the sweat of his brow."

But while they debated, Harvanger had gone over the green, and entered the orchard. He shook one of the trees, and many apples fell, but few were quite mellow or ripe. Then he saw a fine branch, heavy with fruit; and therewith he climbed up, and laid hold of the branch, and shook it. And he thought he heard a noise of thunder, and the sound of a rushing rain.

So he came to the wicket and said: "Did I hear thunder?"

"I know not," said Horn, "unless it may be Goldbeard breaking through lock and bar."

"I deemed there was a noise of rain."

"That must be Goldbeard throwing things on the ground," quoth Horn, lightly.

Harvanger returned, and tugged at his branch until he wrenched it off; and he carried it back over the green.

"See," quoth Bernlak, "here is Harvanger bearing a branch of apples."

And the leaves rustled in Harvanger's ears till he said: "Did I hear men riding?"

"The array of Pike, marching afar off, it may be," said Horn.

[180]

Then they saw the flash of mail, and the colours of banners among the elm trees, and knew that it was truly Pike who followed them. So Harvanger mounted, and all three entered the water of the wide ford, and crossed over towards the great distant blackness of Wildwood.

As they rode their ways, they saw the Silver Knight, standing a-horseback on a knoll. His reins were loose, and there was a strange look in his eyes; but when they would have stopped, he waved them on, and they made no stay. Anon came Pike, bestriding a great bay charger, and his men of arms behind him; and they stopped awhile, to marvel at the Silver Knight, for none had seen him save from afar off, and many thought him but a tale that is told. He called out to them, and said:

"No wise man telleth the wealth of men unknown; he who does so is unwise. I counsel you to return, although I have no reason for giving you good counsel."

They murmured together, but Pike laughed.

"He is but a madman," said he; "for this is the brother of Rafe, who abideth in Greenwood of the north. Sorrow hath distracted his wits."

The Silver Knight gave a great start when he heard this, and answered: "I am a man, and not a shadow. I was born of woman, and am not yet dead. But if I were dead and buried I should

[181]

have more wits to understand wisdom than many who are sane. There is no task harder than to teach wisdom to a fool; for the dog returneth to his vomit, and the fool to his folly."

He turned away then, and they saw him go wandering in and out of the copses, as a man straying idly, and bereft of his senses. But there befel a great debate amongst themselves; for some said he was mad, and some said nay; and others said there was more wisdom in him than in a sane man, as is known from of old. So Pike demanded of his chief counsellor, whence danger could come; and the white-bearded man from whose finger Harvanger had taken the ring, was that man. He besought Pike to return home, for they knew not what lay behind the river, nor where they were, nor what dangers lurked.

Then said Pike, shaking his silky auburn beard: "If I am a fool, I may not amend it; if my judgment is that of a wise man, all is well. Let us go on."

And they went on, till noon was heavy and hot. And at last they ran the three to earth in a glade; and there was scrimmishing and fighting, and many of Pike's men overthrown, until Pike put on his own helm, and called for his spears. But Horn bade fight on, and said that Goldbeard would be with them soon.

It fell out as he said, for when Pike was making ready, they heard a sound, and saw a huge man

[182]

rushing along the ridge with great strides. It was Goldbeard, and he was in a mighty big rage, for his hair was tangled and falling on his shoulders, and his beard was all bristling, and his face red and wrathful. He sprang down the bent, and strode into the dell, and said in a voice like thunder:

"Ho, Pike: thou hast dwelt in the reeds of Mill Weir over-long, gobbling up the little fishes. There never was lightning that made eels wriggle in the mud as the flame of my hurler shall make you wriggle."

And Pike answered: "I never feared God or man."

So he spurred towards Goldbeard; and the sky had been clouding since they left the river, and a heavy cloud was over the heavens. And all at once the sun came out behind its nether edge, and sent a flame of light into Pike's face. Goldbeard reached for the steel hammer that hung at his belt, and raised it to throw; but Harvanger and Bernlak deemed that he never threw it, for then came a jagged bolt of lightning that ran over the ground in blue streams, and filled the dell with blazing fire and pealing thunder; and when it died out, Pike lay upon the grass, and Goldbeard still held the hammer uplifted to throw. They ran forward, but not much was left of Pike; for the flash had melted and fused the mail he wore, and burned him to a cinder. And his folk saw it likewise, and all

[183]

rode back to Whiteways like madmen, recking neither of bush nor briar, nor the pouring summer rain that flowed over the earth. And the tale tells, that the rain made the river rise suddenly; and presently the old weir broke, and let out such a flood of water, that most of Pike's men, as they were in the ford, were washed away by it. So after that, Paranides reigned in Whiteways; and nobody thought the change made much difference.

But those three and Bernlak rode their ways, and entered Wildwood. At the end of the day there was a purple-crowned ridge before them, and trees along its foot. They approached through the tall furze until the purple line grew into a giant land, an ocean of trees. Then Horn said: "My friends, behold—this is Wildwood."

They paused to look upon it, and the surging sea, crowned with foam-crested waves, where the oak and the beech struggled together. In this way they left the homes of men far behind and came towards the Thing which Harvanger should find beyond the Scaur Gap.

## BOOK V.: HE GOES THROUGH WILD-WOOD, AND FINDS THE WILD-WOOD MAID BEYOND IT.

## CHAPTER I.: HOW THEY LAY OUT IN WILDWOOD, UNDER THE FOURFOLD TREE.

IT was a night of hottest August when they made their camp under the edge of Wildwood—those three and Bernlak. All about them was the deep wood, and they were far now from any dwelling of men. There was a great glade in the wood, and in that glade a tree, which Horn said was called the Fourfold Tree, because it seemed four trees, and yet was but one. It fell dark soon after they had eaten their meal, and Orion showed in the coal-blue sky overhead, very large and brilliant.

They were all weary with the work of that day, and soon were sleeping. Harvanger lay with his head pillowed on a bank of wild flowers, as he had lain many a night before, out in the thick woods nigh Greenbank. And with the bloom and glory of that imagination, he fell a-dreaming.

And he saw the Silver Knight walking his horse beside a purple pool, where grew white lilies, and flag-flowers yellow and blue together. Before him went a woman, with skin as white as the white lilies, and her mouth purely pink as the roses in the

[187]

pleasaunces of Whitewall, and her eyes were dark blue, like the flag-flowers. As for her hair there was never any raven quite as black, nor any silk floss quite so fine. A robe of green was upon her body, and the robe was woven with flowers in patterns; but her arms were bare from the elbows down, and her feet from the ankles. Withal, she bore an apple branch in one hand, and on it apples very like gold. Harvanger saw the two of them walking, and wondered in his heart, and was sorry it was a dream.

Then he began to dream again, and there was a fair wooded plain before him; and there was the maid, sitting under a tree and weaving garlands of flowers; but the Silver Knight was not there. So Harvanger watched her, and presently rose up, and went towards her over the long grass, and sat down beside her. And he put forth his hand, and touched the long dark hair that fell upon her shoulders; but she moved not for all that, but went on making garlands deftly with white fingers. Harvanger thought that he was never better content than while doing this; for he sat and watched her fingers move, and her elbow move, and her shoulder move, and he wished for no other thing in all the world but only that. And after a while he thought someone had told him that a hundred years had gone by, and he must depart. But he answered that the time was over-short; and he was not sure that this was a dream.

[188]

It was not long before he began to dream again, and beheld the scarlet towers of Long Whitewall; and he was riding towards it. And a vast army was collected before the burgh. So when he came to the gate, he rode through it, and up to the minster close, which was full of folk. There were Paranides, and the Duke, and diverse others; and the maid standing in the midst with downcast eyes. Then he tried to pierce the crowd, and to gain her side; but Paranides was ever before him, fending him off; and however Harvanger fought there were never any fewer about him, and Paranides was never slain. So Harvanger all but burst his great heart with rage and sorrow, and knew not clearly what hurt him, but it was more bitter than any other sorrow in all the world. And so mighty grew his wrath and hate for Paranides, who would keep him from the Maid, that he gave a cry and sprang up. And it was early dawn, and he had been dreaming, but he had not thought it a dream.

Then said Horn, who was sitting under the tree, watching him covertly: "Art thou hag-ridden, friend, that thou criest out thus?"

"Nay," said Harvanger, "I dreamed."

"And of what?"

"Of the things life is made of: wonder, and joy and sorrow, and love and hate."

And Horn could find no more from him; but smiled, and said he spoke wisely. Harvanger lay awhile between sleeping and waking, not sure in

[189]

his mind what had come upon him. Then he said:
"There are many things left out and forgotten;
and some are kept in that are not needed."

"Which be they?" demanded Goldbeard.

"O, he is waxing in wit," answered Horn, "but
I deem, if I had said that, I should have meant
craft on the one part, and wrath on the other."

"This is a tree of dreams," said Goldbeard,
colouring, "for it is fourfold, as the days of life are
four. One branch is young, and full of shoots,
and one is green and leafy; and one is grey and
dead, and the fourth one is ever-living."

"And that one should be called the Branch of
Love," said Horn, "for birth and life and death
pass by, but love endureth for ever."

Harvanger turned to look at the tree; and it
was the ever-living branch that he had lain under.

All that autumn they journeyed through Wildwood, and when the winter came, they found a
garth in the midmost wood, and dwelt there gaily.
But in the spring of the year the Silver Knight
haunted the wood again; and they followed his
ways, and came at last to the further end of that
mighty ocean of trees.

## CHAPTER II.: OF THE RED HERMIT, AND OF THEIR COMING TO THE SCAUR GAP.

IT was the middle of May when they forded a stream that lay between dense thickets of thorn, dotted with ancient oaks; and lo, there jutted forth a fierce edge of rock, brown below, and blue in the deepest of the pool, but in the dry parts grey and lichen-covered. They marked it, and said that now surely did they draw near to their journey's end. Harvanger's heart beat; and he said: "I know not what we shall find there—but it shall be something strange, and past belief for the wonder of it."

"Yea, mayhap," quoth Horn, "if we have eyes to see, and ears to hear."

All that week they pressed on their ways, and each hour they looked about them, half hoping and half fearing suddenly to see a great marvel. Ever the rock came nearer the ground, and the soil was shallower over it; the brooks foamed over great stones, and fell into hollows, and there was abundance of rock of all kinds. And so the time wore on until an evening, when they ungirthed in a little vale, with the woods rising high on either side; but Horn stood apart, gazing before him.

"What dost thou see, friend?" said Harvanger.

Horn took him by the arm, and pointed; and

[191]

beyond the trees which closed the end of the glade arose a vast line of mountains, blue and dim and terrible in the broad evening light.   Then he said: "Lad, beyond that lies the land of the Three Kings, mighty, great, and glorious; and amidst of it is that which thou seekest."

Harvanger might not sleep for the terror and the hope that were in him, and the presage of a new life that should be more wonderful than dreams. But they journeyed on betimes, and so wore through another day or twain; and then they un-girthed beneath a tall rock, and waited the night through more waking than sleeping.   And before the sun had broken over Wildwood, they arose, and trussed their harness, and rode on through a brook that tumbled amid stones; and now the wood was well-nigh over, so that when they turned about it lay behind them as a cloud; but before them all was broken into a multitude of steeps and scaurs and beyond lay the wide line of the mountains. The dawn spread apace, and as it became light they turned clear of the rough land, and saw the moun-tains stretching east and west, save where, before them, a great shard was pieced out—a huge ra-vine.   Horn pointed and said: "Here is the Scaur Gap."   And well they gazed upon it and upon each other.

So they journeyed on betimes over the stony land that lay betwixt wood and mountain, and at the end of the day they rested in a dale cloven out of the sheer rock. Fair it was, and yet awful, bordered thickly with trees, and cut in twain by a river that welled from the hills, and came down in falls and pools. Yet still the woodland clung to the face of the earth. Horn said, the water was called Doom Water, after an ancient name well-nigh forgotten by the passing of time. All that place was ancient; yea, and the dwelling of men long since gone forth into the wide world, who were strong and all-winning, and yet to whom befel many wonders and haps, both good and evil. A change had come over times and days, and some things were forgotten, or remembered only in books; but the strangeness clung, and it seemed a land where men were not rightly the same as other men, but different, and younger, and fuller of all passion and labour, and wise and glorious.

And when they had eaten, and listened to the half-told stories, and the hints that Horn gave, they went to sleep. But Harvanger rose up after a while, and went to the water bank, and stared into the dusky depths.

So anon he saw a light, and at that he marvelled, and it was in his mind to go thither and behold it. He went up the water bank until he came to a narrow, where the water slid down a force swiftly between high banks; and there were trees all about, and in the stream many branches and logs left by the spring floods; and from bank to bank ran a wooden bridge. Then he passed over the bridge,

[193]

and saw the moon rising over the mountains, a thin crescent arched over with dots of light. He strode on; and now he saw a chapel built of stones, and roofed on high. The door was open, and thence came the brightness he had seen. For in the chapel stood an altar, with many candles burning, and behind the altar, on a red cloth, hung a sword, and beside that were hooks for another sword, albeit none was there. And it seemed to Harvanger that he had known this place of old.

When he turned about, he saw one who was garbed as an hermit, and white bearded; but his face might not be seen, because of his cowl, and his hands were clasped, but hidden with huge sleeves. And he spoke and said to Harvanger: "I am called the Red Hermit. I know thy name and thy kindred, for they have been told to me. Tell me what bringeth thee so far to this place."

Harvanger paused before answering. It was but a year since he had left Greenbank; yet it seemed longer, for he had grown in body and mind, and was no more a boy, but a man, secure of speech and sure of manner. And he felt a little of this, for it was borne in upon him that he knew better what he desired than aforetime, and was not innocent of what he wished to gain. He cast his eyes on the Hermit, and answered:

"So it was, that I dwelt in Greenbank, which is beyond Greenwood, and my mother and my father nourished me to manhood; and that was a dear

[194]

and pleasant world, and all I knew of as then. But they died; and I went forth and departed to seek another world as dear and pleasant. And I come here because beyond this land is one in which there is the Best Thing in the World; and thou shalt direct me thither. I have not found among men that which I desire; nor do I know how to attain it, save here."

The Red Hermit answered nought awhile. Then he said: "Deemest thou not that, by hap, love is a wage earned through deeds? Why should men love thee when thou hast done nought to deserve it?"

"Nay," said Harvanger, "never did I do ought that should earn me love of my father and mother, being but a child. For I think that love cometh more of being than of doing; I was myself, and they loved me; and I them."

"True," said the Hermit. "But tell me, young man; what wilt thou do with the love thou gainest?"

"As I did with the love of my parents," quoth Harvanger; "for we loved one another, and from that all things flowed."

The Red Hermit answered: "Thou hast a sword which is not thine."

"If I knew whose it is by right," said Harvanger, "I would render it again." And he touched Paranides' sword, which was belted round his waist.

[195]

Then the Hermit beckoned him, and he followed into the chapel, and so came to the altar, where the sword hung glittering in the candle light. And the Hermit said: "Hang thy sword by its fellow."

Harvanger strode up, and drew his blade; it flashed and gleamed, and was straight and well-balanced, until for a moment he yearned to keep it. But he hung it beside its fellow, and the two glittered together.

"Choose which of the two thou wilt have," said the Red Hermit. "One is named THE DEATH OF MEN, and the other THE DEATH OF KINGS; and there is power of death in either, and power of rule."

"I will have the Death of Kings," said Harvanger; "for I do not think I shall need to fear any other folk save the mighty." And therewith he lifted it from its hooks, and ran it into its scabbard, and so returned.

"Now thou hast the gift that is won at the Scaur Gap," quoth the Hermit.

"I think," said Harvanger, "that there is more to be gotten than this. I will not believe that even the best of swords can be the Best Thing in the World."

The Red Hermit regarded him intently; then he said: "It shall be as thou wilt. Go hence to-morrow, and enter the Scaur Gap."

So Harvanger issued forth of the Chapel, and

came to the little bridge, where Horn stood pensively; yet neither spoke ought to the other, but they went their ways to their sleeping place, and on the morrow they began to climb the Scaur Gap.

Many days were they in climbing, for the way was rough and steep; and soon they were in the midst of the mountains, with their path no more than a ledge before them, and Doom Water falling and foaming below. And all about them rose up grey cliffs. Three days they climbed; and by then Doom Water was grown small, until they passed the shed of the waters, and beheld the streams flowing westward. All that time they laboured sorely, what with the roughness of the way and the hard fare; but when they had passed the shed of the waters the passage widened into a way between broad hills, and they could often see a glimpse of somewhat beyond, which was green and blue. On the seventh day they camped below a high cliff, and Harvanger reached out his hand, and said:

"We draw near to the dwellings of men."

"Nay," quoth Horn, " there are none here."

"Then white harts haunt the mountains," said Harvanger.

"Thou hast been dreaming, lad," answered Horn.

Said Harvanger: "It is as I say; for surely have I seen a man or a woman in the distance."

[197]

Afterwards they journeyed further downward, and on the road met a bear, and slew it. Then Harvanger said: "Folk dwell hereabouts."

"Then they are since my time," quoth Horn; and likewise said Goldbeard. But Harvanger felt the grip of spring, because he was young; and he took to watching by night. And on an evening he saw a thing that was white under the moon; and a great longing came into his heart. Also, he would fall asleep as he watched, and dream of the milk-white maid he had seen under the Four-fold Tree; and then he mingled the twain together, and shaped a story in his heart, and thought that the maid dwelt alone in the waste; and over this he brooded. It was not long after that they came down into a vale, which Horn said was named Folkvale, because men once lived there; and, indeed, a great doom-ring of ancient peoples lay in it, somewhat fallen, so that the dolmens lay about. Towards the east, the land rose up into a rocky ridge, and Horn said:

"Lo, now we are nigh to the end of our way-faring; for beyond this ridge lieth the best land in all the world; yea, in spring the flowers are knee deep, and deeper; and such abundance of nuts and corn in the fall of the year that no man could starve there, save a devil possessed him. There are lakes and waters, and woodland, and plain-land; there is neither snow nor bitter wind, but fair wind all the year, and bright sun even in winter, and the rain is gentle and kind. And in summer the brake is so thick that it cannot be seen for blossom. It is not a large land, but small, and full of sweet corners, and harmless beasts—yea, a very fair land."

So they deemed themselves well come into it. But at night the moon rose golden and splendid, and Harvanger lay awatch; for his dreams were full as the moon, and as golden, and every hour he expected some wonderful thing to happen. He thought that Way-wise ruled this land as a mighty magician, more wonderful than any woman's son; and he thought that a maid dwelt in the midst of it, in a little house half hidden among apple trees that were now blossoming. He thought he had seen her once in dreams; and she was fleeter than a doe. And then, as he lay half asleep, he thought she passed by quickly, and was lost in the break of the ridge. And he fell fast asleep and dreamed.

## CHAPTER III.: THE DREAM-HUNTING OF HARVANGER AND YOLANDE.

THEY slept that night and there were tall rocks, clothed with moss and bushes, about them, and short smooth grass, and before them the slopes and towering cliffs of the great mountains, and the water that foamed and flowed through

[199]

the vale; a plentiful country and good, luminous and bright.

Harvanger slept there under a tree; and presently he began to dream; and he dreamed that he sat on the edge of a tall bank, grass covered, above the fairest land that ever eye saw. He deemed it may-time—for the moon was bright, and the grass fresh and springing, and the leaves new-grown; and the scent of apple-blossom was heavy in the air. The moonlight fell on the land, and the mist made bright webs of silver that circled round the orchards and trees; very fresh it was, and rich. Strange enticing glades, magical and mysterious, departed on every side; everywhere were long, mist-wrapped vistas, and glades of grass, and tall parklike trees. Never was a sweeter little land than that.

So as he gazed, he saw something white moving. He thought it a deer at first; but presently it moved out of the shadow into the moonlight, and it was a slim youth, carrying a long tapering bow —very deadly and limber, both of them, he deemed. But then again, the youth moved nearer, and turned, and he saw that it was a woman, by shape, and walk, and motion; and when her face looked against the moon, he thought it the maid he had seen in his dream under the Fourfold Tree. He wondered at that with sudden deep wonder and desire. So quietly he slipped over the edge of the bank, and dropped to the ground, and jumped through the bushes and over the silvery brook. He looked about, and saw the Wildwood maid passing on forth by apple trees; and he stepped on very lightly and very swiftly to meet her— none could step more softly than Harvanger, when need was. No twig broke, nor did any leaf rustle; the dew was heavy and deadening on the grass.

So he passed into the little orchard; and the maid had passed in also; and neither saw the other. A curtain of blossom fell in front of Harvanger's eyes, sweet-scented, and most beautiful. But he listened with intentness. . . . And then, after turning round to look at the land, all quiet in moonlight and dew, he stepped a pace or two forward; and before either knew, they had walked sharply into one another, and both recoiled trembling, though neither knew why. Harvanger moved his grasp along the maid's arm; but she glided out like the very light of day, more subtle than a cat—and sped over the grass. He followed, and they ran; he not knowing why, or whereto, or whither. She moved from light to shadow, and from shadow to light, agile, swift, never hesitating, but quick and acute. And Harvanger felt a strange desire grow up within him, so that he followed and followed eagerly, with a little smile on his face; he would not have given up the delight of that chase, nor his pleasure in the swift and agile maid.

[201]

Then after moving in and out of the apple trees awhile, the maid fled suddenly across the glades, over the short grass; but that was a man's advantage, and Harvanger all but caught her ere she turned in amongst the trees on the further side, and so escaped; for a swift woman is swifter than the swiftest man in avoiding and turning and tricking. But Harvanger was never far behind now; and when the maid was forced out of the cover of the trees, they made a hard run of it down into a little dell, where was a brook, and a small lake, and trees thick scattered thereabout; and they ran round the lake, and doubled, and turned amid the trees, and at last the maid, for sheer weariness, had to run forth again for home. But Harvanger grew stronger every moment, and more set on his quarry, and more determined to catch it; not, as then, considering much what he would do with it when it was caught.

Now they came to the upland, and there was short smooth grass there; and they ran around a thicket, and Harvanger saw at last a garth wall, and a quickset hedge, and a gate thereto; also, within the garth, a little house. But before she came to the gate, the maid fell suddenly, and Harvanger fell too, over her, and his mind grew dark awhile; yet one thing he knew, which was, that his hand was upon her wrist. . . .

Then he arose suddenly and ashamed, and glanced about. The maid had arisen, and opened the gate, and leaned upon the gate somewhat wearily, for she was spent. So he sprang up and walked towards her; and true it was now, that she moved not at all, and made no effort to fly. The faint scent of the garden, and the breath of the stirring night air, and the silence of the un-silent woodland—these, and the white radiant moonlight, and the silvery web of the mists, and the deep coal-blue sky, and the luminous shades everywhere, Harvanger did not ever forget in coming days. And he took the maid's hand in his; he never forgot the touch of it, cold and warm at once, and living and shapely and sudden, he looked into her eyes, and she looked down again; but he was dream-bound, and only knew the pain of a vague yearning and a passion that had no end or aim, but was beautiful as heaven.

Suddenly he turned strangely sober, for he was lying on the ground, and the dawn was just spreading a wonderful translucent blue over the east; and near by sat Horn, with his hat pulled down and his cloak pinned up with long golden pins—watching. Harvanger thought he looked as if he knew more than a man, for there was something inscrutable in him; a calm and some hint of a knowledge deeper than he avowed.

## CHAPTER IV.: HARVANGER COMES INTO THE FAIR VALLEY.

IT was a morning of early summer when Harvanger lay between sleeping and waking; he remembered his dream, yet it was not any sudden eagerness, nor any fretful passion, but rather a feeling of peace and certitude that made him presently begin to look forth towards the ridge that he had passed in his sleep, and to regard it as a place that presently he should cross waking. He gazed at it a little while; he would have been at unpeace with himself had he thought that he might not pass it, or that weakness, or any other thing, might stay him. But so sure he was that he would presently attain that place, that he lay and looked upon it, and felt in no haste or hurry. When he had had his fill of gazing, he turned over and began to unbuckle the straps of his harness, which he had worn since that morning at Whiteways. He cast it off and was arrayed only in the dress he had worn of old; and that was a thin shirt of coarse linen, and breeches of the same, that ended above the knee, and leg swathes that ended below it, and shoes of soft leather, laced with a leathern lace. He took also his shepherd's coat of sheep-skin; it was short and armless, to wear in cold weather. He sat and thought over this garb; but his thoughts came to nothing, and were

[204]

only memories, and feelings of being free and at ease.   Then he rose up, and saw the dawn rising over the mountains.   He took a javelin and stepped across the sleeping Bernlak, and after a while was scrambling and climbing up the ridge. At the summit he stopped, and sat down.   It was like his dream, save that now he saw it by day-light; but however long he waited, he spied no one.

He went down the further side of the ridge now, and sprang over a brook, in which grew blue flags, just past their prime.   There also were for-get-me-nots growing in blue masses; and the grass was short and warm to his hands.   He sat there idly, but presently went walking across the vale under the scattered trees, listening to the sounds that were on the wind, the noise of birds, and the rustling of trees.   So long he went, that he forgot how long it was; but at last he came to a shallow lake that shone in the morning light; the swallows were skimming and flashing hither and thither, and turning with a spark of white, and darting back.   He lay under a bank, over which grew wild apple trees, and remained watching the brown water, with its border of sedge, and its weedy rim, and the discs of water lily, and the flies that fell into it, and made rings.   He saw in his mind's eye the water-beetles that would be running about the bottom; and he thought the bottom would be of soft clay.   Then he watched the flowers; and

[205]

looked across the land to the copses that were on every rising ground, growing dim as the distance grew. A deer was on the upland, and a wind-hover hung in the air a mile away. So he turned his eyes upon the wood about him, and searched out every thicket and dimness, but still saw no one. Then he fell quietly asleep.

When he awoke it was high noon or more; the sun was bright on the grass, and the sky full of light; the sun-flecks fell through the leaves and dappled the shade with gold. But Harvanger saw something more than this; for as he lay quietly among the grass, he saw a face that looked forth of the apple-foliage; a very pensive face that gazed upon him with deep eyes. It vanished then, and the foliage rustled; but Harvanger lay still, with ears alert for the least faint sound. There was no eagerness or wonder in him; neither were there any thoughts in his mind. He saw the land and the sky, and heard the birds and the breeze, and they passed before him like pure images, one as good as another; but the face he remembered twice. He turned his eyes further back, to look up the bank behind him; and he saw what seemed to be a slim youth with plentiful dark hair, and a tapering unstrung bow, that had leaped lightly from the trees to the bank, and remained watching, and ready to dart away like a deer. Harvanger knew that while he remained still, so would the other; and he wondered if it would be good to call

[206]

out, or whether it were not best to wait and watch. But he thought that least done may be soonest mended, so he stayed still.

Then that other one stepped afresh on the bent trunk of the tree, and came and looked down. Harvanger knew that it was a woman, for no youth was ever shaped so delicately. And she had a very strange face, broad browed, with a sharp and narrow chin, and very pensive eyes and mouth, half sad, and yearning, and tender. Yet Harvanger thought he must have seen that face before; there was somewhat of expectedness and familiarity in it, as though there were a place in his memories where it fitted perfectly, and was at home; and yet he knew that he had not seen it before, nor any countenance like it; and it was all of one colour, and pale; and her hair was dark and dark well-nigh to blackness. Thus much he saw.

Then he said: "If thou shakest the bough so, apples may fall upon me, and hurt me." And even as he spoke, a small immature apple fell and rolled near him. When he looked, the Wildwood maid was half way up the bank again, and watching.

Harvanger sat on the grass; and there was vexation in him now, lest she should depart altogether, and he see her no more. So he said again: "I pray thee, go not away. For I will

[207]

do thee no hurt or injury. I desire to speak to thee." But, nevertheless, she moved up the bank slowly, watching out of the corner of her eye, and then sprang into the bushes. He remained on the grass, and now that she was gone the land seemed not so good; there was an emptiness in even its beauty, and a lacking as of desire unfulfilled. As he sat discontented, he saw the maid again, issuing into the broad grass beyond the trees. She came towards him slowly, and then stopped. Harvanger very much desired that she would come near; but after a space, she went towards the lake, and was lost amid the trees. Still he watched, and anon he saw her approaching along the lake edge. So she came near, and then stood leaning against a tree; and presently came nearer, and sat down on the grass not far from him. They looked at one another, and it seemed to Harvanger that the craft of the fox was unrolled in him, so that he understood immeasurable things concerning speech and silence. And also he thought that in this woman were things that were in no other, and they were all things akin to himself, and he understood them; he would not have had any gulf between him and her.

He said: "Shall we speak together?"

"If thou wilt," she answered quietly.

"I would that we might talk together often; for I deem that there are many things we might say," said Harvanger.

She said: "There are not many people in this land; I dwell here with no other, and I know not what we should talk of."

They stayed gazing at one another strangely for a little while, and neither knew why.

"It is ill faring alone," said Harvanger; "for presently there is no one but would desire to speak to another, and have that other see what we see, and care for what we care for. Is not that so?"

"Nay, I know not," she answered, smiling suddenly, as though the thought were new, and yet had become true in the moment of his speaking.

"I will tell thee my thoughts," said Harvanger, leaning on his elbow. "It is the trouble of life that we seek to have those who are of like being to us, those who see as we see, and love as we love; because it is good to live among those to whom we can tell our thoughts; and yet withal it is hard to find them, and the search is long, and until we find them there is unpeace with us, or at least a constant hoping that to-morrow may see us find them; we live in to-morrow, not in to-day, and are not wholly content. But when at last we have found them, we are content and at peace; and we at length understand all things, and the trouble of life is no longer in us, but outside us, and we can deal with all trouble that is outside us, and yet be happy; whereas the trouble within us is hard and unhappy."

"Very wonderful things thou sayest," said she;

"and they seem true now; but certainly they were not true yesterday. Why is that?"

"So long as we know not what could be better," said Harvanger, "what is good seems very good; but when we see a better, the good is less good."

"I will think about that," said she.

Said Harvanger, presently: "My name is Harvanger. Hast thou a name?"

She answered: "I am called Yolande."

"Yolande," he said, "dost thou not think it good that I should tell thee what is in my mind, and thou me, what is in thine? For I will show thee many things."

She gazed towards the lake.

"Truly," said she, "it might be good; but I know not why."

"And thou wilt not fear me?" he said; "for indeed I will do thee no evil."

"Nay," said she, "I am not afraid."

Said Harvanger: "Hearken, then. Shall I tell thee a tale?"

She answered: "If thou wilt."

"Of old," he said, "I dwelt in a little house far away in Greenwood; I, and my father and my mother. I loved them, and they me. I lived in the woodland, and learnt the wonder and beauty that was in it; I never tired of the woodland, and of the things therein. Then there came to me a man of wisdom, who spake to me of the Best Thing in the World, and of how it was gained through that change of times and days, and that waning of joy which is called grief. And so it was, that I who had not ever cared to seek the Best Thing in the World, because I seemed to have it, presently lost that which I had; and my father and mother died. So I left my place in Greenwood, and set out to find the Best Thing in the World. And so I have come here to see if it is in this place, or whether I must go yet further to find it."

"Dost thou think it is here?" she asked.

"It may be," said he, "if I look."

She thought awhile. "What would it be like?"

"How should I know?" said Harvanger.

Yolande said: "If thou knowest it not to see, thou wilt never find it."

"I think I could tell it if I saw it," he answered. "Hast thou ever seen it?"

"I know not," she said. "I have never thought of it; it may be here."

"If I find it," he said, "I should take it away with me; and what wouldst thou do then?"

"Wilt thou go away?" she asked.

"Dost thou desire me to stop?" he answered.

Yolande said: "I know not." But he thought she might wish him to stay.

"Well," said Harvanger, nodding his head and his shock of fair hair. "I do not hurt thee."

"No," she said pensively.

He said again: "What dost thou think would be the Best Thing in the World?"

"Yesterday," she answered, "nothing seemed better than this fair land, and all that is in it. But it may be that there are better things that I do not know of."

Said Harvanger: "If thou likest me not, I will go away."

"I will tell thee when that happens," said she gravely.

"Then," he said, "I will be thy friend."

Yolande thought awhile, as if wondering over many things.

"What wilt thou do?" she asked.

"I will lie under the apple trees," he said lightly, "and in the day-time I will look at the land, and see if the Best Thing in the World is here."

She looked at him questioningly, as though still wondering what he was, and whether he lived on the earth or in the sky.

"Of old," she said, "there was never anyone here save me, and Way-wise, who comes seldom. I know not how I shall live with thee in this land."

"O," said Harvanger, "I will go away when I have found the Best Thing in the World."

Yolande still seemed pensive. Then she said: "Truly, it is hard to do new things, and I do not know in what ways I should act. Shall I bring thee food to eat, and milk in a bowl? What will be good to thee?"

"As thou wilt," he said. "I will eat and drink if thou art kind to give. But I can sleep without a roof; for this is a warm land, and I am hardy."

While they were still silent after this, she suddenly rose up, and fled away swiftly; Harvanger thought she moved fleetly and well. So he stayed where he was, and fell to thinking. And half he was glad, and half unglad, for now he began to seek into his soul, and wonder about himself, and be discontented even with the fairness of that fair evening. For he began to wish Yolande with him, and to long after her.

CHAPTER V.: THEY MAKE FRIENDS TOGETHER IN THE FAIR VALLEY.

WHEN the stars grew dim, and the vault of heaven was changing again into deep luminosity, Yolande stood at the door of the House in the Wood, and wavered in her mind between the dream and the reality. It was still a dim and shadowy world, although the bright light— brighter than ever at noon-tide, and purer—was breaking down the dale and creeping between the trees; dreams still lurked in the shadows. And at one moment she deemed that no change had come, but all was as it had ever been; and at another, she knew a subtle difference, and a heightening of life within her. So, after standing in the dawning-time awhile, she passed into the garth and did such things as she was wont to do. There were eggs to be found, if one sought in all the cunning nooks within and without the garth. Some she found, still warm, and stored into the fold of her youth's tunic; and presently came to a long avenue of woodland, where the vista went back into the dusk of the copse. A brook trickled between high grassy banks, and flags grew therein, not yet in bloom. She stood musing again; now picturing herself living through that day as before —but it seemed vague and unlikely; and now picturing herself seeking the lake—but although this seemed to be what would happen, she half hated it, and said she would not go. Yet it was all dreaming, and none of it was very clear. So Yolande returned to the House, and there was a wooden bowl with a handle, full of milk, besides the eggs. She touched neither, but sat down upon the edge of the bench, and mused further. And what was in her mind was the saying of Harvanger, that all people found it good to tell their thoughts to others, and share their heart. And something that was akin to fear came upon her, to think of the going down of the sun, when the blue shadows crept over grassland and woodland, and all was deadly quiet, and none near. For although this had once seemed restful and pleasant, it seemed dreadful now.

The dawn broke apace, and a ray of bright sun gilded the lintel. And then she thought that perhaps it was all a dream, and that Harvanger was a fancy of sleep, and in no wise real. Her heart fell so suddenly that she was fain to gather her thoughts together, and to remember all those things that make a difference between dreaming and waking. And when she had made sure of this, Yolande was glad, and questioned herself no more, but stood in the doorway and loved the dale, and the morning.

And being content with this, and sure, she wished no longer, either to go or to stay, but passed to and fro, satisfied; until unbidden and unrebuked she took the bowl of milk in her hand, and passed down towards the lake.

When she had come there, she saw the water and the grass, and the wild apple trees that were over the bank; it was very fair in the morning. And she heard a sweet and musical sound from the trees, as it were a new kind of bird, and a strange; and Harvanger was high up in a fork of one of the apple trees, whistling, and peeling a wand. Yolande stood beneath, and looked up at him, with the bowl in her hand.

"Yolande," he said, "when I dwelt at Greenbank I knew a tree that was the highest tree in the world; I think its branches reached so high, that one might have caught at a star and held it in one's fingers. Dost thou think so?"

"I know not how far away the stars are," she answered simply.

"Well," said he, "I used to climb up it and swing from little boughs near the top. Shall I show thee, or art thou afraid?"

"Nay, show me," said Yolande, in some wonder.

So he turned round and swung up from branch to branch, until the little boughs gave and bent under him. And so high he went, that at last he was among the smallest branches of all, and sat there whistling. Then he came down again, and stood on the grass beside her.

"See," quoth Yolande, "here is milk."

He took the bowl from her, and said: "I thank thee, Yolande." He looked across it, and said again: "Drink thou first."

So she took it, and drank, and gave it back to him; she did not know how keenly he watched her, nor what strange thoughts passed through his mind. Harvanger made the sign of the hammer over the bowl, and drank it at a draught. Yolande's eyes were on the ground, and her head a little aside. As he yielded the bowl to her, he was smiling.

She said: "Thou art merry."

"Art thou not, then?" said he.

"I am neither glad nor unglad," she answered, gravely. Then she said: "But thou dost many strange things." And she began to smile too, she knew not why.

Harvanger sat down on the grass; and Yolande sat down too, holding the bowl by the handle.

[216]

"Many strange things thou sayest," she said. "Wilt thou answer questions, or would that be wearisome?"

"Ask me what thou choosest," said he. "And as for the wearisomeness, I can walk fifty miles a day."

Yolande twisted the bowl about between her hands thoughtfully. "Hardly do I know what it was that I desired to ask," she said; "but tell me, if all people find it so good to have about them others who are of like mind with them, and to whom they can tell their thoughts—how do they live and devise it so?"

"I deem," said Harvanger, "that they devise it much as the birds and beasts do. For every bird that sitteth on a bough hath its feathered friends to chirp to, and make devices with; and out of those, also his own mate, who is before all others."

"True," she said, half smiling. "But I know not what the world is like, nor did I ever consider it much. And are there many people in the world, or few?"

"Many," he answered. "And they live many together for the most part."

"True," she said again. "That also is something that is true now, but was not yesterday; for even as thou speakest, I seem to remember."

"What then?" he asked.

"It would be the strangest thing of all," she

[217]

said, "to be among folk as many as a tree-full of birds. I know not what it would be like."

"Yea," said Harvanger, "I deem it would be so. Yet the strangeness would not last long."

"Tell me," she said, "are all men and women even as thou and I?"

"Some are, and some are not," said Harvanger. "Some are good and friendly—some evil and unfriendly."

They fell silent awhile.

"It is no less strange to me," he said, "that thou livest here alone. Art thou not afraid?"

"Nay," she said; "I am not afraid. There is no hard season or evil foe here."

"Yet thou hast none to speak with, or be friends with," said he.

Yolande clasped her hands together.

"Half I wish thou hadst never come here," she said, "for thou fillest me with new thoughts that frighten me; and yet I am not sorry. But what shall I do when thou art gone?"

"Truly," he answered. "I fear that thou wilt be very dull." Then he swiftly began to speak of other matters.

"Let us fare about the dale," he said, "and see if the Best Thing in the World be hidden in any corner."

So they left the bowl in the fork of a tree, and walked down by the lake side.

Yolande wondered greatly in her heart. Harvanger was a tall young man, and beautiful of face and form, yet big and strong. He had blue eyes, and fair hair that was soft as silk; and his mouth was kind, yet she dimly saw somewhat else in him; for he walked not as a woman does, but as a man does, and he spoke not as a woman speaks, but as a man speaks.

"Tell me, Yolande," he said; "didst thou grow up wholly alone in this place?"

"Nay," she answered; "there is one who comes, and speaks to me, and teaches me how to devise; once every year he comes, and brings with him strange things from the world beyond. He hath to name Way-wise the Ancient. He is a man too."

Then he told her what he had known of Way-wise; and she thought of that, but did not clearly understand what it might mean. Speaking idly in this way, they came down beyond the lake, and there she beckoned him aside.

"Go not yonder," she said, "for a bear liveth in the wood."

"That is no great danger," said he.

"O," said Yolande, "he comes forth sometimes; but unless he be disturbed, he does no evil."

"Then we will pass him by," quoth Harvanger. So they circled round that part of the wood; and went on. And there were nests of wild bees, and

honey-combs that Yolande knew of; and a little
burgh of rabbits, and haunts of deer; and places
by streams that were fair and sweet to walk beside.

"One could live well here," said Harvanger.

"There is nothing that is not in this land," she
answered.

"And even the Best Thing in the World may
be found in it," said Harvanger, digging his javelin into the turf.

"Wilt thou find it?" she questioned.

He said: "Of a surety, Yolande, I shall not
go hence until I have gained it; for it is in
my mind to gain it, and from that I will not
budge."

She smiled, and said: "Thou art of a fixed
heart."

"So are all men of valour," he answered.

"What is the mind of a man, then?" asked
Yolande.

Harvanger said: "To pursue, and to seek, and
never to cease until the sought for thing be attained. That is the mind of a man. But what
is the mind of a woman?"

She answered: "I do not know; for there
seems nothing in my mind save to live, and to be
content."

And even as she said this, it seemed the shal-
lowest of things, and content seemed as far off as
knowledge of what would be its shape. And for

a little while her mind was clouded with a new sense of despondency.

But Harvanger gathered such reeds as he could find, and showed her how a pipe could be cut from them. So he cut a pipe, and they sat on the bank of a stream while he played it, and entranced her with little tunes till she was smiling at him with a measure of wonder.

"Very many strange things thou doest," she said.

"I will show thee many more," he answered. Then he taught her how to play on the pipe.

When it was high noon, they found their meal in the wood, of wild honey, and berries, and eggs; the land seemed the richest in the world, and as Horn said, no man could starve there save a devil possessed him.

In the evening they returned again, and at the end Harvanger said: "Yolande, are we good friends?"

"Truly," she answered, "I like thee well, and fear thee not."

"Then," said he, "clasp thy hand in mine; for that is an ancient custom between friends."

Yolande gave him her hand, and he held it a little while.

"I deem," he said, "that I shall find the Best Thing in the World."

So in a few days that passed, they ranged the
[221]

dale in all parts, and sometimes went so far that it was night before they returned. Yolande knew every way and corner, and every thing that was in the dale; but beyond the borders she would not go. And when those few days were over, her mind was troubled within her, and she knew not why. For Harvanger was subtle, and keen as a hawk, and Yolande understood nothing of her own mind. He sat in the apple tree on warm nights of June, and kicked the branch. He desired Yolande; yet content was far from him. She was strong and swift, yet like a doe of the wood for mingling of tameness and timidity. He began to doubt his own mind in the evenings; but in the mornings he never doubted. Also he wondered and wondered at her, and sometimes thought her no woman at all, but a wood-dame of the fairy folk. And on the last evening he said:

"Yolande, are we better friends than before?"

She said: "We are no less, I deem."

"Well," said Harvanger, "that is good." And he kissed her. But this also bred discontent in him, and a little of anger; and on the morrow she came not. That was not a happy day for Harvanger; he lay in one part of the woodland, brooding over he knew not what; and Yolande strayed in the dale elsewhere, and pondered over she knew not what. So they were not happy. But in the evening she came softly and observed him, and departed again. As for him, he began to fear her a little; because he desired her, and yet could not ever tell her what that meant, any more than a child. And between one half-truth and another, they were tormented with things they understood not.

So Harvanger took his javelin, and in the early morning fared away swiftly eastward up the dale. Great joy it was to him; he sang as he sped through the glades and over the grassland, up towards the hills. He went far and fast, until he was beyond those points that Yolande never went over; he exulted in his strength, and never stayed until he was high up in the hills amongst the chasms and torrents. And when night fell, he slept there, whether the wind were cold or warm.

But Yolande, like a moth, presently came to the candle; and found Harvanger departed. And then her heart was heavy, and she was less happy than before. The next day she went fearfully, and still found him not. Then she knew that he was gone, and she sat under the apple trees, and there was no good thing left in the world for her, and the sun was gone out. There seemed no thing so desirable as he, and his playing on the pipe. She knew nothing, save that she was unhappy because he had gone.

## CHAPTER VI.: OF HARVANGER'S GOING, AND RETURNING, AND HOW HE FOUND THE HOUSE IN THE WOOD.

WHEN the sun rose over the hills in gold and crimson, and glorious dawn, Harvanger stood high amid rocks, and looked over the fair dale. And suddenly the discontent and vague fear fell away from him as a mantle cast off, and a cloak whose tie is unloosed; and he knew of nothing else save a passionate longing that rose within him as the dawn in the sky; and it was as glorious as that. He gazed over the dale with a joy that was sadness; for great joy and great sadness seemed to be one in his heart. He thought of Yolande, and desired her so utterly that there was room for no other thought in his mind, but only the turn of her head, and the pensiveness of her countenance, and the step of her walking, and the divine smoothness of her skin. And with that, desire and longing of love came upon him like a flame, and sorrow that he had left her, and self-reproach. So he had not seen the dawn rise, nor the sun lighten the dusk of the dale, before he was speeding down the hill paths again, swifter than ever he had come. He went by the narrow ledges, and by the broad ways; and he sped by bank and thicket, as swiftly as a strong young man might go; he came down again into the valley be-

[224]

fore the noon was gone past, and hastened, never resting, by the water-courses that flowed so quietly, with such clear trickling of water, from pool to pool, and under foxglove-covered banks. And he never ceased nor tired until the afternoon, when he came to the apple trees by the lake, and flung himself on the grass. But the dusk was coming, and the quiet of evening approaching; it lay over the land with stillness, and hushed every sound. He sat there with a measureless sadness and hope in him; for Yolande was not there, and almost it seemed as if she had never been, nor would ever be. There seemed a desolation come over the beauty of the spot; and he was alone there. And yet he said in his heart that never should Yolande be in any place, and he not go to her, and seek her; for he knew that without her he could no more exist.

And when he had thought these things, he rose up again, caring for nought but to find her. He sprang up the bank, and stood there, looking about him. Yea, his heart grew strong when he thought that he should find Yolande. He knew whence she came in the mornings; for from his perch in the trees he could see far and wide, and he knew the ways she came from, although not the paths she came by. So he went on and up the grassy slopes of the fair valley, where all the trees moved softly in the quiet-tide of the early evening. And at last he came to the stream that flowed past the

[225]

House of the Wood; it fell down a long bent,
tangled with trees and underbrake; and he could
find no way to gain heart of the wood. Pool
after pool it came down, foaming lightly over the
green rocks, and falling into stilly brown pools,
where lurked speckled trout. Reeds grew along-
side it, and blue flag flowers were open and in
bloom. So when he could find no other way, he
waded into the stream, and breasted up it from
ledge to ledge; for nowhere was the water deep.
In this way' he reached the top, and forced his
passage through the reeds and flags, and so reached
at last the level bank. Rabbits scurried under
the brake and the dusk of the wood; but after he
had rested a little, he went on beside the stream,
until he saw the garth, and the House of the
Wood. It was not large, and apple trees clustered about it behind, and their boughs touched
the roof. Very swiftly he sped on, and came to it.
Nought he saw thereabouts; all was quiet. But
when he came to the door, he saw Yolande; and
her head lay upon the corner of the rough table,
and her hair fell heedlessly about her, and he knew
not whether she were weeping or not.

Then his heart melted within him, for sorrow
and love, and pity and self-reproach, and he
dropped his javelin and sprang to her more swiftly
than a panther springs. He knew little what he
did, or meant to do, save only that his heart was
melted with love; and he had caught her, and

[226]

knelt beside her, before he had reckoned up one thing or another.

"Yolande, Yolande," he said, kissing the whiteness of her arm. "Yolande, I am here; I have come back; I will not leave you with my goodwill. . . ." And he said many things that did not greatly differ; and when they both woke from that sudden trance, scarcely they knew what had befallen, or where they were; for he kissed her, and smoothed her cheek, and she neither forbade nor avoided, but lay in his arms gladly, and knew of nothing else.

And he said: "Yolande, did I do wrong to leave thee? Didst thou think I had forgotten thee, and gone away?"

"What else could I think?" said she. "O, go not away, for the land has changed, and I fear the great stillness of the evenings, and the darkness of the night."

He said: "Yolande, never will I go away, not even for pretence; for when I came to the apple trees there was nothing but a desolation and an emptiness without thee. Let us be friends, for indeed I cannot do without thee for a friend."

"Fair boy," she said, "neither can I do without thee; for I fear the land, and it is dreadful and lonely, and thou art the only one to make it friendly again. Go not away."

"Yolande," he said, clasping her afresh. "I love thee, and I desire thee; there is not anything in this world that I desire more. And thy friend will I be for ever, and go not away from thee; but if thou diest I will die, and wheresoever thou goest, I will go, and thy friends shall be mine, and thy foes my foes; for I desire not anything save thee and thy friendship for ever. Nor shalt thou go from me; for thee I will have, and nought else."

So when they had said these things, scarce knowing that they said them, but speaking from full hearts, they fell quiet, and the sudden fear and joy went. They stayed, holding each other's hands, until the fear returned, and then they clasped one another again, and so remained long, speaking no word. And it was as Yolande had said, the dread of the great wilderness had come upon her, which once had been so friendly, and she yearned for what might fend off the loneliness of it.

And they parted no more, but were content to be together.

The dusk closed in upon them, and Yolande stood up and smiled suddenly, as though a ray of sun had fallen upon her face. And a very great and sweet dread fell upon Harvanger, when he saw her gazing forth over the dimness. Slim she was, and agile as a doe of the wood, and in his heart grew up passionate love, and desire, and fear, and tenderness, and he seemed to himself grown to the stature and strength of a giant, and no more a boy at all. And most of all a watch-fulness grew in him, lest even the trees and the grass should rise up to do any hurt to the dearness of Yolande.

And as for her, she was aware of new things and of old; she moved to and fro lightly, and yet surely, and knew that as yet there was no to-morrow.

CHAPTER VII.: THIS IS THE NEXT PART OF THE TALE OF HARVANGER AND YOLANDE IN THE FAIR VALLEY.

AT dawn Harvanger arose, and thought that so many years had passed that they might not be counted. For all things were grown dif-ferent, and were no longer the same; yea, the land itself had waxed in beauty and gloriousness of ripening summer, and his heart with a gladness which had no name. And there was Yolande, asleep on the fur of a bear, and her face against the soft shag of it, a flower fresher than lilies, and more precious than gold. And at that he took three steps forward, and knelt over her, and kissed her hair, and said: "Yolande, Yolande, I have loved thee of old, and in dreams which I had for-gotten, but seem to remember now. It is long since I began to love thee; so long that the years may not be numbered; and now we may never part again with my good will."

[229]

He lay there awhile, pondering these things strangely, and marvelling how swiftly time leaped upon time, and days changed upon days, and old things into new, which were both different and not different. The dawn was past, and the hill-side was in golden sunshine; and now the slope lay green and clear, topped with its thickets, and below ran the sweet water between its flowery banks.

He turned his eyes again to Yolande, and now the sun was beaming in, and falling upon her, so that she began to awaken. She opened her eyes, and moved her head; and presently she and Harvanger mingled their glances, and she became clearly aware. And for a little time she did not move, but lay watching him with eyes that smiled, and yet questioned. None the more did either move; only they looked one at the other. Then Yolande stirred and arose, and paused on the edge of her couch. She cast back the scattered length of her hair, and again looked at him, smiling pensively.

She said: "I have dreamed."

"Of what didst thou dream?" asked Harvanger, quietly.

Yolande did not answer, but turned her eyes forth of the house.

Then said Harvanger: "I bid thee a good day, Yolande."

"And I thee," she said. Harvanger knew that she was bidding him also a subtle defiance; but

[230]

he forbore to say or do anything as then; he watched, and remained quietly. For now he was assured that they would never part again, and he knew that her good will therein was no less than his; yet she would flee from him as swiftly as a hare doubles from the hunter. He pondered over this, until he smiled, and then she smiled too.

While he searched in his mind for the right word to utter, a shadow fell upon the floor, and he looked up and saw Way-wise. And at that, Harvanger sprang to his feet. But when he thought of all that he had long since devised to say to Way-wise, it was as nothing; for he knew that he was a child, and as clay in the hands of the potter. There was a flash as of sunlight in the one eye of Way-wise; and his step was so quick and his form so straight that none might ever approach him. From him there ran a stream of consuming energy. He stepped into the doorway and so stood, gazing at the two with a hawk's eye that yet had a smile in it, and friendly irony. Then Harvanger saw Yolande, still sitting on the edge of her couch, and they both looked at Way-wise hopefully, without fear, and yet with a little guiltiness of soul.

"What," said Way-wise. "So thou hast come over the Scaur Gap, Harvanger? What has fallen of thy quest?"

"Thou art a good prophet, Way-wise," answered

[231]

Harvanger; "a mighty man of wit thou art. But what shall I desire more than what lieth to my hand?"

Way-wise took a pace to the couch, and sat confronting Yolande. She drew herself back, and smiled and avoided the searching question of that very keen glance.

"Hast thou any fault with me, Yolande?" he asked.

She said: "Nay, none."

"Have I been thy sufficient friend?" said he.

"Truly," she answered; "I deem so."

He paused, and seemed to question both her and himself.

"Yet," said he, keenly, "I have laid a heavy yoke on thee, Wildwood maid. Dost thou not think that I have some right to make demands of thee, seeing how much I have given thee?"

"Yea," she answered, quietly.

"Well," he said, "listen. I will give thee a choice; for I am the task master of this world, and none who work my will, or share in what I give, may avoid the fine I levy upon them. I will not say but that some have cursed me for this. Yet thou, even as they, may not go free of scot. It is not appointed."

"Ask, and I will answer," she said, in a soft and even voice.

"Then," he said, "I appoint that this shall be the last day when thou and Harvanger dwell together. And for the rest, thou shalt live as before, happily, and without more than thou hadst of old, or less.",

Yolande gave a little sigh, and lifted her elbows. Then she said: "I will not make that choice, for I am a woman."

"How long hast thou known that?" demanded Way-wise, smiling.

She coloured, and made answer: "I deem that some knowledges come from within, and when they arise, there is no need for the telling to come from without. Thou canst not tell me that I am not as all women, Way-wise."

"Nor will I try," said he.

"Good friend," she said, "I know well thou art understanding. It may be that thou knowest the minds of all who speak to thee. So if I am a woman, do not ask me to be ought else."

Way-wise said, with great gentleness, that shone also even from his hawk eye: "Yolande, I will never devise any evil for thee, save what thou devisest for thyself. If I give thee a gift, it shall be even as thou hast demanded of me, good or evil." Then he turned half round towards Harvanger.

"Wilt thou make the choice, Harvanger?" he said. "Wilt thou suffer this to be the last day of thy tarrying here with Yolande?"

"If I am to speak my mind," said Harvanger, "I will not suffer it. For there would be no evil

[233]

in the world so great as that. So the choice is made, on my part, Way-wise."

Yolande sat with eyes averted to the wall.

"Very valiantly thou speakest," said Way-wise.

"I speak as a man will," answered he, somewhat proudly. "I know not the inner heart of a woman, but if Yolande will assent to this, and if she desireth it, and if no hurt shall fall to her of it, I will fear no thing, that I may always be her friend, and possess her."

"And dost thou not fear that I may lay a heavier yoke on thee, Harvanger?" quoth Way-wise. "For thou hast not yet heard what other choice I give thee."

"I care little," said Harvanger, "for the loss of the Best Thing in the World cannot be compensated for save by the avoidance of the worst; and that itself would be the worst."

"Ho," said Way-wise; "thou art growing older, Harvanger, than when thou wert in long clothes."

"I have learnt from a shrewd counsellor," said Harvanger.

Way-wise nodded. "Yolande shall make her choice, now that thou hast spoken."

Said Yolande: "Dost thou think, Way-wise, that my mind changes so readily?"

He smiled, and answered: "Truly, no."

She was vexed, and gazed first on one, then on the other, with heightened colour.

"Listen, Yolande," quoth Way-wise, in his

certain, harmonious voice; "thou hast come to a
fork in the ways of life. Thou canst not have
happiness without paying scot and lot; it is not
appointed so on the earth. Then thou shalt
choose what strife or innocence shall be thine, as
the scathe of happiness."

"Is no one ever quite happy?" she asked sweetly.

"Yea," said Way-wise, "those who pay for it."

"I know not what penalty may fall upon me,"
she answered, clasping her fingers tightly together,
"but if Harvanger desireth me for a friend, I will
even be so, and remain so all my days. So I will
not take thy first choice, Way-wise; withal, I
have not heard the other, nor care to."

"Many a woman speaks thus, and rues it,"
quoth he.

"Then I will rue it," she said, "if need be."

"Thou art a fool, Yolande," he answered.
"Thou hast never seen any other man but this;
nor dost thou know him deeply."

"That is at thy door," she said, quietly.

"Thou art waxing in wit, as he is," quoth Way-
wise, laughing out. "Truly, great things are be-
gotten between a man and a woman."

Said Yolande: "I am not able to shift from one
point to another, as the wind does. I am steady
of mind. This may be good or evil, but it is as
I say."

"Yolande," said Harvanger, "if thou wilt be
my friend through this life, I will be ever thy

friend; thou shalt lack nothing that I may give, for there is nothing in the world dearer to me than thou."

"I believe it," she said, "and I am glad."

So Way-wise, after he had looked from one to the other in silence, spoke, and said: "As the choice is, so shall it be. And look to it that ye go not back on it, even in folly and waywardness. Ye have chosen the greater thing, and the happier and wiser; but it is bought with a price. For those who love much have understanding of the greatest knowledge; they apprehend the divine things, and share therein. Happiness may be bought with innocence, for even as the beasts are happy in being no more than beasts, and free from the trouble that is the price of the highest joy, so may men be. But those are wisest and most seeing who choose the happiness of knowledge, and pay for it with long labour and steadfastness. Now," he said, "choose."

They both rose up together, and Yolande suffered Harvanger to take her into his arms.

"Way-wise," he said, "there is no thing greater than love. I will not part with Yolande; but in life and in death I will keep her, and she shall keep me. Demand what thou wilt, and I will pay that price gladly."

And Yolande yea-said that, without speaking; for her eyes spoke for her. Way-wise sat with one leg hooked over the other, and his chin on his wrist, gazing at them. He seemed content.

"Listen," he said, "and I will deal out doom. Thou shalt go back to Long Whitewall, Harvanger, and rule that land, for much it needs a man fit to do the will of the wise to it. I give thee no wisdom but thine own, nor any help save what thou hast already earned. Neither will I ever help thee. As thou art, so thou shalt stand, and what you two shall become, that ye shall bear with. For no man may be made what he is not; on thine own legs thou shalt verily stand. It is ruled that none should have great gifts and not use them. They who would keep those gifts hidden, presently find them gone. And on that day when thou art tired of love, or tired of the price, the other shall be lifted off thee of thine own will. Now the doom is dealt out."

Harvanger smiled and said: "Thy dooming is passing light, good friend."

"No doom is heavier," said Way-wise.

"I know not what thou art saying, whether one thing or another," answered Harvanger.

"No man of wisdom ever thought otherwise," said Way-wise. "For he is a fool who only saith one thing, when he may say two together."

"Truly, I deem it so," said Harvanger.

"And therefore," quoth Way-wise, "all wisdom is a riddle to be read; and out of it the wise man readeth the justification of his wisdom, and the fool the justification of his folly. As their perception is, so they read the riddle of existence; and as they are, they judge themselves."

He mused a little while; and they looked upon him quietly, and with a little wonder. Then he rose up, and put a hand on each of them.

"I deem ye will do well," he said. "So I will not come to you again. And if I have done a good deed, the reason shall not be told before you yourselves perceive it. All things ye shall comprehend when comprehension cometh; and before then, it cometh to none."

He kissed Yolande on the cheek, and strode through the door, and was gone; nor did they ever behold him again. So they remained standing a little while together, without speaking.

## CHAPTER VIII.: THE TALE OF HARVANGER AND YOLANDE IN THE HOUSE IN THE WOOD, AFTER WAY-WISE HAD LEFT THEM.

A LITTLE while they stood together, hand in hand, not sure of what had befallen them. Then they turned towards one another, and so stayed a little, still hand in hand; and they wondered in their hearts what was to come, and yet were not troubled, for they knew that whatsoever it was, it would be good. Presently Harvanger stooped and kissed Yolande, and again they stood, until she loosened her hands, and stood alone.

[238]

So he said: "Yolande, art thou afraid?"

"Of what?" she asked.

Harvanger was silent for a little; for the sun shone in at the door and the light was broad over the fair world; yea, the earth was singing one great paean of life and joy, and the birds were in the wood, and the bear-skin was as gold. And as he looked upon all these things, he knew that Way-wise had priced love at a little price.

"Come," he said, holding out his hand again. She took it, and they fared out into the garth, and through the wicket gate into the field, and so came upon the wide stretching hill-side, where the deer were coming again in the morning. They sat down upon the grass. Yolande swept her fingers through the long blades and the flowers, while he lay not greatly thinking, but still with a keen sense in his heart. Then he turned round and stretched his hand forth near her.

"Yolande," he said smiling, "thou knowest nothing of love."

"None the more knowest thou," said she; and they both smiled together.

"Yet we may find out," said Harvanger; "and from no other will I learn save from thee."

She said: "I have dreamed."

"And what dream was that?" he answered.

"I dreamed that we stood together in the house," said Yolande, "and Way-wise came to us with deep questionings and devious sayings; and from

[239]

me he wrung what I had in my heart, although I had made up my mind that it might not be said; or perhaps I did not know it was there. I forget. But how shall I forgive him that?"

"Truly," said Harvanger, "that dream came also to me. And his devious wisdom told me what I had always known, but had never thought of; that the strong lover is the world's ruler."

"Then mayhap it was not a dream," she said.

"Does that matter?" said he. "What should we care, Yolande, whether it be dreaming or waking? Shall we not discover for ourselves what it was that Way-wise taught us? What dost thou know of love?"

"What dost thou know?" she said with spirit. So they both sat on the grass defiantly, and began afresh where they had left off.

"I know this," said Harvanger, "that I love thee, Yolande; and I love thee whether thou likest it or not. And I will not go away; for I have found the Best Thing in the World, and it is called love. Also, I will pursue thee from world's end to world's end, and attain thee by force or fraud, and by persuasion or strong hand. This much I certainly know of love. Now tell me what thou knowest."

"Nay," she answered, "I will learn from thee at present. Perhaps thou knowest more than that?"

"Of a truth," said Harvanger, "I know more."

"Then tell me," she said.

"I know also that I love thee," said he.

She said: "Thou hast already told me that."

"Nay," answered Harvanger, "this is a new sense and meaning. I love thee once and I love thee twice; and once and twice are not the same."

Then the sundog caught the sun, and a shadow flitted across the coloured grass. Yolande smiled, and said: "When that is told, what next?"

"What more is to be told?" he asked idly, and yet with a spark of fire in his eyes.

Yolande answered: "I know a little of love also; and I will flee from world's end to world's end. For I hate what I have said, and I will not forgive Way-wise."

"Flee, then," said Harvanger, pulling the grass up suddenly in a handful. "Flee, Yolande; for wherever thou goest I will go."

She said: "I am not happy."

Harvanger looked at her, and said: "I am happy enough, because I love thee, Yolande. I am well content."

She sprang up suddenly, and turned away by the edge of the wood; and as she passed the brow of the hill, he was pacing a step behind, and never further. There was a certain glory in his face; the long hair ruffled behind his ears, and glowed like pale gold. And now there flashed through his mind all the words of Way-wise, double-edged,

[241]

that every man should read according to his wisdom. Not only did he comprehend what then he heard, but Yolande's mind was become his mind, and he saw through her thought with supreme certitude and triumph, as though he had become a master among men. He had no more doubt in his heart than fear in his body. All things were revealed to him by an inward sun. So he paced on behind Yolande, triumphing in that he knew, and understanding what was in his heart, yet unspeaking, and not minded to speak.

So they came to the garth gate, and she turned to him and laid her hand on his breast, as if to fend him off. She passed through the wicket swiftly, and it caught behind her passage.

Harvanger vaulted the gate lightly, and Yolande felt her feet suddenly slip from beneath her, and she was lying on the grass with him kneeling beside her, and her hands clasped in both of his. She closed her eyes, and then opened them again. Her hands sought his shoulders, and rested there, half in clasp, and half in defence.

"Listen, Yolande," he said. "This is appointed by the gods of this earth. I love thee, and thou shalt not go from me, nor will I go from thee. For wheresoever thou goest I will go; and I will hold thee and possess thee for ever and ever and ever. Mine thou art, and shall remain; there is no man need be so hardy as to dispute that possession with me; for that I will go through fire and water and battle. Yolande, Yolande," he said, "I possess thee." And he kissed her lips and face; her heart beat against his clasped fingers; there seemed no limit to the great force of that love. And yet his heart melted for Yolande, and he yearned over her with a tenderness that felt like grief.

He said again: "Listen, Yolande. We will go amongst men-folk where our place is; we will set love as a jewel amid the gold of the world's faring. And I will make all women wish to be thee; I will not let it be said that any woman has a nobler lover than thou hast. For here we might love our life long, yet lose that best of love which is won in the midst of the world and its strife. So we will go; and for ever we will love one another, and we will spread that love among all folk." And he said again: "Art thou content, Yolande?"

She said: "I am content."

So that day, and for many days after, a new life came to them; for now each knew the heart of the other, and they were at peace. And a great peace it was, in those early days in the Fair Valley; they drew closer together, and were afraid no more. Also, they were happier, and had no more fear one of the other, and that made them kinder; and they walked through the wild grass-land, and in the woods, and by the apple trees, fearing neither themselves nor others. They crowned one another with crowns of flowers, and rested in the evening-tide, speaking of things strange and familiar, and happy in the first peace of love. And on that day Yolande looked into the eyes of Harvanger, and said:

"True it is, that he who best loves the one, will love also the many and the all, in ways of wisdom."

He answered: "I love thee, Yolande; and I have found the Best Thing in the World."

"And when," she said, "thou hast done the bidding of Way-wise, then love shall be complete between us; although I do not know how that will be."

She looked at him again.

He said: "My friend, I can give thee nothing that I do not give thee; and thou canst give me but one gift more. I am content that thou givest it at thy good pleasure; for I am ever thy friend, and I will not take from thee anything without perceiving thy will in it."

"I am glad," she answered pensively; "and now all is well between us, and I am happy."

# BOOK VI.: THEY SAIL THE SEA IN THE BLUE SHIP.

## CHAPTER I.: THEY GO SOUTH OVER THE MOUNTAINS.

NOW tells the tale of that little campment at the foot of the hills, where Horn and Goldbeard, with Bernlak, waited out the time till Harvanger should return. It was a clear evening in August, when the air was still, and the thick, dark foliage moved but little, that Goldbeard saw a tall man, with a javelin in his right hand, and a cloak over his left arm, come over the ridge and stride up the hill. Straightly and stark he stepped, looking to one side and the other with wide clear eyes. Horn heard the step, and said: "Surely I deem our stay here drawing to its close."

"And I deem the ending better than the beginning," quoth Goldbeard, "as every tale should go."

But they said nothing until Harvanger flung his cloak on the grass, and sat down with them.

"So swiftly goes the time," he said, "that I thought I left you yesterday; but it is longer than that."

"It is indeed longer than a day," said Horn.

Harvanger turned his eyes upon them, and all four were well content.

[247]

"For myself," quoth Goldbeard. "I thank thee for keeping us here. I have eaten in the shade, and slept in the sun, and been at peace. And these three things come not always."

"And I," said Bernlak, "have hunted that Goldbeard might eat, and sung that he might sleep, so I am merry of mood. I desire only that I may presently fight; for I am growing fat."

"I," said Horn, "have watched the land by day, and the heavens by night, and pursued thee with hopes and wishes. And that is good."

Said Harvanger: "Truly, ye have without doubt found good things; and I exceed you all, for I have found the Best Thing in the World."

"I pray thee tell me that tale," said Bernlak, "for it is a thing I have never found yet, save in books, and in my friends."

Harvanger answered: "I have bought it with a price. Wilt thou help pay it, messire?"

"If it be not gold," quoth Bernlak, "I will help. I have all things save gold and a wife."

"Then thou art free from the root of all evil," said Goldbeard.

"And from the root of all good," said Bernlak. "For love and money do much, if not all."

Said Horn: "Goldbeard is prattling of the market-place. He has been asleep so much, that he is no longer able to keep quite awake."

"Nay, go to," said Goldbeard. "My wisdom is of the green fields. I shall remember it soon."

"Hearken," quoth Harvanger. So they hearkened to him, and listened to his words. "Bernlak is a wise man," he said; "for he alone, of all men, told me most nearly what the Best Thing in the World would be; and his wisdom came true."

"Harvanger," answered Bernlak, "thou art a princely man. I deem thee a man of noble birth, whether rich or poor. And be sure that I will ever be thy friend, and the friend of whomsoever may be passing dear to thee."

"No otherwise I thought thou wouldst say," said Harvanger.

"Now, if it seem good," quoth the King's Son, "tell us for whom we shall battle. Like seeks out like, as I have learned; and the Best Thing in the World to thee will not be less noble than thou."

"That is true," said Horn.

Said Harvanger: "In the fair valley is a wood, and in the wood a woodland maid. And she is my friend for ever; and when I am Duke of Long Whitewall, I will set a ring on her finger, and part from her no more."

A little silence befel after he had spoken those words; and they gazed at him with keen, bright, smiling eyes, but said nothing as then. But they all wondered, and meditated in that brief space, for a sweet miracle had come to pass, and that had happened to him which they would have wished for him, had they thought of it; but it was too great for them to have thought of. And whereas he had left them a handsome boy, he came back as one on whom the sun of Heaven has shone, and in whom the light of God has been litten; or so they deemed, while they looked.

"Duke thou shalt be," quoth Bernlak. "For my freedom, my father shall give thee five thousand spears of Varraz; glad he will be to give them."

"And I," said Goldbeard, smiting one palm on the other, "will bring thee seven earls, and the sea-wolves of the North, who worship Blade-bearer the One-Handed."

"I will counsel thee wisely," said Horn. "When thou art ready, we will seek the Ocean-sea, and a Blue Ship shall be there for thee."

So that night they held counsel, under the black sky and great stars of summer; and the cool wind blew gently upon them as they lay and talked in the dusk. There was a great bar of blue in the west, that lingered long after nightfall.

It was still August when Horn, Goldbeard, and Bernlak rode by the woodlands and glades, until they came to the bank of a stream where the water flowed broadly over pebbles, and made a musical sound. Very gay was Bernlak; he laughed and sang, and curvetted about on his great white horse; there was no man gayer on that summer morning. Goldbeard stalked on beside him, sometimes laughing and sometimes speaking.

"Of a truth, messire," he said, "I understand not why thou shouldst sing so much of love, when thou hast no lady."

"I love all women," said Bernlak.

"It is in my mind," answered Goldbeard, "that those who love all women are apt to love no one of them more than any other."

"Is that a fault?" demanded Bernlak.

"I will wait until thou hast a lady," quoth Goldbeard, "and then confute thee out of thine own mouth."

"Thou art wrong, Goldbeard," answered Bernlak. "He who loves all women, in any courteous sense, will love one more than he who despises all save one; for he may in his heart presently despise her too."

"Well, I will not say nay to that," answered Goldbeard. "But as I have known men, they most often learn to love all women because they love one; not one, because they love all."

Bernlak said: "Our father Adam was the first man of courteoisie."

"He let a woman persuade him," answered Goldbeard.

"He might have done worse," quoth Bernlak. "But I deem him courteous, because, rather than be no true fellow of Eve, he ate the fruit and fell in company with her. Had he been a burgher," said Bernlak, "he would have reckoned the price.

[251]

I think well of Adam, in that he followed Eve."

"Thou art a heathen, thou knowest nought of scripture," said Goldbeard, laughing; "and what thou dost know, is false."

"My grandfather," said Bernlak, "was King of Varraz, and a right noble man. He hated all priests and burghers in his life-time; and was wont to say that he could read the scripture to better purpose than any priest."

"Well, he might have done that," said Goldbeard. "I know not."

"He would have done that," said Bernlak, "because no good thing is so well read as when a man of courtesy readeth it."

Then he began to sing a song aloud, as they passed under the spreading trees.

Therewith Horn reined in his horse, and said: "Ho, I think we shall see Harvanger soon."

And as he said this, they saw Harvanger crossing the stream lightly on the dry stones, where the water fell over a ridge. There came one after him, who seemed to be a slim youth with a bow. They stood on the bank together, hand in hand, and looked towards the three with shaded eyes. Yolande feared somewhat in her heart to see these strong men; very strange and mighty they looked, but her spirit grew lighter when she saw that although they were noble of bearing, and such as it might be good to have for friends, they were not

[252]

like Harvanger, nor was that in him abated, which made him beyond all others, and the beloved of her heart.

Harvanger held out one hand and said: "Formerly I was one; now I am two; yet I will not take less friendship than before. I will ask twice as much."

"It is not hard to give that," said Horn. "It should have been given for the sake of the gift." Then he said again: "I perceive that you will both be dear to me, and no one less than the other. If I have left any word unsaid, I will say it now."

He gave them both a hand, and gazed at them.

Then Harvanger said: "Indeed, thou givest me all I could desire of a friend."

So he turned to Goldbeard, and said to him: "Goldbeard, thee also I can trust."

"Thou shalt never rue it," said Goldbeard. "For ye shall remember me as a friend."

And when it was the turn of Bernlak, he stepped forward and kissed the hand of Yolande, and spoke: "Madam, thou shalt have no friend more ready than I, for I will fight thy battles when thou needest it, and be no less a friend to thee than to Harvanger."

In this manner they made their pact in the woodland; and afterwards fared down those steeps eastward, towards the sea.

Many days they went, along that stream which,

in the Fair Valley, flowed past the House of the Wood. While they were by it, and could hear it babbling, and see the clear pools and green banks of it, Yolande felt the change not greatly; for it seemed a living link, and a strong grasp on ancient familiar things. So they went down through the bosom of the mountains, and through the broad defiles and by the hill paths. They saw towering pikes far away on either hand; snow-capped hills, white even in August. Yet they themselves came near none of these great wastes. They followed the tumbling, splashing downfall of Yolande's stream, and left it but seldom, and then for but a little while. Now it sprang in one plunge over the brow of a cliff, and flowed away beneath; now it flowed smoothly over fine pebbles, and between flowery banks; and again it would leap from pool to pool down the manifold rock steps of some deep vale, lingering in blue chasms like a serpent unready for the light, foaming crystal clear over the smoothed edges, and spreading out quiet and lucid basins, where the trout lurked artfully amid the weed at the bottom, plain to see. Yolande loved the stream, for while it was near, she seemed still in the Fair Valley, and at home. Then they left the great hills, and passed through the lesser hills; there were upland forests of oak, and vast steeps, unwooded, bare, and sere, that rose up in one long line above them; but still Yolande's stream. And it grew greater, for many small streams and mountain torrents fed it, and it bid fair to become a goodly river as it went musically forward. Yolande saw all the world, for ever one or another there was, to show her all that eyes could see; between them, they encompassed the half of knowledge. So she was glad of heart; and although there was in her some of that fear and sorrow which comes of leaving that place where one has lived long, she would not have gone back without a desolation greater still. She and Harvanger each loved the other more every day. The longing and desire of love never went from them. As the river grew and deepened, so did their love; until by when they had reached the sea, like the sea it had become infinite and without end. But Harvanger knew not whether Yolande loved him less or more; and she knew not whether he desired her more, or less. Yet she, jealous of her own eyes, lest they should cry her heart's thoughts abroad too swiftly, loved him more, and learnt from Bernlak. Bernlak was little loth; he told her tales of the great world; he described to her the world of men and women, their doing and thinking, their work, traffic, and war, and their comings and goings. He sang her songs also; yet she liked best Harvanger's reed pipe. And as for Harvanger, he was never far from her, and his hand often sought hers, and hers rested very gladly in his.

,

## CHAPTER II.: OF THE BATTLE BETWEEN HARVANGER AND BERNLAK IN THE WOOD.

BUT as yet Harvanger was not wholly happy; for now that they had left the Fair Valley behind them, and were drawing near to the great world, and its fierceness and violence, a little spark of foreboding began to grow in his heart; he would wake up in the early morning, sometimes, and toss and fret impatiently, or sit watchful and thoughtful because of some vague and hateful dream-fear that he should lose Yolande, or at least, never find her; and other dim discomforts of the like sort, that mostly vanished when the sun rose. They made him a little unhappy and fearful, and a little inclined to suspicion of everything and nothing, so that he looked with over-keen eyes on even small things; and it destroyed for a while what would else have been the bloom of perfect content in those early days.

They rode the hill paths and the mountain passes; a quiet journey in which Harvanger was never far from Yolande, but rode side by side with her mostly. Yet he was not content (who once had thought that less would content him), but chafed and watched still; why, and for what, he could not tell.

One morning he had lain awake until the dawn

had flushed, and the birds aroused themselves. Then he rose up swiftly and cast the scarlet belting of the Death of Kings over his arm, and strode down to the river, near which they were lying. His way went through birch glades, where the first blue of the daylight was beginning to make the shapes of things clear. It was most sweet and delightful in that early morning, yet was he weighted with some apprehension. As he walked the dawn grew; tongues of heavenly flame floated under a dome of sapphire, and all was wrapped in one ecstasy of colour; and the birch woods rolled away before and behind, and the crags showed here and there a piked grey shoulder, and the river gushed and flowed.

So he swam in a deep pool, scattering the lurking trout, who retreated into the amber-coloured hollow under the rocky bank; and presently returned, and cast the belting of his sword over his arm again, and went back. He had not gone far up the glade when he saw something white gleam, and although he knew of nothing, and had no clear thought in his mind, he turned fiercely and suspiciously, and crushed across the bracken, treading it down under foot.

Then suddenly he saw Yolande and Bernlak, walking in the wood together; and clear as the dawn itself, he saw them standing in earnest converse, holding one another's hands. A cloud came over his heart; it seemed like death, for this was his

[257]

dream-fear become real, and it was very bitter to him, and exceeding grim and hateful. And he could see himself now in coming years with that bitterness and loss still in his heart; for he knew that nothing could salve him for the loss of Yolande, nor was there anyone in the world as she was. There was something else withal that grew in him, that he had not known before; great anger and wrath, so that his heart grew clear and hard as a diamond is, without shadow or softness in it. In Bernlak's visage, too, when he saw Harvanger, there gathered an image of the same thing.

Yolande glided away suddenly and swiftly. Neither of them looked after her, nor noted when or where she stayed her footsteps. Harvanger drew the Death of Kings out of its scabbard, and threw the sheath into the bushes, and Bernlak also drew his sword; and they moved silently into the clear sweep of grass, with no word to each other; and then they began.

It was a stern fight, but not a long one; and it was a wonder that they did not kill one another before its brief span was over. Bernlak saw again the height and strength of Paranides opposed to him, and the fierce blue eye and terrible reach of arm; but it was a young Paranides, active and fresh and full of energy, as quick on his feet as Bernlak himself was, and taught by him. Yolande watched them with a wonder and terror that went beyond music and dreams; she had never seen or thought of this before, but she understood it now. She feared, lest they slay each other, and delighted, that they should do this for her; she remembered the strange fancy that came to her in sleep, of one in silver and white, who carried her on an arm through roaring flames, and between fierce men, and she crying out with joy at the flames; but she did not know when that was, nor if it were true or a fantasy. She saw Harvanger cast Bernlak over into the bracken, in some way, and put a foot on his neck; and then she glided quickly beside him again.

Bernlak neither spoke nor smiled, but closed his lips; and it was not Yolande he was thinking of, but his own grief that he, who had never, since his days of squirehood, fallen before any man, even before Paranides, should now be overthrown by a boy. There were tears of grief and mortification in his eyes, when he thought of so bitter an end to his fame.

So he asked nothing, and Harvanger, in the hardness of his heart, would most likely have given nothing; and although no two men had loved one another more than they, the stroke would have been given and taken straightway, had it not been for Yolande.

Two small and strong hands suddenly closed on his wrist, and held it; and there was a countenance at his shoulder at which he started a little aback.

She said: "Harvanger, do not be angry."

"Yolande," he answered, "it is not anger I feel so much as fear."

"Be not afraid, then," she said, drawing his arm to her, and laying her cheek against it.

"Then," said he, "I shall never be afraid, for and can never have better reason."

"Bernlak is thy good friend," she said. "Do not harm him."

The mood began to pass from Harvanger as swiftly as the clouds of a summer storm vanish after rain. Yolande's touch, and her eyes looking up at his, almost made him think he had been bewitched in those moments; and yet again, not quite, for the shadow of the fear was still upon his mind. Presently he withdrew his foot from Bernlak's throat, and stepped through the bracken to his scabbard. And when he had picked it up, and had sheathed his blade again, he stood for a moment considering. Now Bernlak also had risen, and Yolande stood a little way off, leaning against a tree, and watching them with grave and interested eyes, but not speaking.

As soon as Bernlak stood upon his feet, he perceived that he had done wrong, and unwisely; and he saw also that no such great harm had befallen him as he had thought. Rather, he began to feel pride in that he had taught Harvanger so well in every way, and made him so expert a man of arms, and so sharp on the point of honour. And Harvanger likewise remembered that Bernlak had been

[260]

his master in courtesy, and was a man noble and generous.

Bernlak said: "I see now that I have a good pupil, who has learnt well, and does as I would have wished him to do."

"Messire," answered Harvanger, "remember that the Best Thing in the World is not worthless, that it can be let go by default."

"That is true," answered Bernlak, "and so I deemed. Yet thou needest not to fear for what is safe, as that is."

Harvanger said: "In courteous words, at least, I shall never be superior to thee, although I will try."

"So far as I am concerned," said Bernlak, "I will abide by what thou wilt in these matters."

"Then we shall remain good friends," answered Harvanger.

When he had gone, Yolande said: "Sweet my friend, thou art angry and despondent. Yet I know not why thou shouldst be so."

He answered: "How could worse ever happen, that I should feel it more?"

"I do not know what has come to pass," she said, "save only that thou art angry. Tell me what I have done, that it should be visited upon me."

"Truly, I cannot say," said Harvanger. "It may be that I was wrong, but I deemed——"

[261]

"What?" she questioned, laying her hands upon his.

"O," he answered fiercely and discontentedly, "I thought it was true, as I had feared, that thou didst love me no more, or that thou wert being enticed from me in ways thou couldst not foresee or understand."

Yolande thought awhile. "Canst thou not trust me?" she said.

"It is hard," he answered, "and very hard; for thou art too dear to me now for peace or trust. And why should I trust thee, Yolande?"

She answered: "I do not know how there could be true friendship or true love without faith, and those who have faith in each other have also trust. If thou lovest me, trust me as I do thee."

"If I cared nothing for the Woodland Maid I would never mistrust her again, Yolande," said he. "For often I dread and fear beyond words to lose thee."

"Sweet my friend," said she, "have I mistrusted thee? Did I not stake all when I left the House in the Wood?"

"O," he answered, "what is there for thee to fear? Could I ever play thee false? Thou knowest, Yolande, that I could not do that; thou holdest me in bonds too strong."

Well she knew that; yet it was happy to hear it again. Then, after hesitation and seeking words, she said: "Have I not more fears before me

[262]

than thou? For all my days I shall dwell behind
secure walls, and in safety; but thou wilt be open
to many dangers. If then I can be of quiet heart,
canst not thou be also?"

He said: "It was not that which I feared; for
although such a parting as that would be sad, and
not easy to bear, yet it would be but little beside
losing thy love, which is immortal, and is not
broken by death. It was rather that some craft or
beauty should persuade thee or entrap thee, and
we be left afterwards with the delight of our hearts
destroyed; and dost thou deem I could think of
that, and not be quick even against my friends?"

"Dost thou deem I have never thought of it?"
she answered quickly. "Have I never been jealous for thee, and foreseen strange and as yet un-
heard of things to guard me against for thy sake?"

"I know not," he said. But with the talking,
his fear had largely slipped away and vanished.
"Only, I feared. Thou wouldst not desire me to
be indifferent?"

"Nay," she said. Then, after she had waited a
little moment, Yolande said again softly: "Thou
hast not yet asked me what happened?"

He flung away suddenly a pace or two; but he
was smiling when she looked at his face.

"Nay," he answered: "I will not ask thee
questions. . . . Forgive me, Yolande. Perhaps
I shall often do wrong, and speak foolishly, and
oppress thee with jealousy."

"Thou wilt learn how to trust love," she said.
"Well," said he, "I will say no more."

CHAPTER III.: BERNLAK GOES BEFORE
THEM INTO VARRAZ.

A S for Horn, whatever he knew, he said nothing; he neither advised nor reproved, nor
even showed that he perceived ought.  To him
came Bernlak in the afternoon, while they were
resting.

"Horn," said Bernlak, "I desire to know
whither thou art intending to go."

"That is for Harvanger to settle; I but better
his devices," answered Horn.  "Yet I deem that
we are going to the sea, there to wait until such
time as may bring us the friends we expect."

Said Bernlak: "Two paths lead hence.  One
goeth to the sea; but the northern path to Varraz.
To-day I shall follow it, and seek my own people."

Horn studied him a little.  "I deemed not that
thou wouldst leave us," he answered.

"Nevertheless," said Bernlak, "it is best that I
should do so.  I will speak to Orvan my father,
and request from him the spears I need to fulfil
my promise."

"Thou art free from that promise, if it irks
thee," said Horn.

"I thank thee, Horn," answered Bernlak, "but
it irks me nought at all.  I will ride towards Var-

raz to-day; and to-morrow ye shall follow me, and dwell there until all is ready. I deem ye will need some time of rest and thought before starting on the great journey."

"We will do so," quoth Horn. "I shall be well pleased to see thy people, if they are as thou art."

## CHAPTER IV.: THEY CROSS THE FORDS INTO VARRAZ.

IT was late summer when they crossed the broad heaths, that were covered with bracken, and found the road into Varraz. The rounded hills lay on either side; down the valleys ran the brooks, and there was a faint heat-mist that hovered over the lowland, yet was never seen near. A still and quiet country it was, wholly waste of men-folk. Here and there in the wilds rose up some steep hill, crowned with a jutting crag of rock; and far off, from whence they had come, were tossing dark pikes, looming and sharp. Yet between them and Varraz the hillsides were long; grass and bracken covered the soil, and wild sheep and deer started up afar off to stare at them. They passed this, until one day they came to a good road that dipped between high banks. They went down this passage, and Harvanger, who rode first, threw up his hand, and gave a shout of joy. Then when they came up to him, and had ranged themselves by his side, they perceived why he had shouted.

[265]

Under the hoofs of their horses was a strand of loose pebbles; and beyond lay a broad and shallow river, flowing gently and softly along, with little ripples on the surface. And there was a staked ford, and the stone tower of a ford-watcher on the further side of the river. And even beyond that lay a rather bare country, rising into high hills far off; in the midst were steep knolls, of which many were covered with clustering houses, and crowned with the tall battlements of a stronghold. And as they looked they saw all the land.

"What dost thou perceive, friend Horn?" quoth Goldbeard.

Said Horn: "I perceive herds, and men that guard them. Also I see tillage and woodland; but not over much."

"I deem this one of those upland countries that are poor in world's goods, but rich in men," said Goldbeard. "For I have noticed that those lands that are rich in goods are mostly poor in men."

"True," answered Horn.

Harvanger said to Yolande: "Behold, Yolande: this is Varraz; and here we enter the world."

She clasped her hand in his, and set grave eyes upon the land; for it brought nearer the days that were coming.

"It is but bare," she said.

"A land wealthy of men is never poor," said Harvanger. "For better is a desert with love and valour, than a rich country with evil folk."

She began to smile suddenly and sweetly, and turned her head towards him as he sat in the saddle.

"It is strange—about folk," she said.

"In what way, heart's-beloved?" said he.

"If all men were kings," quoth Yolande, "all men would be happy."

"Thou art wise, Yolande," answered he. "But tell me why thou sayest so."

She said to him: "The evil of the world comes from that some men are weak, and go beneath the yoke of others; and hence come many ills that seem of another nature."

He answered: "That is true; but since it is so, let us make the yoke easy. The good of the world cometh from that some are strong, and can devise and contrive for others."

Now Horn began to enter the water; it flowed around the fetlocks of his horse. So they made the fording, and came to the tower of the watcher. There they saw a man armed, who spoke not.

"Ho, friend," quoth Horn, "tell us where we may find King Orvan."

Answered the watcher: "Go whither thou wilt; he is there. Many a foe hath found this out."

"That is a good name to give a king," said Horn.

"In Varraz," the watcher made answer, "we give a king the name that he makes for himself."

"If I were a king," answered Horn, "I should

desire to have my people speak in this manner."

"If thou were King of Varraz," said the watcher, "thou wouldst get it, desire or none."

Horn said drily: "Sharp tongues dwell in a secure kingdom."

The watcher said again: "Many questions are made by those who are wise. I meant no ill."

"Tell us then," quoth Horn, "where we may find Bernlak of the High Marches."

"I know not," said the watcher, "save not in the High Marches. The world is his nest; his nest is the wild places of the earth to him."

"He flung a shoe, three miles back," said Horn. "So he passed here yesterday, if I am wise."

"Dost thou see this hill?" quoth the watcher, lifting his hand to point.

"Truly, I see it," answered Horn.

He said: "That is Varraz the city. Go thither."

"We thank thee," said Horn; and rode on.

Presently Horn let Goldbeard lead, and turned his horse to ride beside Harvanger and Yolande.

"Listen, Woodland Maid," he said. "Shall I tell thee a little wisdom?"

She said: "It will be as easy to me to hear as to thee to tell."

"The man who is courteous in humiliation is the most courteous of men," he said. "Regard him well."

"I will do so," she answered.

[268]

Again he said: "Valour is common to women and to men; but the valour of a man lies in what he will do—the valour of a woman in what she will bear."

"I will consider it," she answered.

He said yet again: "When thou holdest Long Whitewall in the palm of thine hand, remember that it is a love-gift from the God-folk. Treasure it truly and dearly."

"I will try to do so," said Yolande. Then she looked at Horn and smiled; and he smiled too.

He said yet again: "It is easier to control a horse when thou art in the saddle. Thou shalt make it go thy way when thou art ready to go with it."

"Most understandingly thou speakest," said she.

He said yet again: "Kings rule men-folk; but women rule kings."

"Why?" she asked.

He answered: "Because they are women. Never forget that, in love, women make men as the mould shapes the metal. When thou goest to Varraz, Woodland Maid, thou wilt see a little of the world of folk. Cast thine eye therefore upon the women of it, and test their wisdom with thine own."

"I shall know thy wisdom more perfectly when I have followed it," said Yolande.

"That is true," quoth Horn; "and wise. Wis-

[269]

dom is the simplicity of wise people. I will give thee no ill counsel, Yolande; for thou and Harvanger are dear to me. Thou knowest not the power that thou wilt possess; and I wish thee to find out. For great it is to conquer a kingdom; but greater to rule one. And in ruling, a woman is often supremely wise." Then he said: "Think not, Woodland Maid, that I tell thee of anything new or hard. I but tell thee of what thou already knowest."

"Yet thou hast said I knew it not," said she.

"We do not always know what we know," said Horn; "and this most when we are among things new to us. True it is, Woodland Maid, that thou knowest all I have told thee; but I deem it well to tell thee, lest thou shouldst think that thou knewest it not."

"I will look into my own heart, then," said Yolande, "and remember that the wisdom of the woodland is the wisdom of the world."

"When the country mouse came to town," quoth Horn, "it deemed that in this strange land sweet was sour, and water ran up hill. But soon it learnt that wisdom is always wise, both in the north and in the south; it but changes its lesser manners."

"A man may change the sword for the spear," said Harvanger, "but all battle goeth by courage and craft."

"Keep that in mind," said Horn.

[270]

Then Harvanger whispered to Yolande: "I will love thee in the country and in the town."

She looked up at him, and answered: "I will love thee in the town as in the country."

So long they rode their ways, that they came towards Varraz the city. It was ever in full view; but slowly they approached it. And when they were near, they saw a company coming against them; right well it was armed, in mail of steel, and bright coats and bardings. They drew up to let the company go by; but when it had come to them, it stopped, and two men sprang down and walked towards them; and one was Bernlak.

He doffed his plumed bonnet courteously, and spake to him who was by his side: "Messire, behold my friends, I pray thee love and entertain them, as they have me."

Then said Orvan: "Know for a truth, fair my son, that thy friends are ever mine, and as truly welcome to me as thou art."

Yolande looked upon the lords of Varraz around, where they sat on chargers of white, and cream-colour, and black; and upon Orvan. Most small men they seemed; yea, beyond belief; and yet sturdy, and strong of visage, even as Bernlak was. Orvan was but a little man beside Harvanger; his hair was white and bushy, his beard grey, keen eyes he had, dark as night; and a face broad above, and sharp below. He was a most courteous man, and fair spoken; it needed not any

[271]

great craft to see in him the sire of Bernlak, for they were wonderfully like.

He stepped up to Harvanger, and said: "Sir, you are wholly welcome to Varraz; both thou and thy friends alike. I beg you to abide at my house, for I desire to speak with you, and to have your company."

"Messire," said Harvanger, "there is no man now alive whose company I will more readily accept than that of Bernlak's father. And thou shalt know that he has been our friend; and we seek no payment for love."

"That is courteously spoken," said Orvan. "And thou, too, shalt know that in Varraz, love is paid for with love, even as hate is by hate."

He turned therewith to Yolande; his dark eyes flashed through her as the swallow flies in June. "Madame," said he, "my lady has sent these words by my tongue; but they are hers and mine. Thou art welcome to Varraz, and in Varraz thou shalt never lack friends while life endures."

Then Yolande remembered what Horn had said concerning him whose courtesy was greatest among men. She answered quietly: "Very great is your courtesy. I thank you, and also him who has spoken well of me."

"Thou speakest well for thyself also, madame," quoth Orvan, sweetly.

So they entered into Varraz through vast gates;

[272]

and they rode up the steep streets, where every man and woman wondered at the tall fair men, and the slender dark Yolande; and they entered the house of Orvan.

And there they stayed through autumn and through winter. Often Harvanger and Yolande paced the embattled terraces of that strong burgh, and looked out over the land. It was but a day or two after their coming that the Queen sought out Harvanger.

"Sir," she said, "I have a woman to show thee that thou hast not yet seen."

"Madame," answered Harvanger, "save thyself, I have never yet beheld but one woman."

"Thou shalt see another, to-day," quoth she. "Come."

Greatly wondering, he followed her where she led. There was a long room, where she mostly sat, and thither she brought him, and took him to the largest window, where a woman sat in a long gown of green, with a golden girdle and a chatelaine hung by a golden chain. She looked not at Harvanger, but away from him, and he marvelled and waited, and approached her a little, until she turned; and it was Yolande.

Presently he took her face between his hands, and said to her: "Heart's-beloved; indeed I have never seen thee before. But what thinkest thou?"

"Dost thou love me?" she asked.

[273]

He answered: "I love thee, Yolande; and in some way I love thee more, although that seemeth to be impossible."

"It is a change of times and days," she said; "yet with the crown the king is made; he feels a king then, even though he were one before."

He laid his hand caressingly on her shoulder. "Yolande, Yolande," he said, "I perceive that I love thee much, and that Long Whitewall shall fall swiftly. Now we are in the world."

That winter was a winter of counsels and devisings. It was in March that they held their last great feast in Varraz; and when it was ended, Orvan set his hand to the Loving Cup.

"Ye lords and men of gentillesse," he said, "hear my words. A week from now these our guests and well-beloved friends shall depart from us, upon a good and courteous undertaking from which, I trust, great honour may be obtained. We know that Paranides and the Duke have worked great evil in Long Whitewall; for they closed the Mill Weir to us, and destroyed our people who journeyed thither. And that was scathe to us, who are but a poor folk in world's goods. Six thousand spears of Varraz shall go hence, and my dear son Bernlak, who was evilly cast into prison by the Duke. And I trust that ye who go will remember us, that we wait eagerly to hear of the courteous and honourable deeds of arms ye

[274]

shall do. And let no man return to us until he has in such wise done, that the name of Varraz is honoured and well-regarded, as much amongst our foes as amongst our friends." Then he held up a green scarf that was worn by Yolande. "This," he said, "Bernlak shall wear for me. Do honour to it."

## CHAPTER V.: THE SAILING OF THE BLUE SHIP.

THE tale tells that they came to the great sea on an early morning of springtime. For they passed through the woods and the grass-lands, and it was night when they camped by the sparse, wind-blown trees that lie near the sea—bare they were, save for a few leaves that streamed on the breeze, and they leaned away from the south, whence the gales blew. It was a starry, fine night; the sky was blue as a coal, and lit up with a mist of stars, and brilliant, glittering jewels that hung low on the sky-line. Not yet had they seen the sea; but they heard the distant sound of it, not loud, although they were near; because the weather was quiet. Yolande wondered greatly what it should be like, and listened to Goldbeard's tales of it; for he had fared oft on the sea, in storm and calm, and knew much of its ways and manners, both the beauty and the terror of it, and the harsh north and the warm south. And Harvanger wondered too; for they were woodland folk, and not of the sea, as Goldbeard and Horn were. Thus they slept that night happy and unfearful, and eager as children to set their eyes upon the great sea.

A little after dawn they arose, and gathered together their gear. Horn led them to the waste by the sea-shore; for all the woods ceased nigh the salt spray, and there was stubby, knotty grass, and a wild waste of bushes, and gorse. Over beyond they saw nought, but only a white emptiness, for the mist lay thick on the water. They came to the edge of a low cliff, bordered with bushes; parts of it had slidden, and parts had been eaten away by the sea. Below them they saw a stretch of sand, ribbed and streaked with weed; and a line of glassy water that spread smoothly, and came and went; and a line of foam that curled and broke. They looked on this together. The sound and the scent came up to them.

"The sea is strange," said Yolande.

"Thou hast not seen it yet," quoth Horn; "for the mist lies on the water. It will rise before long."

Then he led them over the grassy waste along the cliff edge. It was warm, and the young leaves were growing, and the sky overhead was pure blue. A gull came over the mist, with its cry; and was gone again, floating strangely down to its

[276]

nest. Also, rabbits flashed in and out. They came presently to the shelving of the cliffs; and then they were going over large pebbles. Yolande stooped to pick them up; they were white, and blue, and red; some were purple. And there were many shells among them—small shells of all colours, as yellow, and white, and clear red, as many as grains of sand.

"Thou shalt find better than those, anon," quoth Horn, smiling.

She answered: "These are the first I have seen. I will take them to me for luck. Lo, I take the things of the sea."

Then they came to the line of sea-weed, and to the hard sand beyond; for the tide was low. So Yolande took of the sea-weed—it was of all colours save blue. Therewith Goldbeard stalked out of the mist.

"I think I have heard the bell," he cried. "Say thine adieux, Yolande, and thou Harvanger. For soon we shall be on the sea."

Then after they had bidden farewell to those of Varraz who were not accompanying them, they walked on over the sand. Goldbeard was deep in the water, up to his knees, listening. As they waited, and hearkened, lo, the sound of a bell floated through the mist; and the mist was curling and rising. Goldbeard put his hand to his mouth, and cried "Ship ahoy."

There came an answer out of the fog, and the noise of men rowing; and a boat came forth of the mist. Men were in her.

"Are ye of the Blue Ship?" demanded Gold-beard.

"Sir," they answered, "of no other. We shall presently bring you aboard."

Into the boat went Harvanger, and Yolande, and Horn. Harvanger and Yolande felt strange in the boat, and gazed at it; but Horn was well at ease. Goldbeard pushed off and sprang in after, and they were on the water, with the mist around them, and waves dancing up, and winking at them, and flowing on to break at the beach. Also, they felt exceedingly hungry.

When they had rowed in this manner for a space, they beheld something huge in the fog, that loomed up on high above them. Yolande slipped her hand within that of Harvanger; for neither of them knew but that this might be a whale, or a sea-serpent, or some monster of the ocean. But Goldbeard took a boat-hook, and rose up in the bows, and called aloud; and a voice answered. He caught the gangway with his hook, and made fast the painter.

"Behold the Blue Ship," said he. "And this is the road to Long Whitewall."

There was a man with a grizzled beard, who looked down at them. Harvanger pressed the hand of Yolande, as she withdrew it; and Gold-

[278]

beard lifted her in strong arms, and climbed the ladder. Him Harvanger followed, wondering at the heaving and dipping of the ship, and so they came aboard, and stood all on the deck, with the mist curling and rising about the tall masts, and clearing swiftly. And in no long time it had risen and gone; and they saw the wide sea about them, smooth and streaked with currents, and ever restless, ceaseless, moving, murmuring; and the cliffs, and the mightier dark cliffs, like great mountains, that arose far away on the north and the south.

Most wonderful of ships was the Blue Ship; it was large, and tall, and blue. It had a mighty poop and great castlings, and masts that touched the sky, and sails with figures on them, as a rising sun, and a brown serpent on a yellow field, and other devices. It had streamers, and banners, and all sea-gear. Many days they sailed in that ship, for the ship-master was expert and wise, and he knew Goldbeard well. Harvanger soon learnt the ways of it, for the ship-master was nothing loth to tell him thereof; yea, he thought, and said, that no man was a man of full understanding who knew nought of the sea; "for," quoth he, "in the sea is more wisdom than ye shall pick up on land; the land is firm and unchanging, but the sea changeth from hour to hour, and is as a living thing to be watched and understood. Those who are of the sea-folk are the best of all men."

[279]

And whether this were so or not, they found great pleasure in learning and perceiving all things, and being taught the wisdom of the sea. And in this way passed many days, as they sailed to Long Whitewall.

On the fifteenth day the sea was running high, and the Blue Ship beat north, and beat west, and tossed and dipped with straining cordage in the strong gale that drew from the south. The sun shone over the sea; the white horses came and went; the wind never lulled, but blew steadily, fluttering every loose thing and all but taking away the breath of those who faced it unaccustomed. For here Horn looked to meet Blade-bearer. It was towards evening when one in a top cried out to those on the deck. Harvanger caught Yolande by the hand, and led her to a corner of the poop. There was a speck of gold far away, that burnt steadily, and went, and burned again, and slowly grew larger.

"What is it?" she asked.

Said Goldbeard: "Golden prows come over the sea."

"It is the longships," quoth Horn.

Said the ship-master: "Sirs, I have done as ye bade me do. I hope no hurt comes of it."

"Nay," answered Goldbeard, "nought save good."

[280]

"Well," quoth the ship-master, "I trust in God. For I have no love for the sea-wolves."

The wind freshened during the afternoon, and the sea waxed high. And ever the golden speck drew nearer, and others arose behind it. And an hour or so before dusk, they could perceive the longship approach them. Its huge sail had a drake thereon, curling and biting with open jaws, and on the poop was a mighty man in gear of scarlet, steering with an oar. Long and low was that ship, and deadly to see; it rushed through the water swiftly, and was well manned.

Goldbeard arose, and cried over the water. "This is the Blue Ship, and I am Goldbeard the Hurler. What ship is that?"

The man who steered gave over his oar, and came to the bulwarks.

"I am Sea-Drake the Earl," he cried, "and this is my ship Sea-Drake. Well-pleased is my heart to see thee, Goldbeard. Come aboard, for I would speak to thee."

Goldbeard yea-said that; and Sea-Drake took his oar again; and presently he saw his way, and shot his longship down athwart the stern of the Blue Ship, and Goldbeard sprang lightly down into the waist. And before they knew, the longship was high above them on the crest of a wave, and far away. The ship-master liked this little; but he granted that the sea-wolves were expert men of the sea. So they passed the night; the Blue Ship with lanterns hung out; but the longship showed no light, and when the dawn came, it was still nigh them, sweeping through the water like a water-serpent, swift and steady.

"Sir," quoth the ship-master, "I will give thee a word of wisdom. Thou art in luck if the Seven Drakes are thy friends; but build not over much on that. When their turn is served, ask them not too nigh thee. They are perilous folk."

"I deem it so," quoth Harvanger.

With the dawn, they found the sea full of the longships; Horn knew each leader of them.

"That is Shell-Drake," quoth he, "and that is Fire-Drake; and Wood-Drake is yonder, and by him is Holm-Drake the Earl. Blade-bearer sails with one or the other, I know not which. We shall learn when Goldbeard returneth."

When they had broken their fast, Goldbeard was on the deck of the Blue Ship again, and he drew them aside, and spoke thus: "The fire is up, and over the land. Sea-Drake telleth me that the war is well afoot already, for Bernlak and Yvain have forced the passages of the river at Mill Weir. The day after to-morrow we shall enter the outer port of Long Whitewall, where it abuts on the sea. Have thine arms furbished, Harvanger. Thou wilt have no great foe to fight at first; but Paranides is coming with the Companions, and when he joineth the Duke, the fight shall be sharp.   Also I have heard strange news."

"What is it?" quoth Horn.

"Well," answered Goldbeard, "I know not if it be true or no; but they say that the King of the Romans is abroad, with a mighty big battle behind him.   As to this, we shall see."

So they turned their ship towards Long White-wall; and Harvanger laid out his arms in order. Yolande sat by and watched him.

# BOOK VII.: OF THE COMING OF THE KING OF THE ROMANS, AND THE WEDDING OF HARVANGER.

CHAPTER I.: THEY COME TO THE PORT OF
LONG WHITEWALL.

NOW the Blue Ship came on a morning
to the port of Long Whitewall. The
land and the dawn rose together.
There was low-lying land over the
sea, blue and green and distant, and fair sea-water
between this and them. But the sea-rovers were
clean gone away, and the ocean was bare of their
craft. So when they had made their way into
the river's mouth, they saw the port before them;
the finest of noble wharves and sea-harbours, with
steps of glittering stone, and gabled houses, and
fortalices, and bell-towers, wherein the bells rang
and chimed. Many masts were there, and gay
banners; and within and without the town were
trees and orchard closes. Thus Harvanger looked
again upon Long Whitewall, from the deck of the
Blue Ship.

Yolande also looked upon it, and now she grew
pale as she saw. She turned to Harvanger, and
gazed upon him, where he stood beside her. There
was mail of white steel upon him, and armoury
of blue and gold, fair to see; the Death of Kings

was belted to his side, in a scabbard wrought by strong men of Varraz, for Orvan had given him such gifts as a king gives to those that he loves. His bright hair was thick, and the sea-wind stirred it; he smiled as he looked over the sea, and the men of Varraz were gathered here and there in array of war, seeming nothing loth nor unhappy.

Then he stooped and said: "What art thou thinking of now, Yolande? Yet I think I know."

She turned away again, and breathed more freely; but again she turned to him, and said: "Tell me what is to come now?"

He answered: "First, Yolande, I who was a boy am to be a man, and a ruler of men."

"O," she said, "I perceive now that it is true; thou art become a king, who before wert but my man and my fair boy."

"I love thee ever, Yolande," he made answer; "then and now, and throughout this life, and the next."

He smiled afresh upon her; there was no fear, nor shadow of sorrow upon his countenance. He said again: "And thou, who wert but a maid, and a white fawn of the woodland—thou art to become a woman."

Yolande looked over the sea, and smiled a little.

"Since thou hast become a man," she said, "I will become a woman, and keep thee company."

He took her hand quietly, and turned clear

[288]

blue eyes to her. "Have no fear, Yolande," he said; "for I desire thee to look upon me, and find me a man. I desire that thou shalt see me to be no weakling nor unable one. Therefore have no fear; and we shall enter Long Whitewall, and the tale thereof shall be told for many a day after."

She heard these words, and in her heart spoke and said to him, that whether he were victor or vanquished, she loved him; but these words she did not speak. Instead, she whispered: "Let me see thee act well, and be the first of men."

With that they ceased speech, for it was not yet time to speak. The Blue Ship ploughed through the waves, and the men of Varraz gathered in the waist, all armed and well-appointed for battle. A mighty little wood of spears they made; they were not many, but they were expert men and hardy of heart and fierce, for Orvan himself had chosen them. The ship-master held the tiller, and cried aloud his commands. There were musicians who made music; and the water lapped, and the cordage sang, and the sails thundered as they were drawn or changed, and the music beat over all, as they drew near the port, and beside the glittering steps thereof.

Then Harvanger drew on his gloves of steel, and stood before the men of Varraz, and spoke thus, in a voice not very loud, but clear: "Messires, I will not bid you be valiant, for I have heard so much of those of Varraz and known so well what manner of men they are, that I deem you more likely to need the curb than the spur. Therefore, I say, let us remember well that we are few, and guard ourselves well and wisely; and let us so comport ourselves, that we need the less help that may take from us the honour of this battle. For we are alone in this ship, and Long Whitewall is the mightiest burgh in the world, and the home of valiant men. Presently we shall disembark on these quays, and do what we may to achieve the port. So we will say our farewells to the Blue Ship, for whether we win or lose, we shall need it no more."

They all yea-said this, and no more words were spoken. Harvanger kissed Yolande on the cheek, and then the steel hid his head, and was laced on. He stood by the gangway as the Blue Ship loosed and furled all her sails, and slowly drew against the steps. Therewith he ran down the gangways, and was the first to set foot in the port of Long Whitewall.

## CHAPTER II.: HERE IS THE TALE OF THEIR TAKING OF THE PORT AND THE BATTLE IN THE MARKET-PLACE.

IT would be over long to tell of all they did that day, for so many deeds were done, that no book could contain them all. The Blue Ship seemed to come out of heaven, and no man of that town knew ought of one thing or another until

they saw the strange men of arms who stood by the
gates, and entered the fortalices, and spoke proud
words to the lords and governors of the burgh.
When they had disembarked their horses, they assembled on the quay, and unfurled a banner that
bore a sun gold upon blue, and they sounded a
trump, and so rode through the streets in order,
until they came to the market-place.  Harvanger
sent those who seemed good to him to seize each
great gate of the town; and swiftly this was done,
and no man might issue or depart, nor come or go
to Long Whitewall, that lay eastwards over the
plain country.  And when this was done, he bade
all folk seek their homes; which also was done,
since none of them knew what thing to do, nor
whither to go.  They were as sheep without a
shepherd, and in no wise eager to do battle for
what did not concern them.  Then Harvanger
came before the lodging of the lord who ruled the
port for the Duke, and bade a trump be sounded.
So they parleyed, one sitting on his charger below in the market-place, and the other overlooking
him from a bay window.

Said Harvanger:  "Sir, I bid you to understand
and take notice, that I seize upon this port as a
prize of war; and from henceforward it belongeth
to me, and I rule in it.  For this I am willing to
give account to whomsoever may account demand;
yet if I may give thee counsel, but a little word,
I would counsel thee to ask no account of me, lest

I give it thee, and more than thou lookest for into the bargain."

The governor answered: "I hear thee well, and take the notice thou givest. Tell me thy name."

He said again: "I am called Harvanger from Greenwood."

"With thy courtesy," said the governor, "I will now depart to my breakfast."

"Wilt thou not hear what further I have to say?" asked Harvanger.

"I would do so," quoth the governor, "if thou couldst give me any reason therefor. Or thou canst leave word with the porter."

Harvanger smiled, and cast his eye upon the men of Varraz, who smiled not, but looked most black, thinking this great discourtesy. And after a little, he turned his horse round, and spoke to one and another, and ordained their work for them; and these knights of Varraz rode round to the fortalices and lodgings of the burgh, going wheresoever they could find those that they sought; and they went to the deans of the crafts, and the leaders of the quarters, speaking to each the word given them, and bringing back the answers they got. So a little before noon, Harvanger had their answers given him, and bade the trumpet be sounded again.

"Sir," he said to the governor, "I trust that thou hast had a good breakfast."

"I have had a good meal," said the governor, "and I spent the rest of the morning in visiting my armoury, and speaking to my gentlemen. I fear that thy company will be but a short pleasure to us."

"Truly," said Harvanger, "that may be so. Now I bid thee hearken again. There is no man in this port who will fight for thee, save those that are in thy lodging: and I know that thou hast but few men here, for the greater part have gone hence to the war. Therefore spare thyself, and thy men, and if thou wilt fight, on thine own head be it."

"I thank thee," quoth the governor; "and as for the time, I will choose it myself."

Now Harvanger bade the approaches of the market-place to be closed; and they shut the streets with wagons, and beams of wood, and chains; and they bade the folk shut their doors and windows that looked thereupon. The governor had called upon the crafts of the people, and they made excuses; and he had sent to the lords who dwelt in the burgh, but when they saw how things were going, they made no answer to him; and he had bidden riders go to the Duke, but all were taken at the gates by the men of Varraz. So when he saw that the burgh was wholly quiet, and would not move for him, then at last he bade his doors be flung open. It was towards the

[298]

fourth hour after noon when the gates of the courtyards were unlocked, and opened upon their
hinges.

Forth then came the knights of the Duke; there
were about twenty lances, with esquires and pages;
men all armed in mail, and bright in armoury.
Of the men of Varraz there were nearly as many,
and they were ranged up under their banner in the
midst. And so there was a short space of crying
and challenging, and seeking out of one another,
and blowing up of trumps; and when this was
over, the battle fell to and lasted until night, when
Harvanger called for torches, and it went on by
the light of them.

A fierce and deadly battle it was, and many
men met their bane in it. But in the end, the men
of Varraz prevailed. Harvanger was the first of
them all, and the tallest man there; and when he
had finished with his enemies, he struck into the
battle afresh, and helped one man and another.
And soon such of the men of Varraz as had done
likewise were also free; so that when the torches
were brought, they shone upon ruffled heaps of
armoury that lay about the market-place, and a
small array who fought in a corner, half in the
dark. Some had cried quarter, and these were
saved; but the knights of Varraz had little mercy
on the rest, nor was much asked of them. So it
fared on to midnight, when the fighting dropped
away, and the torches went out one by one, and

the moon rose over the houses, and cast a faint light into a square that was quite empty.

## CHAPTER III.: HERE IS THE TALE OF HOW HARVANGER'S RULE OF LONG WHITEWALL BEGAN IN THE PORT.

HARVANGER and the men of Varraz entered into the Governor's lodging, and found it a strong house, and well garnished. And none opposed them. So they cleared their disarray, and slept awhile; and in the morning stirred early. Harvanger bade the men of the burgh assemble to hear him; and also he bade to him the gentlemen of the city. And the knights who obeyed met him in the hall of the Governor's house; they sat on benches by the table, and behind him were men of Varraz.

Then he said to them: "Sirs; I perceive you to be a gallant and honourable company; nor do I think it would have been easy to encompass this port had ye been in my way. Some of you I know, and some of you I shall know anon. Ye have not had a Duke over you such as it is meet for you to have; nor do I see why ye should undergo labour for him, who hath ever set men of other lands over those who were born in this country. Neither is it time now to begin; for in a short time I shall show you ten thousand sea-wolves who desire to speak with his friends. Will ye that they

[295]

come here first to speak?—or will ye that they find no friends of the Duke here to speak with? As for myself, I say nothing; ye shall decide this matter."

They looked sad enough, but spoke with one voice; and that was the voice of him whom men called the Kinglet, and he had been one of those who had kept Alyot Courtain from breaking the lists against Bernlak aforetime.

"Sir," he said, "thou sayest well that it would have been a hard matter to encompass this burgh had we been assembled against thee. Nevertheless, thou hast done a bold deed; and most of us deem that the Duke can fight his own battles, since he himself thinks so. For ourselves, we will not fight either for thee or against thee, so long as thou bringest no scathe upon the land."

Said Harvanger: "O, I promise that. And if ever I attain my desire, ye may be easy of mind concerning what shall follow."

They thought well of him, they knew not why. It was in their mind that he was a bold and a calm man, and kingly of manner; and if he came to be Duke, they thought it not the worst of things that could happen.

Then Harvanger came to a window, and found the leaders of the folk assembled beneath in the market-place; there were not many, because the approaches were still held by men of Varraz, but still a goodly number.

[296]

"Good people," said Harvanger, "I bid you pay heed to my words. Ye have long had a Duke in this land who careth little for you, and whose rule is the rule of Companions and outlanders. Great evil has come upon the land in his time, and the time of Paranides the Burner. There is no man here who knoweth not what things have come to pass; for Greenwood is full of more than deer. I am come hither, not to destroy your customs nor take your goods, but to cast down him who hath oppressed you. I bid you tell me, therefore, whether you are minded to fight for the Duke, or to rest content in me. And what you shall require of me, I will listen to."

They heard these words, and also they looked upon Harvanger; and they were well disposed to regard him, they knew not why.

"Sir," they said, "thy words are fair. Give us surety that we shall not suffer as to our customs."

"I bid ye hearken again," quoth Harvanger. "All your ancient customs I grant to you and confirm to you; and I make promise to you that none shall suffer without sentence, and none be hurt save in justice."

"These are excellent words," they made answer. "We have had but orgulous speech of the Duke; and little justice or regard of our customs. Wilt thou also give us surety that the Duke shall not visit this upon the heads of us, and our wives, and our children? For thou art not able to do this; but the Duke will do so."

"I bid thee hearken to my words," said Harvanger. "A great battle of the men of Varraz is coming from Meadham and Whitewaterford, seeking Paranides. And Paranides is seeking the Duke, and the men of the Duke are seeking him, that they may overthrow the men of Varraz. And to prevent them I am bringing the Seven Drakes, who desire to speak to the Duke and his friends. If they find my friends here, they will pass by this burgh; but if the Duke's friends, I fear for you."

"Sir," they answered, "do as ye will. We are wholly content."

So they departed; and in this way began the rule of Harvanger in the land of Long Whitewall.

## CHAPTER IV.: HERE BEGINS THE TALE OF HARVANGER'S DEPARTURE FROM THE PORT, AND HIS APPROACH TO LONG WHITEWALL.

IT was not long before tidings of these deeds reached the Duke's ears; and they were heavy tidings to him. Harvanger set a knight of Varraz to rule the port; and to his care he gave Yolande. He said: "Heart's beloved, the time is near when I may speak with thee. But as now I go to make it nearer."

So Yolande stayed at the port, with the women
that had come with her, under the care of that
knight of Varraz; and when the news of the coming time came to the port, greater each day, the
ladies who were of the burgh burned to see her;
and they truly did see her, and spoke wonderful
things about her, some true, some more than true,
but none less. And from that day forward grew
the tale of Harvanger and Yolande; of which, as
it was spread abroad, there were marvellous and
beautiful things not told here.

So Yolande, knowing it not, also began her days
of rule over Long Whitewall. They thought her,
as they thought Harvanger, strange and noble and
well-regarded; they would have hated her as a
lady of the burgh, but they liked her well as a
queen of the land.

Now Harvanger took his lances of Varraz forth
of the port. The Duke shut the gates of Long
Whitewall, for he had long since sent out his battles to meet Paranides; and Paranides was coming
from the south, swift as might be. Harvanger
entered the villages of the folk, and sent word all
over the land of his coming; there was none who
desired to hurt him, nor any to fight against him.
To him came many men who hated the Duke, and
many who feared Paranides; and so the days wore,
and his company grew ever greater, until the men
of Varraz were but a part thereof. Thus he drew
towards Long Whitewall slowly, and stayed near

[299]

it; until at last he heard that the men of the Duke were returning, and Paranides had crossed the river, and was coming with them; but of the sea-wolves, no word he had. And on a day, he saw the banners of the Duke set up on a hill over against him, and a multitude who came with them, earls and knights of Long Whitewall who held with the Duke; and the black and yellow banner of Paranides stood before a battle that gathered nigh the river. Then Harvanger's heart beat, and he knew that he should have to fight these great battles alone.

But while the evening was yet young, Bernlak and the men of Varraz were gathering brush-wood for a beacon-fire over the river; and the next morning, golden prows gleamed over the sea. They saw them coming at the port, and eagerly spread the banner of the new Duke. And all that dawning-tide the black longships sped swiftly into the river's mouth, like dragons of the ocean-sea; Sea-Drake, Fire-Drake, Wood-Drake, Holm-Drake, Land-Drake, Drake-Seeker, Shell-Drake—all these sea-rovers came into the river's mouth, swift and eager for battle, each with his fleet. They set the first ship to shore, and the first man to stride over the plank was Blade-bearer the One-Handed.

CHAPTER V.: HERE BEGINS THE TALE OF
HOW PARANIDES MOVED INTO BATTLE;
AND THE WHOLE TALE OF THE BATTLE
WITHOUT THE BURGH.

WHEN the dawn had flushed and spread, and
died into clear day, Paranides marshalled
his array between the blackberry bushes and the
orchards. The sun was still behind the dark
woods; but it arose every minute. His banner of
yellow, with the ravens displayed thereon, floated
in the wind, and before it sat he, on a great black
destrier, a mighty man and fair and well-beseen.
On the left, near the river, were the gentlemen of
the Duke, and the guardians of the burgh under the
Duke's Seneschal; gold upon crimson was their
banner. On the right were the Companions; and
these were the men most to be feared. Harvanger drew up the Knights of Varraz, and those who
cleaved to his banner; they were not many, but all
valiant men. He bade his banner be unfurled,
and so rode to and fro before them, armed in gold
and blue, with his fair hair tossing in the wind.
He spoke to the men of Varraz and thus he said:

"Messires, he who strikes first is commonly he
who strikes also last. We will not delay, for it is
in my heart this morning that we shall fall on
swiftly and ask peace of none. I bid you lift up
your hearts and be bold as lions; and let us see

[301]

who amongst us will do the most valiant deeds, for this day will go well with us, and I shall forget none that I see do honourably."

Their marshal answered: "Duke, deem no task too hard for us. Sound up thy trumpets, and we will keep our breath for the onslaught."

And in this manner began the battle.

CHAPTER VI.: HERE BEGINS THE TALE OF THE ONSLAUGHT OF HARVANGER.

NOW the helms were closed and the shields were set, and the lances feutred in rest. The trumpets were blown, and the men of Varraz moved over the grass together like a thundercloud. Harvanger rode on before. So swiftly they went down the little steep and up the hill between the blackberry bushes; they spurred on faster, until Harvanger came to the banner of the Duke, and then was a seeking and a mingling and a halting, and then a mighty sound that filled the air. Many men were overthrown; horses galloped away without riders; there were no few who fled away, to return afresh. The onslaught and the battle moved over the ground, and left it trampled and spangled; it passed beyond the orchards, and there the fiercest fight was waged. The men of Varraz cast down all who opposed them, and pursued on, and struck down those who would rise up, and scattered them abroad, to right and to left.

Many fled; then the Duke's battle was broken up, and in disarray.  There were those who came to Paranides, and told him these evil tidings.  He answered: "Ye have done ill: but I foresaw no better.  I trust that we shall soon remedy this."

At this pass he wheeled about the nearest battle of his Companions, and said to them: "Sirs; follow me, and do your best."

So they moved along the river bank, a gay company, and Paranides led them; and Alyot led the third battle round on the other side.  Harvanger called the men of Varraz together, and said: "Let us now accept this encounter that is offered us by Paranides."

## CHAPTER VII.: HERE BEGINS THE TALE OF THE ONSLAUGHT OF BERNLAK FROM THE WOOD.

THUS stood the fight, that the Duke's battle was broken up, and Paranides came to its help; and Alyot sought to strike in on the flank, and drive the men of Varraz into the river.  But whilst they were for a little while at pause, and passing words to and fro, and ordering themselves aright, they saw a huge fire over the river, and a smoke that swept up therewith, from dry bracken of the wood.  Straightway came a mighty press of men, that filled the bridge, and drove before them the few watchers that were set to guard it.

[303]

Then the press burst over the mead and the clear field, a great battle of fresh and strong men; and the foremost to win through was Bernlak. They came with loud shouts, and burst in upon Paranides like so many devils; he had no more than time to face round and meet them before all the meadow was full of the men of Varraz, and no man knew his right hand neighbour from his left. They were all mingled, the yellow Companions, the crimson clad men of the Seneschal, the dark little knights of Varraz, and those many of Harvanger's who bore all armouries under the sun. Now the fight grew and waxed hot; never was such an overthrowing and a casting down. Between the orchards and the river were done the mightiest deeds of arms that day.

When Paranides saw how subtly he had been entrapped, he acted as a wise and valiant captain. He was the first of all his men, and the strongest of arm and heart. He plunged into the crowd trampling down whomsoever came in his way, and crying his cry of: "Saint Mary—Saint Mary of Long Whitewall." The yellow Companions fought well; they were hard and most fierce men; but no less well fought the little black devils of Varraz. Bernlak saw the flame of Paranides, and the struggle around him, and how he smote down on the right hand and on the left. He pressed towards him, crying out his cry of "Varraz," and overthrowing all that would stay his course.

And now came Harvanger likewise on the other side, bright with gold, and shearing down with the Death of Kings. Around these three the fight grew ever greater. Many men were unhorsed; and these wandered about fighting on foot. On the outskirts was the trampled ground, well sprinkled with those who had fallen. Men on foot battled under the trees, and over the meadow; they ran down after the great fight, that now struggled and poured forth beyond the orchard, into the dale, and so out into the clear country beyond. Bernlak drove the Companions before him; Paranides held himself like a lion; Harvanger's battle was driven before both, till it found itself in the little dale, and there he led it on afresh. So there the three came together again. Paranides beheld a little man on a large horse, and the blue armoury of Flacandrin, sprinkled with golden tears; and he saw the Seeker after Strange Deeds again, and the thunderous strokes with which it smote down. And straightway he beheld also a tall man in mail of gold, who pressed through the battle towards him; his shield was shorn away, and its bearings defaced, but Paranides knew that this must be Harvanger. At last they all locked; scarcely could any man, save those on the outskirts, do more than keep his horse on its feet, and himself in its saddle. Bernlak drove down like seven furies, and Harvanger waged his war up like an angel of battle, and they were all crushed together

[305]

and swaying perilously. Those who slipped down rose up no more; they were whelmed under the horses and the fighters. And as yet Alyot held his hand. Still Paranides strove to break up the lock. He set his strong hands to the haunches of the horses near him, whether they were of friend or foe, and of his own party or the other. Some rolled down; others rolled over these; there was dreadful work done there; but still Paranides cried, "Saint Mary of Long Whitewall," and had no time or thought to fear the issue.

Then swiftly he saw one who lifted up his horse, and showed hoofs of gold; and Bernlak thrust in on the left even as Harvanger worked his way in on the right. Paranides saw them come; all about him the yellow and the black were mingled with the dark colours and the many colours; none knew who was on his right hand or his left, or before or behind. Paranides cried: "To aid! To aid!"

Then the two swords crossed before him. There was a man who struck at Harvanger; but he was overthrown before he could strike, and he who overthrew him was cast down, and he who cast him down was hurt and left. Bernlak was fended off by a lance shaft, until some man of Varraz cut it through with an axe; but this man vanished under-foot, and the Companion who slew him was himself slain. None of these things saw either. Paranides smote fiercely at Harvanger, and then saw no more; for Bernlak gripped the Seeker after

Strange Deeds, and smote him so fierce a stroke that all grew dark to Paranides; and Harvanger struck him down upon the bow of the saddle as by a thunderbolt. Bernlak caught at Paranides' embroidered belt, and pulled at it; it came away. The Companions sought to save him; Bernlak to thrust him down. Then came Alyot out of the emptiness, with fresh lances of the Free Companions; they heard his trumps blowing, and the cry of his onslaught. Swiftly he came, and drove all that battle before him like sheep; those who fought went fighting, those who were too tightly locked to fight went as they were; and by this time, there were not many who knew whether they themselves were alive or dead, and on their heads or their heels, nor any other thing whatsoever. But they kept on fighting.

## CHAPTER VIII.: OF HOW YOLANDE CAME TOWARDS LONG WHITEWALL.

A T that dawning tide two men strode up the steps that led to the house in the port where Yolande dwelt; and they sought out Yolande. When she saw them, she said: "Ye are most welcome; as ever ye will be."

Horn answered: "Yolande, we desire that we shall be those who first shall take thee into Long Whitewall. Wilt thou come with us?"

"It is over, then?" said she.

[307]

"Come and behold the end of it," quoth Goldbeard.

"At least, ye have news?" she asked.

"Truly," said Horn, "we bring the news that
Blade-bearer is on the land. Is not that enough?
Didst thou fear, Yolande? Have no fear at all;
for no men in the world are there able to cast
down the sea-wolves."

She said, half sighing: "I will come. Why
should I not come?"

Horn nodded quietly. And when he had
spoken with the knight who acted as master of the
port, he and Goldbeard fetched a horse for Yolande, and took as guardians three gentlemen of
Varraz. So they rode out in the morning, and
came towards the river.

When they had come there, Yolande saw beyond
the trees and the orchards, over the fair bright
grass and cornlands. Far away she saw something
that made her pause; for there sprang up the
mighty spires and towers of the great burgh, en-
circled in their ring-wall, bright in the morning
sun. She looked at Horn.

Said he: "This is the burgh that is thine, Yolande."

She answered: "I think I dream. I shall
awake."

"It is a dream that will last long," he said.

So then she turned, and perceived a coloured
and manifold line of men, with seven great ban-

ners planted before them; a vast battle they were, of foot men tall and strong. Before each banner stood a great man garbed in scarlet, with wide raven pinions spread abroad from his helm; they leaned on great axes, and long bright swords of war; they were Sea-Drake, and Fire-Drake, and Wood-Drake, and Holm-Drake, and Shell-Drake, and Land-Drake, and Drake-Seeker; and before them all flew an eighth banner, and there stood Blade-bearer the War-King. He leaned upon a bare sword, and his hawk-like eyes moved neither to right nor to left, but gazed keenly forward. Thin lips he had, hard gripped together. He was slim, and tall, and terrible; a very engine of war. From head to foot he was in scarlet, and against his side rested a round red shield.

They passed by these sea-wolves, and Yolande remembered the words of the ship-master who sailed the Blue Ship. Horn turned his eyes to her.

"Fear not," he said, "for these are our friends."

Now Yolande came near to where Paranides' banner had flown; and she saw the press and the strife between those of the Burgh and the Company, and those of Varraz and the land. This she stopped awhile to behold.

"Tell me," she said, "how it goeth; for I know not whether well or ill."

"There are more of the Burgh and the Company," said Horn, "and they are valiant men; but those of Varraz and those who are of Harvanger's

[309]

battle, are no less valiant, and they are captained by valiant leaders."

Now they saw a battle that rode round a small hill; the thunder of the horses shook the ground, and before it rode bright captains whose armoury was fresh and undinted, swiftly over the green grass and past the dark woods. Closely and well rode that array of spears, and they smote and scattered the battle that was waging war, and drove it before them. And as the fight fluttered, Yolande saw a man on a tall horse, and he glittering in gold, who was the fiercest in the press, and first to rally those who fled. Said Horn:

"Let us knock on the gates of Long Whitewall."

## CHAPTER IX.: OF THE ON-FALLING OF BLADE-BEARER THE ONE-HANDED.

WHEN Blade-bearer saw the falling-on of Alyot Courtain, his eyes changed, and he drew in his breath and moved.

"On, banners; now for the Drake and the Burgh," said he.

He lifted up his great red shield, and it went forward like an August moon, plunging past the bushes and the knolls; on he went, never pausing or looking back, but with his blade held low and pointing forward. After him rolled the battle-

[310]

array of the sea-wolves, and the Seven Drakes who led the banners.

Paranides was looking at the blue sky; for the press had gone far away from him. His helm had been torn off, and many a buckle and chain had been snapped, and his harness was ragged and broken. And after a little while he turned on his side, and saw the on-coming of Blade-bearer. Blade-bearer was running afar off, yet swiftly. Paranides felt for his sword; but no sword was there.

Then Paranides, helpless and swordless, turned on his back, and thought of how good his life had been, and how little he had gotten of it that he could carry thence with him. So he composed himself quietly, and thought again that none may be wiser than it is given them to be. Neither did he hope for ought, or repent of ought; only it was in his mind that he would wax in wisdom in days that were to come otherwhere. And Blade-bearer saw him, and knew him, and slew him as he ran past; and that was the end of Paranides the Burner.

But Blade-bearer sprang on; and now he came to the edge of the battle, where it was fought in the fields by the river. The sea-wolves closed upon the press; and that was the end of the old Duke's rule in Long Whitewall. Their double-axes smote down the horses, and cleft the helms of the riders; they burst like a storm-cloud upon the flank of

[311]

Alyot's array, and drowned it as the floods drown the land in winter. Harvanger and Bernlak saw huge and flaxen-haired men amongst the struggle, and One who cleft a lane as the reaper in the fields, and cried: "For the Drake and the Burgh, the Drake and the Burgh." Now befel nought but the flight and the pursuit; for the Companions had no longer any to lead them. The flight scattered across the fields, and amid it were the well-horsed men of Varraz who galloped and smote, and the shielded axe-men who slew and spared not. There was a trail of yellow and crimson over the meadows; those who could, begged quarter of the men of Varraz, and the knights of the land who cleaved to Harvanger; some leaped into the river; some fled; and some were slain as they fled, and some as they fought. And this is the end of the tale of the Battle without the Burgh.

CHAPTER X.: IN WHAT WAY WERE WRITTEN THE CHARTER, THE TITLE, AND THE BULL-OF-BLESSING OF THE NEW DUKE.

HARVANGER sat on his horse beside the orchards, from which the blossom had as yet hardly gone. He held in his hand the helm he had taken off, and his fair hair was ruffled and wet. It was not long before one came, and sprang from the saddle, and approached him; one who was battered and befouled, but smiling and whole.

"Harvanger," quoth Bernlak, "I shall be the first to hail thee as Duke of Long Whitewall; and here is a line of thy charter, thy title deeds, and thy bull of blessing." And he stuck the Seeker after Strange Deeds into the earth, where it stood.

"To thee, Bernlak," answered Harvanger, "first of all men the Duke returneth thanks. Here is another line of my charter, my title, and my bull." And he stuck the Death of Kings beside the other sword.

Then came sundry of the men of Varraz, and anon many of the sea-wolves, of whom the first was Blade-bearer; and they stuck their swords into the ground round about; and so were written the charter, the title, and the bull of the new Duke, with the Seeker after Strange Deeds and the Death of Kings cheek by jowl in the midst thereof.

"Harvanger," quoth Blade-bearer, "tell me whether I have done to thee all that my brother Goldbeard promised on my behalf."

Harvanger answered: "Thou hast done all. I thank thee. And if ye will, ye shall march through the treasury of the Duke, and each take what a hand can carry away with it."

"Nay," said Blade-bearer; "this sunrise I came; this sunset I go. There is a north wind. The ships shall go on the wings thereof. Farewell."

And it was even as he said; for as night fell, the sea was clear of the longships. Neither did

they ever come again to the land of Long Whitewall.

## CHAPTER XI.: OF THE OPENING OF THE GATES OF LONG WHITEWALL.

THE next day, about the third hour, there
came one in gold-inlaid mail, with his head
bare, and he approached the western gate of Long
Whitewall, up the long grassy slopes that fell away
from the burgh towards the sea. And from the
gate came many folk; a bishop with crozier and
pall, and the crafts of the people, with banners
displayed in order. They saw Harvanger and the
men of Varraz, and Harvanger saw them.

He paused, and awaited their approach. And
when they were near, he perceived that first of all
others strode two men, with a woman walking between them; the men were Horn and Goldbeard,
and the woman was Yolande. But she had her
eyes cast down, and looked not at him, for all the
intentness with which he looked at her.

Then Bernlak, dismounting, slipped his arm
through his reins, and spoke, saying: "Messires,
and ye good people, I present to you him who is
your duke. And if ye desire to see his charter,
his title, and his bull of blessing, it is ready for
you to see." And he stuck the Seeker after
Strange Deeds into the ground.

Then spoke Horn, and said: "Sir Duke, and

ye messires of Varraz, and lords of this land, I present to you the folk of Long Whitewall, who are issued forth to welcome you. I bear the keys of this burgh, and its sword of Justice. Sir Duke, hearken to the words that Long Whitewall speaketh to thee through my lips."

"I bid thee speak," said Harvanger.

"Thou shalt slay no man; thou shalt harm no woman; thou shalt preserve the ancient customs of the burgh; thou shalt weigh justice in an even scale, and know not the great man from the small man. If thou wilt do these things, thou art welcome. Declare thy will in this matter."

"It is my will," said Harvanger, "that no man in this burgh shall suffer, and no woman be grieved; I will weigh justice with truth and true measure, and mine eyes shall never see the great man or the small man, but only him who does evil or good."

"Here are the keys of the burgh," quoth Horn. "I yield mine office of Seneschal to thee."

Harvanger remembered the Seneschal who fell one day beneath the Hermitage in Greenwood; it seemed long ago. But he touched the keys, and said: "Messire Bernlak, for this time take these keys, and the keep of the burgh, to lock and unlock."

Bernlak thought that he would have liked them passing well once, when he could not attain them; and that too seemed long ago.

Then said Harvanger: "I bid the folk come near, and let each who can speak for others set his hands in my hands."

So they filed past him; and swore each the oath of homage, these men of the folk who could speak for the folk.   And about noon, they marched back through the gate, with the Bishop last; and after the Bishop rode Harvanger the Duke, and after the Duke, Bernlak the Seneschal, and after Bernlak, the men of Varraz, like a moving forest of spears.   Thus they came into Long Whitewall.

## CHAPTER XII.: OF HOW THEY RODE TO THE DUKE'S PALACE.

THEN the bells were rung, and the trumps of the men of Varraz were blown, and there were many people in the streets, and many at the windows; but the Duke and the men of Varraz rode on through all, like towers of steel.   They came past the houses and the booths; they rode up the cobbled streets while the bells swung and rang, and the trumpets blew.   There was a man with a bow who stood in the street, before other of the folk; a stout and red-faced woodlander.   When Harvanger passed him, this man sprang forth, and lifted his hands.

"Duke, Duke," he cried; "a boon of justice."

"I will give thee justice, Roger," quoth Harvanger, "and all those of the Spotted Deer."

[316]

Roger of Coldhaven would have stooped and slidden back into the crowd, but might not. He stood up again and said: "I know not how thou knowest me. But I shall hold thee to thy word."

"March before me, friend Roger," said Harvanger.

"I have a woman with me," he answered.

"Bring her too," answered Harvanger.

Straightway he saw a woman dressed in black, who stood at Roger's side. She would have moved with him, but when she had seen Harvanger, she touched his stirrup leather.

"I know thee," she said. "Thou art the boy whom we found in Greenwood when Rafe was slain."

"I know thee also, Queen Kate," answered Harvanger. So they walked on together before him; and she was behind Yolande; and they were much alike in some ways. Harvanger saw this as he rode.

## CHAPTER XIII.: OF THEIR COMING INTO THE DUKE'S PALACE.

THEY went by the sign of the Chanticleer, where once those three and Bernlak had dwelt; and they entered the precincts of the mighty palace which the Dukes of Long Whitewall had built for themselves of old. Now it was all but empty, and swiftly it became full.

Harvanger said: "I see that I shall have but little sleep awhile yet; for many things are to be done. But come ye, Horn and Goldbeard, and thou Bernlak and ye lords of Varraz; I will sit in the pleasaunce where we played the three games of old."

That fair garden was still beautiful. The roses were not yet in bloom, the crocuses had gone only a little while before. Harvanger sat in the pavilion, and said again to Roger: "Now speak."

"Lord," quoth Roger, "whereas ye are now sworn to observe the laws and customs of the burgh, I present to you this dame, who claimeth a right of justice at your hands."

"Then let her speak," quoth Harvanger. He sat very still; he neither moved, nor uttered any word; and likewise sat Horn and Goldbeard. So the tale was told, of Paranides, and Kate, and Rafe, and Yolande.

CHAPTER XIV.: HERE BEGINS THE TALE OF PARANIDES THE BURNER, AND OF RAFE AND KATHERINE WHO DWELT IN THE FAIRFOLDS.

THIS is the tale that Kate told. "Long ago, men came out of Greenwood, tall men and fair, with kings amongst them. They were fierce, and of heathen customs, and they built the first burgh of Long Whitewall. They were ruled by a woman, but because the folk had lived a life of battle and bloodshed, it was their custom to marry the Queen to one who might fight her fights, and rule the burgh and the folk for her. In her and in him dwelt the luck of the burgh and the folk, and from them it flowed; and in those ancient days began the May Day custom of Long White-wall. For on May Day, whosoever was of the folk might challenge the King, and sit in his seat if luck favoured him; so that no weakling ever reigned in the burgh. But none might challenge save one who was of the folk, for they would not suffer an outlander to rule them.

"Now many tales might be told of Long White-wall, and of its people, but when many years had gone by, there had come a change of days, until of that ancient folk but few were left, and a small dark people dwelt there. Yet the customs did not cease; for though they were few, the ancient folk might yet fight for the Dukedom, and in days when so few were left that to see one was a wonder, there came a man to Long Whitewall who was called Paranides, and was of that folk. It was bruited abroad that he had agreement with the Devil, and had fetched from Hell one of the two swords that had of old stood in the sanctuary of the Kings of the Burgh. At least, he overthrew the champion of the Duke, and displayed such skill and strength in arms, and such address in playing the games, that on a May Day he stood in the

[319]

shoes of those who had gone before him, and demanded his forfeit. They would have resisted him by craft, had he been a weak man; but he was the captain of a Free Company, well able to enforce the rights he claimed, and therefore the Duke had no choice but to fulfil the custom as had before been done, in old·times.

"The Duke's wife was dead; two daughters remained to him, of whom the eldest was called Katherine, and she was the Luck of the Burgh, and the inheritor of its rights. But Katherine would not wed Paranides; and it may be that the old Duke was of foresight, and did not go further out of his way than need be, to compel her. For thereby the title of Paranides was weakened, and the Duke held his own against him. Thus, in such a case the matter rested a short while; but Paranides ruled the land, for if he were not the Duke, he was no less. And already he had begun to rule evilly, although not so evilly as in after years.

"Now Paranides set his heart upon Katherine, and strove to win her; but she hated him. There was a man named Rafe; he was the lord of the Fairfolds, and a man frank and rich in world's goods. His fathers had been long in Whitewall; they were great and ancient of lineage, and strong men and brave. This man loved Katherine, and she loved him; and it came to pass that they were wedded. Paranides did not forgive them this; he was their enemy ever after.

"So strong was Paranides in those days, that his will was never over-set in the burgh. Those who strove against him came to evil ends. There were at first many men of ancient lineage who despised him, and many who were his foes; and these, in one way or another, were at the last all overthrown. Some he entrapped, so that they destroyed themselves against his craft; and when at last they gathered together, he destroyed them in war. None was so great or so reputed but at last Paranides mastered him, and made him of nought. And most of all he hated the proud men of the land, who were fierce and haughty and frank, and never bridled their tongues, but spoke of Paranides what their hearts conceived; and that was not happy for him to hear.

"Now when a year was gone Kate bore a daughter, so Paranides judged that his own title grew less and less firm. They held a parliament that year in Long Whitewall and therein Paranides made claim that Katherine had not obeyed the custom in that she would not wed him, but had wedded another. He alleged that since this was so, they must remedy it; and he claimed that she must be parted from Rafe, and their marriage declared void and of no effect.

"A crafty man was Paranides; but Rafe and his

[321]

friends had taken deep counsel, and this was the defence they made.    They claimed that the marriage
should hold good, but that since Katherine had
failed to fulfil the forfeit, she should no more be
the Luck of the Burgh, but that this should fall
to her sister, who should then be married to Paranides.    But Paranides claimed more than this; for
he required that all Katherine's daughters should
be put clean out of the succession and the right.
They answered him, that this was not just, until
he himself had a daughter in whom the descent
might continue.    Therewith was he ill content,
and they broke up without a decision.

"Now when this came to pass, Paranides made
his resolve to take by force what he deemed his
rights.    So he caused Rafe to be put in durance of
the Duke; and that same night he burnt the house
of the Fairfolds, and all that was therein.    But
Rafe and Katherine fled, and dwelt in Greenwood,
until the day when Rafe was slain.    It is truly said
that the old Duke connived, and helped them, so
that Paranides' title might continue in debate.
Thus he held on to his Dukedom until now, and
never could Paranides gain it.    For unto this day
no certain agreement has ever been come to concerning it."

Now when she had ended, she said:    "I do you
to wit that I am this Katherine.    I have shown
you my descent, and what rights belong to my

daughter, according to the customs of the Burgh which ye have sworn to observe. And I will bring witness that it is all sooth, and verily as I have declared."

But Harvanger said: "Let those who are here withdraw, save Horn, and Goldbeard, and Messire Bernlak; for I desire to take counsel."

And when those four were assembled in close council, Harvanger said: "I have heard a tale which so pairs with this, that the two together make but one tale."

"That may well be," quoth Horn.

"I knew Rafe and Kate of old," said Harvanger, "and I heard him tell of the burning of the Fairfolds. And he said that his child had perished therein. Hence, where is Katherine's daughter?"

"What was the name of the child?" asked Horn.

"It has slipped my mind," answered Harvanger, knitting his brows. "Whensoever I think, I can only think of the name of Yolande."

Bernlak smiled; but Horn said: "What is wrong therewith?"

Harvanger looked at him suddenly.

"I knew Rafe's brother, James of the Fairfolds," said Bernlak. "He it was who was bereft of his wits, and wandered in Wildwood. He was a worthy man of his hands, and few cared to undertake him."

"What hath become of him?" demanded Harvanger.

Bernlak said: "I can tell you that. He fell when we of Varraz forced the passage of the Mill Weir and drove Paranides from Whiteways, on the road hither. He was of our company."

"Is that all?" asked Horn.

"I took over such effects as he left," answered Bernlak. "There was a cup and a ring among them."

Harvanger bade them be sent for; and when they came, he took them into his hands, and knew them again. He turned to Horn.

"To whom do these belong?" he asked.

"To those whose names are written on them," answered Horn. "I will give you good counsel: show the cup and the ring to the dame."

So they recalled those who had been sent away.

"Dame," said Harvanger, "where is your daughter, on whose behalf you assert these rights?"

"Sir," she answered, "I do not know. I thought her dead, but now I hear that she may be alive, and in that hope I came to preserve her rights."

"What was her name?" he asked.

She answered: "Her name was Yolande."

He said: "Who was at the Fairfolds with her when the house was burnt?"

She answered: "James, the brother of Rafe."

Then Harvanger put the ring into the cup, and held out the cup towards her. She changed countenance suddenly, as those do who are taken un-

[324]

awares between sorrow and joy; but presently she said:

"The cup is Yolande's cup, and the ring is his."

Harvanger rose up and said: "Now the tale is fully told, for I saw Rafe slain; and I knew him who took Yolande beyond the Scaur Gap, and there I met her, and here we have cast down Paranides, and avenged Rafe. If you will come with me, madame, I will show you one who may tell you more."

## CHAPTER XV.: NOW HARVANGER CLAIMS THE MAY-DAY FORFEIT.

HE brought her within doors, to Yolande. "Dame," he said, "I present to you her who I think is your daughter. Whether this be so, thou shalt thyself try; and I will leave you to it."

Kate turned to Yolande, and there were tears in her eyes: "I pray thee love me if thou canst," she said, "for I have loved thee always, near or far: and thou art verily Yolande, unless I dream."

They approached one another, and held hands. Yolande gazed at Kate with strange, wide eyes.

"Madame," she said, "it will be easy to love you."

"Oh, it is nought to thee," said Kate.

They thought over this for a moment, still holding hands. Then the fear that it might mean

[325]

nothing to them, because of too long sundering, moved both women, and their eyes changed.

"It may mean much to us when we have forgotten how long we were sundered," said Yolande. And they kissed, half timidly, hoping that this might be true.

"Art thou happy?" asked the one.

"Most happy," quoth the other, "for he whom I love, loves me."

Said Kate: "Thou lovest him, and he bestows on thee many things. What hast thou to give him?"

"Myself," answered Yolande, meekly, "for nought else have I."

"But," said Kate, "wilt thou not like to give him some great thing equal to the things he gives unto thee?"

"Madame," said Yolande, with glowing eyes, "I should rejoice. Tell me if thou knowest of any means by which I may do it."

And when Kate had told her, Yolande rose swiftly to her feet, and kissed her, and said: "Let us go forthwith, lest another minute pass, and it still remain undone."

So Kate knew that she had no more to fear, but was secure of her daughter for ever.

Thus they came into the garden: and before all those present Kate said: "Sir, this is my daughter, whose right I have claimed before you."

[326]

Harvanger stood up, and said: "Listen to my first doom of justice. Whereas the dame Katherine failed to fulfil the forfeit bidden by custom, we doom that her own rights were voided thereby, and were carried over to her daughter. And since I am the May-Day man in whom rest the rights won by myself, Horn, Goldbeard, and Bernlak of Varraz, I claim Yolande therefore as my forfeit, in place of the false forfeit offered me before."

And therewith they were all well content.

## CHAPTER XVI.: NOW BEGINS THE TALE OF THE COMING OF THE KING OF THE ROMANS.

WHILE they sat at meat that night, a man rode into the city, and sought the Duke. When they showed him Harvanger, he said: "It was the Duke I sought."

"I am the Duke," quoth Harvanger. "There is none other. That which thou wert before, thou art now. I bid thee speak."

And when the man was convinced that these words were true, he spoke his message.

"Sir Duke, I am one of those set to watch the tidings from the north. There are a hundred thousand men who already force the passes there; and he who leads them is the King of the Romans. He is the wisest of all captains in this world; he marches in a crow's line, and none know his coming till he is upon them. To-morrow he will be here."

"To-morrow," said Harvanger, "we will receive him."

They slept ill that night, all save Harvanger; for none knew what to-morrow would bring, and yesterday was still upon them, so that they were disordered and disturbed, and men had not yet fallen into any accustomed place. But Harvanger was calm; he feared nothing, and knew not why.

And on the morrow morning he arose, and flung open his window, and looked over Whitewall. And when he had eaten, he called Bernlak to him.

"Forsooth," he said, "we have as yet no might to man this city. Go therefore, King's Son, and set thy Knights of Varraz at every gate, and leave every gate open; and set them in every court that opens upon the market-place, and close the doors. And let it be spoken to the people, that they abide within doors, and issue not forth on pain of death. This is my will."

And as he said, so it was done.

At noon, Long Whitewall was still. There were mailed men at every gate; and every gate was open. The pigeons wheeled in the market-place; but it was empty. None knew that behind the gates of the courtyards stood the mailed men of Varraz; for the gates were closed. And there were priests and canons within the Minster, but the doors were shut. So at noon there came a man, and looked at each gate of the burgh; and shortly there came the mightiest wood of spears that the sun ever looked on. It came by every road and path, and it glittered like a many-coloured dragon. And there came tall men in armoury, who stood before the open gates marvelling, and a trump was blown before them.

Then cried one: "Greatly I wonder at this; for it seemeth a city enchanted."

Another said: "Bring this word to the King."

Straightway strode out a man of Varraz.

"Sirs," said he, "I think I heard a trump blown."

"That is true," they answered. "We blew it."

"If ye desire entrance into the city," quoth he, "enter—for the gates are open."

At this they wondered exceedingly, and deemed some trap hidden beneath it. But when they had brought word to the King, he came, and looked on the city.

"Let us enter," he said.

CHAPTER XVII.: HOW THE KING OF THE ROMANS FOUND THEM IN THE MARKET-PLACE TOGETHER.

HARVANGER looked again over the city, and saw that the men of the north were before it; and he too wondered. Then he held out his

[329]

hand to Yolande, and said: "Yolande, let us go together."

"I will go whithersoever thou goest," said she. So they passed hand in hand across the stones of the market-place, and stood upon the steps of the Minster; they two alone.

They waited in the stillness, quietly, and not speaking or moving. Yet in some way each knew the whole mind of the other, from the moment when they first stood there, to the moment when they saw the approach of the King. They knew that they loved one another, and that there was nothing that either would not give or do in that great love; and so clear their minds were, that there seemed no need for any words at all, but all was clear and perfect and golden as sunlight, without wavering or apprehension in it. And they seemed now to belong to that place; not that the past days were any the less dear or well-remembered, but that the present seemed born complete and anew, and they were in their true and eternal place, whence none should ever put them forth. So they stood; and his strong brown hand clasped her small hand confidently.

They saw riders pass through the streets—great and splendid men, armed and accoutred in stately harness; men helmed and crested, and capped with nodding feathers of blue and crimson and gold. Their horses paced along; and yet more came, and ranged themselves down by the houses that were shut; never was such a stately display of strength and magnificence. And presently they saw a man walking; he led a horse by the bridle. His arms were plain and weather-worn; he had a helm of gold, but his côte-hardie was of linen. Yet on this was broidered the single headed eagle; so they knew it to be the King.

He motioned men still with his arm, and looked across the market-place. He shaded his eyes with his hand and gazed. Then when he saw Harvanger and Yolande, for a little while he was still; but anon he dropped the bridle from his hands, and came slowly forward over the deserted place. Harvanger saw him clearly. He was not old; he was a young man, and not great of body. He had the eyes and the brow of a King, hard and stern, yet not cruel. Those eyes were sad and questioning at times; and at others, strong willed and fierce. He seemed to be one who had been born to power, and loved it, and was a ruler of men; but also he seemed one who wished for things that he had never attained, and sought something that he knew not surely of, but could expect and hope for, yet never reach, until the hoping and expectation grew dissatisfied. He was a man given to brooding, unless he forgot it in action.

He came near, and tarried in his steps, as though with wonder; and he came nearer, and again tarried; and at last he came to them, and

[331]

said: "Ye are the first folk I see in this burgh,
big as it is. Tell me who ye be."

"I am the Duke of this burgh," answered Harvanger. "I am here to bid thee welcome."

"Truly," said the King, letting his eyes flash
wanderingly over the houses, "I have heard much
of the Duke of this burgh; but I deemed him an
old man, whereas thou art young; and an evil one,
whereas thou seemest not evil; and a weak one,
whereas I perceive thee to be of some wisdom and
valour, if I am not mistaken."

"I have been the Duke here two days," answered
Harvanger.

"Wilt thou tell me of that?" quoth the King, in
a very friendly fashion. He seemed to be willing
to speak and be spoken to, as though he suspected
a hidden wisdom. Yet it might go evil, if he
found none.

"If thou art ready," said Harvanger, "I will
give thee meat and drink, and the like to thy lords;
and I will answer all questions that thou mayst
desire."

The King nodded, and looked at him.

"I will as ye will," said he. "But tell me why
I find thee here in this manner. Hast thou no
men of arms?"

"I have many, whom I will show thee," said
Harvanger. So they went down the steps together, Yolande still holding the arm of Harvanger, until they came to the first court gate. Har-

vanger knocked, and those within drew bolts; and the doors were drawn, and within sat in their saddles a company of the mailed men of Varraz. The King looked upon them, and noted their arms; and so they walked round the market-place, finding behind every court gate such a host of Bernlak's men. The King came at last back to the steps. "I perceive it to be as I thought," said he, quietly; "thou art a man of calm and wisdom, and withal of friendly mind. I hope we shall have some speech together, for I am fain of thy company." Then he glanced around strangely, for all was still and empty. "Art thou happy?" he demanded, in a somewhat rough voice. "Nay," he said again, "thou shalt answer that anon. It is in my mind that thou wilt say Yea. Well—I will speak to you both."

## CHAPTER XVIII.: THE DISCOURSE WITH THE KING OF THE ROMANS IS HERE TOLD OF; AND OTHER MATTERS.

"ALL that thou sayest I will hearken to and answer," said Harvanger. "I will not conceal ought, nor make ought what it is not."

Said the King, somewhat doubtfully: "Thou wilt be a great Duke if thou doest that; for it is the weakness of rulers to hide and falsify, and make men strive together to their own hurt. Men deem kings mighty and all-powerful; but that is because they comprehend not the state of a ruler of men. None is so feeble as a king. He who made his will prevail without falsehood would be the mightiest of kings." Then he looked keenly at Harvanger, and said: "Tell me this. Art thou strong in thy burgh, or wilt thou need to pay the tax of fear and falsehood and double dealing? Tell me, for I am also a King; I will tell no tales."

Said Harvanger: "It is as thou wouldst think. I am a Duke of two days; I know not yet what is in the mind of the people. Yet those who hate me may strive against me, and those who love me may strive for me."

"Dost thou not fear for thy rule?" quoth the King.

"Thou seest I do not fear thee," said Harvanger.

"Thou hast no cause to do so," answered the King, moodily. "Thy men are well placed around the market; and also, I have learnt that it is not well to be too hasty in setting up and casting down rulers. A king needeth all the friends he can get. But I have seen a black-man who had lions in a cage. He went in and dwelt among them, and caused them to leap through hoops. Such as that," quoth he, grimly, "are kings. We dwell in cages of lions, and cause them to do tricks. It is an ill business."

"I know not why any man should be a king, then," said Harvanger. "He might be a hind, and happier."

"At times I have thought so too," said the King, "but at other times, not. For when I have pondered over the matter, I see not how I should be any the happier away from the things I was bred in."

Harvanger paused, and then said: "That I can perceive. I fear that thou art unhappy."

"Truly," answered the King, "it is so. Yet again, why should I trouble mine heart? Thinkest thou that there is any happiness for men? Often I deem there is none. I seek for those who are happy; but I find them not; only I find some who are glad, yet whether it lasts for always, or goeth soon, I cannot tell, nor whether it be true, or an illusion of simplicity."

As he spoke these words, he looked at Yolande; and her dark eyes were fixed upon him strangely. He was stirred at heart, and a new sense came to him.

"Let us go to the house of the Duke," said Harvanger. So they went slowly up the steps, and presently sat at a table. There was wine and fruit thereon, and the King set his helm on the table, and his hand to the wine which Harvanger presented to him.

[335]

"I thank thee for thy courtesy," he said. "Let us speak again. Art thou happy? And thou, madam?"

"I deem that we are happy," said Harvanger.

"On what account?" he asked, smiling faintly.

"On the same account that thou art not," answered Harvanger.

"I know not what it is," quoth the King. "I am unhappy because the world seems so. Doth it seem happy to you?"

"Yea, truly; most happy," quoth Harvanger. "When the moon rose over the burgh, I saw one who kissed a maid. What wouldst thou have seen?"

"My own heart," said the King. "For that was what thou sawest."

"Ask me a fresh question," said Harvanger.

So they sat, the three, around the board, and forgot all else save this quest.

CHAPTER XIX.: HOW THE KING OF THE ROMANS ASKED WHETHER MEN ARE HAPPY.

"I WILL that ye shall tell me," said the King, "whether ye are truly happy."

"We are most happy," said Harvanger; and Yolande yea-said that without speaking, for her eyes and her smile spoke in place of words.

[336]

"Tell me also, then," quoth the King, "what it is like to be happy."

"I should deem that thou knewest that," said Harvanger. "For if thou art unhappy, thou must needs know it by its failing from that which thou knowest to be good. Is not this so?"

The King toyed with the cup he had drunk from; he rested his arm on the table, and gazed searchingly at Harvanger with keen eyes.

"Well," he said, "that is a subtle word, and it may be true. Yet I will tell thee also, that I know not surely whether I am happy or unhappy. At whiles I am persuaded that it is an error of the understanding, and that I am happy without knowing it."

"I see not how that could be," answered Harvanger, gravely.

"Nay," quoth the King, "thou art not expert in the hearts of men, whereas I, although not old, am well read in them. I tell thee, Duke, that many men are in the world who are divinely happy; but because they have never had sore trouble or grief, they know it not, and are of the opinion that they have many set backs and injuries. This is true also of women. Therefore, although I am often filled with sadness and vain-longing, I perceive that I may be as these are, and happy, albeit I know it not." .

"That is true," said Harvanger. And he could not avoid smiling to think of this.

[337]

"So I desire thee to tell me what it is like to be happy," quoth the King. "Then I shall know better, whether I am or not."

## CHAPTER XX.: HARVANGER TELLS WHAT IT IS LIKE TO BE HAPPY.

"I WILL tell thee then," said Harvanger. "When the happy one waketh in the morning, he perceives the sun to be shining and warm, although it be mid-winter. He is glad to be awake; the world is full of the fair sun, and birds singing; in every thing, however small, he sees great pleasure, and is well content to see them. His heart is full of knowledge that the most desirable thing in the world is near to him; he labours and rests with his heart singing as a bird, and there is laughter in his soul, even if his face be stern, and his mind hard with forethought and provision. There is delight in the morning, so that he wishes it never to pass; and there is delight in the noon, so that he longs for it to last for ever; and there is delight in the evening, so that he would well keep it, and not let it go; and yet the time passes, and for all his longing he is not sorry, for he knows that to-morrow will be as happy. And when injury or evil befalls him, he is unafraid, for he believes that it will pass away swiftly; and in difficulty his heart is high, and his

[336]

eye keen. There is no soul so steady and unwavering as his. He is keen of eye because he is not enshrouded in any mist of ill-content; not being overwhelmed with fear or doubt, he has time and peace to see truly. And most of all he sees in every moment a Heaven; he sees the exceeding splendour and delight of the earth, so that those who are his friends, and are not happy, are amazed at him, because he seems to see what they cannot perceive to be there. Yet I deem all this but ill-said. If I were wise, I would speak to you wonderful words; albeit even then it would be less than the splendour that is."

"Wilt thou not also tell me what it is to be happy?" said the King to Yolande.

"Nay," she answered, "I am not expert enough to do that; for a woman's happiness is as the sun, and the sun no man may measure in words."

The King seemed to understand this. He sat gazing at them.

"Now I will tell you," said he, "what is in my mind. How know ye but that this is illusion and deception."

"I know not, nor do I care," answered Harvanger.

"That is unwise," said the King. "Ye may be entrapped by the unforeseen truth."

"Nay," said Harvanger, "my heart speaks to me. I know not, in any shape of words; but I know as the sun shines. How knowest thou, O King, but that the sun of spring is illusion?"

"Then ye think yourselves to be happy?" demanded the King, grimly. "Have a care. It may be that ye shall awake from that dream, and find the world not as ye thought it. It may be that this is fleeting, as a sun ray on a cloudy afternoon."

Harvanger smiled upon him sweetly; he smiled upon him with the wisdom of a young god.

"Well," quoth the King—"speak. What hast thou to say?"

"It is not happiness that is illusion," said Harvanger, "but unhappiness. I am awake, King; I see truly and clearly; thou art sleeping and dreaming; thou art in a glamour where all is false. And this I know as surely as that I am bodily awake. When thou dreamest, thou art sore oppressed with the evil of it; thou deemest it real; but when thou wakest, dost thou not know the truth? And I tell thee, that I am awake. I am filled with the joy of the earth."

The King turned the cup over, and still he gazed at Harvanger and Yolande.

"How dost thou attain happiness, then?" demanded the King. "I perceive now that I am more unhappy than I had deemed; and I desire to attain content."

[340]

"I attained happiness," said Harvanger, "by the gift of God."

"As I attained Kinghood," quoth the King, wryly. "They crowned me in the cradle, while yet I clasped a wooden horse to my breast. Is that all thou hast to say?"

"I never desired to be happy," said Harvanger, "nor do I think that even now I desire it."

"I understand thee not, by Heaven," said he. "Dost thou verily despise the joy that is thine?"

"It is above all things sweet and delightful," said Harvanger. "But it is not the sweetness that I desire, nor the delight."

"That is a strange saying," quoth the King. "I pray thee tell me more, for thou art full of wisdom."

"It is easily said," answered Harvanger. "Thou desirest to be happy. Give me, if thou canst, two handfuls of happiness."

The King started, and said: "Nay, it is not a thing to be given in handfuls."

Harvanger took both hands of Yolande, and set them on the board, and clasped them about with his stout hands.

"There," he said, "I show thee my two handfuls of happiness."

Yolande let her hands stay there, but she looked at the King without seeming to look.

"Thou desirest happiness, King," quoth Harvanger, then, "but thou desirest no thing before another. Desire Heaven, and nothing but Heaven; or desire earth, and earth before all else; or desire love, or riches, or honour, or fame—and then thou wilt be happy, for thou wilt strive after these things, or one or the other, and never cease from the pursuit, but be bound up in it so that to thee there shall be nothing in the world save that. Then thou wilt know happiness; greater or less, and noble or less noble, according to thy wisdom. Find the Best Thing in the World; happiness flows from that as from a full fountain."

## CHAPTER XXI.: CONCERNING THE BEST THING IN THE WORLD.

THE King said: "What dost thou deem to be the Best Thing in the World?"

Harvanger answered him: "The love of her whom I love; for there is nothing to be set beside that."

"Desirest thou nothing else?" demanded the King.

"Nothing else," answered Harvanger again. "For while I have that, the world is delightful and happy; I will sleep hard and live hard; I will journey between the ends of the earth, and strive with the great ones thereof. Whether I am rich or poor, and great or weak, becometh of nought;

I am full of pride and carelessness, and of kindness and peace, because I love her who is my Love."

The King said nothing, but once more he gazed at them both very strangely. Then he rose up, and took his helm in his hands again.

"Never yet did I meet two such as ye be," he said. "I would face all the hosts of the Sultan sooner than a man so divinely mad; and thou shalt be my friend for ever, lest thou be my foe." He spoke half in jest, and half in earnest; yet the earnest was more weighty than the jest. "I have kept my lords waiting over-long," he said. "Let us issue forth, or they will be ill content."

## CHAPTER XXII.: OF THE KING AND HARVANGER.

SO they issued forth into the market-place; and it was well they did so, for the lords were growing ill at ease. The King went pacing over the stones. The single headed eagle displayed itself on his back and breast; the sword hung from his side. He walked thoughtfully, with his head bent. When he came to the great men, he aroused himself.

"Sirs," he said in a hard voice, "extend your reverence unto this my friend, the Duke of this burgh. He has welcomed me as befits a man of wisdom and honour; he also biddeth you to his table this night. Thereto I consent. Let us be of sure heart and sweet words before the folk of Long Whitewall. Also, I shall this day send letters to my father, praising the honour and courtesy I find in this place, and the excellence of its rule."

He ceased then; but from that day Long Whitewall was held in honour at the King's Court, and in the court of his father; and no man was so bold as to set his foot across its borders, save in peace, except he defied both the Duke and the King together.

And the King, before he departed, set the coronet on Harvanger's head; he filled Long Whitewall with splendour, and gave Harvanger a coronet set with jewels, and arms worthy of a great Duke. And the last thing he did was to marry Harvanger and Yolande; they were wedded in the great Minster, as none were ever wedded before, and such men were there as never before had assembled together in the burgh. The fountains ran with wine, and so glorious were those days of state and splendour, that they were never forgotten. With which this tale runneth to a speedy end. But it tells lastly of what was said between Harvanger and Yolande on the morning and the night of their marriage, which now shall be spoken of. For what they saw and understood was more than that which others did. So here is the tale of the

[344]

speech between Harvanger and Yolande, and the tale of their wedding.

CHAPTER XXIII.: HERE IS TOLD THE TALE OF WHAT HARVANGER AND YOLANDE SAID TO ONE ANOTHER ON THE MORNING OF THAT DAY.

IT was on a fair morning of June that Yolande arose; and there were not many thoughts in her mind, but there were many things in her heart, for this day was the last of the old life with all its strangeness and familiarity, and the first of a new that would seem no less strange, and yet wholly familiar. Sunshine was in the air; the flowers were bright and sweet. She looked forth of her window, still in her bed-gown, and she saw one who sat in the pleasaunce with a flower between his fingers. And that was Harvanger. Then it came into her mind how little of that day would be hers and his, and how much taken up with deeds and words for others; so when she was attired, she went down a narrow stair of stone that ran in the wall, and out through a door into the garden. He was hidden from her by the foliage and the flowers, and she came upon him suddenly where he sat thinking. His face did not change; for indeed, Harvanger was the least of all men given to any sudden changes of countenance; but there came a

[345]

light into his eyes, and into hers, and he smiled. He drew her to him, and kissed her; and then sat with his arm resting on her shoulder, gazing over the pleasaunce, where a young thrush was seeking and finding. So they stood a little while. Then she said, questioningly: "What is in thy mind now?"

"Very many things, heart's-beloved," he said; "thoughts of the old and the new, and things past and present. Here where I sit was the pavilion pitched; here Horn played the game of chess, and I riddled with the Duke's daughter, and there Goldbeard threw the black-man who wrestled. There is no man so mighty of his limbs as Goldbeard. And now I am the Duke," he said, "and whereas I came here to seek the Best Thing in the World, here also I attain it." He turned his face and smiled to her.

"Tell me this tale," she said.

He sat with his hand still upon her shoulder, and the flower between his finger; and he told her all that tale of the Spotted Deer, and the May Day games in Long Whitewall, and the Battle in the Lists. He told her too of the great digging of Goldbeard, when they pierced the wall of the Doleful Tower and found Bernlak therein. All of this she listened to; and at the end, smiled.

They looked about the garden a little; then both rose up, and he put his hands on her shoulders, and she her hands on his. They paused a little to think of what first to say. Then she said: "Most strong hands thou hast—as strong as a lion's paw."

"Is that so?" said he. "They are thine, Yolande. And thou—small white hands, and strong too."

She said: "And most mighty arms thou hast; I am but small."

He looked at her, till she closed her eyes, still smiling.

She said: "Thou art a mighty man, Harvanger. Thou growest stronger day by day. No man in Long Whitewall has now such height and strength."

"I am of another breed than they," said he. "I am of the fair folk who came from the Scaur Gap—those who built the Doom Ring where the pass shelves into the vale. And thou," he said, "I deem thee the fairest woman in this world; and I have found the Best Thing it has to give."

She said: "Tell me about that too."

"Well," he answered, "I found the world sweet and wide. I entered into the wonder of it, and yet was not of it. For I was of another breed than this folk; they were of the soil, and where they lived they had grown up closely, each with his fellow and friend, and memories of youth and childhood. Each could speak gladly: ' this house my father built; in that house dwelt my mother ere ever she was wedded; there she sat in her girl-

hood, and wove garlands in the fields. This orchard my grandfather planted; that I have
watched and tended in my boyhood. By this lane
I went to meet her that I loved; at this tree I met
her. These are my friends; these are the ancient
places of my youth; I am knit into the life of the
folk by many bonds and memories; my kith and
kin are abroad in the land; wherever I go, I meet
my fellows; every bank and lea is mine, and well
beloved.' Thus they might speak. Into this life
and this land I came; I could see its fairness and
its distance. Though I walked amid the flowers,
I knew them not; each face was strange to me;
no man called to me over the way, nor did I ever
say in my heart: 'I will pass up this road to the
old house I remember, and speak again to my
friend, my kinsman.' So my heart hungered for
that unknown thing which should suddenly knit
all these things together for me. The gods gave
me an egg; but they gave me no salt. All things
were before me, yet I longed for one thing also,
that should flash all with that new and unknown
delight that binds our life into one."

She said softly: "I know, I will tell thee; when
I was young, the vale was mine; I knew each bird
and beast, and loved them. I knew the vale passing well; it was full of friends to me. At every
dell and copse I remembered how happy I had been
there; all was my well-remembered home. What

thou hadst not, I had. I was not alone, for I had myself."

He said again: "Heart's-beloved, they laid many hopes before me. I could have been rich, save that I perceived that it was not riches which would make me strong. And I could have trod in Paranides' steps—for he meant me well, and would have made me great. But I saw that any or all of these things might be mine; I held them so well in my hand, I was so close to them, that I understood that they were not my desire. When thou art hungry, Yolande, thou dost not seek for ought save to eat; when thirsty, to drink; thou wilt not seek to remedy hunger and thirst by that which is not their true assuagement. Is it not so? A man can be hungry of heart; and then his wisdom telleth him, 'not this, not that, not the other—I desire what I know not, but it is not this.' So I fared to the Scaur Gap. In that vale," he said, "I saw a woman. She was garbed like a youth; there was a question in her eyes; she bore a tapering unstrung bow. My heart fed on her as a roebuck at the streams; in her company I knew that I was content. With her, all the world became clear and good—there was no salt lacking in it. And while she was with me, and I delighted in her soul and her body, and all that was her, every other thing was tinged with a like pleasure."

He drew her to him suddenly.

[349]

"I know," she said.  "There came a fair youth into the vale; one who was glorious as a young god, and lay on the grass with fierce and joyful eyes.  In him there was no doubt or hesitation; he seemed to speak to me without words, and say: 'Behold me; I know my own heart; I am one who never swerves.  I will race in the mountains, and shout; I will not turn aside, I will show thee things divinely pleasant; things to laugh at, and things to treasure for ever.  Behold me; I am strong; I am fierce; I am friendly of heart.'  So I fled away."

"Why?" he asked smiling.

"It is a woman's way to do so," she answered simply.  "I saw him, and I thought him a god, and I fled swiftly.  And then," she said, "all the memory and delight of the vale faded; it became as an old garment no longer pleasing to us—a thing without life.  I became as a hare that is hunted, and finds its home stopped.  Oh, I longed and longed for the joy that was gone; I feared and dreaded the vale, because it had become empty, and as the world was to thee.  When I wandered in it, I should no more have delight; I should sit and weep for my young god who was not there with fierce and friendly eyes.  So I went back to him; and he was there; and as often as I departed, fear came; and as often as I went, dread."

"Why?" he said, moving his arm on her shoulder.

She answered:   "O, it is a woman's way to do
[350]

so. He would have sought me, and seized me, and looked at me with those fierce and friendly eyes, and I should have choked, and my heart would have stopped; I should have cowered on the ground for fear of what he might do to me, and of myself. O, O, O," she said, half laughing and half crying, "what would I have done if he had followed me so?"

Harvanger smiled too. "I think," he said, "that there was one who stood on the mountains, and hungered for the sweetness of the Wildwood Maid; and he fled down the mountains like a deer, until he came to the House of the Wood, and there he found her whom his heart desired, and he wrapt her into his arms, whether she would or no. And he said to himself: "Though the heavens fall and the earth vanish, I love her, and I have spoken; and it is done now, and what is done cannot be undone. So it was then accomplished, and peace came to him."

She said: "Truly, it is so. For when it was done, I stood up and said in my heart: 'I know it is done, and I am glad. I do not fear any more, because now the golden horror had come, and it was joyful. I am broken, and caught, and humbled and a slave; I am glad, I am glad, I will look at him now with clear eyes, because what is done cannot be undone.' "

They stood a little while without speaking, until Harvanger laughed a little laugh of joy, and said:

[351]

"If thou fleest, Yolande, I will seek thee as the hunter seeks the quarry. My heart's-beloved, I will grasp thee and attain thee, and then I will be kind; for my heart yearns over the exceeding fairness and pleasantness of thee. This is the heart of a man; thou art most fair; thou art clearer than the mountain waters, and more sweet to my soul than flowers. I desire only that we may love and be of one heart until the day of our death, and longer than that; longer, because one life is not long enough."

"Fair boy," she said. "I desire always to be in thy love. And now thou shalt have the uttermost I can give; take what thou wilt, for I know that thou wilt ever be kind."

They fell silent again; but he pressed her hand; and the thrush still sought and found on the grass.

## CHAPTER XXIV.: OF THE GREAT GLORY IN THE MINSTER.

AT the noon of that day, they arrayed Yolande for her bridal. And very fair she looked. There stood a mighty concourse in the ancient Minster of Whitewall; and in the midst was the Duke, Harvanger, in a long robe of blue and gold, and his sword by his side. There were crimson shoes upon his feet. Then entered a great procession of churchmen, with crucifix and incense; they bore in their midst a canopy, under which walked the King and Yolande, and they passed through the Minster slowly, with music, until they reached the choir. Harvanger stood waiting quietly, with blue eyes that saw little of the deeds done, and ears that heard little of the words said. He was thinking of the slim youth with the tapering bow, who looked out from the foliage of the apple tree. And he saw one very queenly and gloriously arrayed, who stood away on the other side of the choir; his heart stirred, and he wondered and smiled. And Yolande saw and heard but little more than he did; for she was dreaming of the fair young god with fierce and friendly eyes, who lay in the grass and beckoned her to unknown and strange wonders. Then she saw the tall and stately man who stood beyond her quietly; his hair was of gold, and his beard of gold, and he stood unmoving and unhearing. And her heart too leaped; she wondered, but could not smile. And there they were wedded and crowned, and borne forth of the Minster; and many men paid homage, and many women their reverence; and they sat together at a board, where was a large cup of gold; and Harvanger sat with a cup in his hand, and Yolande with her hands in her lap. And this is all they knew of how they were wedded, for they saw and knew nought else. Let those who saw more, write of how it was accomplished, and of the tall harper of the King, his breast scored with armoury of many colours, who stood up and sang the long

[353]

tale of the Dukes of Long Whitewall and the May Day men. And lastly there came a time when doors closed behind them, and they clasped hands in an awful and beautiful stillness, and dared not unclasp them for long.

CHAPTER XXV.: HERE IS TOLD THE TALE OF WHAT THEY SAID TO ONE ANOTHER, IN THE EVENING; AND THE TALE LEAVES OFF.

THEY passed out of bright light, and the presence of many people, and the flame of gay colour, into the dimness of that room. A little faintness came over Yolande; it may be, because of the dimness after the light. There was a long window, half flung open; the crossing of the leads showed against the moonlit sky, and a soft wind came through; there was but a blue dusk and coolness in the room, and she saw amidst it the wide canopied bed where they should lie for many and many a year to come, through storm and sun, and peace and war, and sorrow and joy. It was in her mind to sink down and rest her face upon it; but as she stood, she heard only the little faint sounds as Harvanger drew in the latch-cord sharply, and quenched his candle. He was at her side in a moment. They clasped hands in the dusk, and saw each other's faces in it; and so stood awhile. Then he whispered: "Come to the window."

So they went to it, and he undid the other latch
of the casement, and pushed it out; all the great
flowery pleasaunce lay below, bathed in blue dusk
and silvery moonlight. Beyond rose tall spires,
and quiet gables, amid a bushiness of summer
foliage. There was a radiance in the sky, and a
little star or two, half dimmed by the moon.
They sat down in the casement, where there were
cushions, and looked forth. Harvanger gathered
her little by little into the might of his arms; and
the Woodland Maid rested there in peace.

He whispered softly: "Now I have all—all.
What thou didst promise me in the Fair Valley
thou hast given me, Yolande. What shall I give
thee?"

She said: "Love. Love me ever as now."

"Is that all?" he asked. "Heart's-beloved,
I love thee as thou lovest me; it is easy to love.
But thou givest me so much, and so sweetly, that
I grieve because I may not give thee a gift equal
to it."

Yolande did not answer to this; so he said again:
"I will be ever thy lover, Yolande, and thy master
and thy servant, and thy shield and thy sword;
and all that a man may be to a woman, I will be,
because I love thee. But how may I speak of
that? I know now the wisdom of Way-wise."

"And what was that?" she asked.

He said: "He appointed us effort and rule;

since love is so sweet and tender, that it would soften us into sickness of heart, save unless we are busy with deeds and the outward world. And also, because it is so sweet, that a sacrifice must be made, lest men become as gods."

"Very wise thou art," said she, softly, and knew it to be true.

"To some is given one kind of labour," he said, "and to others, another kind; and we make love quicken the labour; for if thou smitest with a sword a great stroke, and it smiteth only air, hardly shalt thou save thine arm whole; but if it reacheth its billet, there is neither hurt nor jar in it. Love needeth labour for its body, to inhabit; lest, like a soul that hath no body, it be blown before the wind."

"Most wise thou art," she said, smiling. They clasped their hands again.

"Very fair thou art, Yolande," said he, passing his arm round her neck. "God devised the greatest wonder in the world when he devised women; and thou art of all women the fairest." Then he said again, after a little while: "I have arms of brass, and a body of fire immeshed in steel; thou canst not flee or escape, nor avoid me. Lo, I have thee, and I will retain thee; thou art mine, and mine, and the whole of my heart loves thee, Yolande."

She cried out softly, and said: "O."

He unlocked his arm a little, and stirred her hair with his hand. "Did I hurt thee, Yolande?" he said. She nestled up afresh, and answered: "Nay."

He said: "Dearer thou art than myself; thou art so fair and so sweet to me, that what thou wilt I will forego, and take only what thou wilt give; not for that I desire it not, but for that I desire more that peace and gladness shall be in thee, Yolande."

"I believe thee well," she answered, kissing the hand that lay on her shoulder. "And because I believe it, I am not afraid."

So after this, they looked over the garden without speech; but in their hearts were many thoughts.

They rose up presently, and knelt together on the cushions, and looked forth together, with their elbows on the sill. Harvanger spoke softly in her ear.

He said: "Very fair thou art, Yolande, and most fair; thou hast a soft cheek, and thou art strong, and supple, and smooth. There are many ways of love; there is a way of waiting and a way of refusing, and a way of taking and a way of asking. And sometimes love lies in speech, and sometimes in silence. We have wandered in woods, and journeyed by mountains, and stood in walled burghs, and sailed on the sea; and I have fought for thee, and pursued peace for thee; I have carried thy cup, and loved thee in all things. And

[357]

even so I will do to the day of my death; I desire only that I may be thy lover and friend, in small things and in great, and in one as much as in another."

She answered: "I desire only that thou wilt love me, in any way that is good to thy heart."

"Heart's-beloved," he said, "I am wishful that thou shouldst know I love thee in all ways. Most fair thou art, and my soul longs for thee, and hungers after thee; but it is thou that I love, and not only the fairness of thy body. But I love thy fairness because it is of thee; and thou lookest out upon me through thine eyes, and thou shinest out upon me through the fairness of thee; therefore I desire these things also."

Yolande trembled a little. She answered: "Thou art true and wise; thou art my young god. But in days to come I shall be old; and wilt thou love me then?"

He said: "Then, no less than now; thy soul is dear to me, and it is thou that I love. I have won thee, and loved thee; and I desire that thou shalt never deem that I loved only thy body."

"And some day we shall die," said she.

He answered: "I will love thee then. So sweet is love, that it lasteth for ever; it is stronger than death. Have no fear, Yolande, that we shall lose one another; for those who love have ever known that death could not part them. This gladness and good of love we cannot let go. For

[358]

when I saw thee first, it was as though I beheld one familiar to me; I knew that I had loved thee of old; and had but found her who for a little while had been parted from me. And if now I went forth of the door, and presently returned, it would be no otherwise than as it was in the Fair Valley. For there I remembered, and was glad to meet thee again."

Yolande rose up from the window, and stood with her hand raised to her hair, pensively. Harvanger passed his arm around her, and said: "Dost thou deem that now I love thee?"

She answered smiling: "O, young god, all thy words are feeble and foolish, but sweet to hear; I know that thou wilt ever be kind, and a true lover, and for that, no words I need, save for pleasure."

He kissed her; and so they passed into the dusk of the room again.

And here stops the tale of Harvanger and Yolande; a long tale, that never began, and never ended. But if any *be* curious, there is this to be said, which is not part of the tale: Harvanger grew into a great and a mighty Duke, who ruled with a strong hand and a wise; and he and Yolande were ever lovers, and they had tall sons with chestnut hair, who were as good and valiant men as *ever* lived.

Of this tale, therefore, we tell no more.